MILKY TRAIL TO DEATH

STUART G YATES

For Georgie, who left us in the early spring of 2021.
You were so very special, and so deeply loved.

CHAPTER ONE

He came into the town at the back end of a hot, physically draining day. The heat continued to pulse through the thick air as it had since he set out, so hot that his sweat evaporated as soon as it appeared. His canteen of water was empty, his horse bedraggled and close to collapse. The mare needed rest and sustenance and so did he.

A gnarled old man was just shutting up the gates to the livery. He turned and frowned at the stranger's approach. Blowing out a loud sigh, he reopened the gate. "You'll be staying long?"

"A couple of days."

"You were lucky to catch me. It's late." He looked to the slowly darkening sky for a moment before returning his bleary, watery eyes to the stranger. "You look all done-in, boy. You been riding far?"

"Far enough."

The old-timer shrugged and waved the stranger in. "All righty, if that's how you want it."

"That's how I want it."

"All righty. Go and stable her inside and I'll see you in the office." His eyes narrowed. "For payment."

"Two bits a day," said the old-timer moments later when the

stranger stepped into the office. "That includes feed and it's a good deal."

"Never doubted it," said the stranger, snapping down the coins on the top of the desk separating him from the old-timer. He watched the man scribbling something in a dog-eared ledger. "That's two nights, just in case."

"In case of what?"

The stranger drew in a breath. "I need to stay longer."

"You want board there's Miss Bessy's guest house. She provides a comfortable bed with a fine breakfast and dinner."

"That's your recommendation?"

The old-timer sat back in his chair. "Mister, it's all we got. This ain't exactly the liveliest town in these parts."

The stranger tipped his hat and turned to go.

"It's second on the right," said the old-timer. "Tell her Destry sent you. She'll give you a discount."

Pausing at the door, the stranger considered the old-timer with keen interest. "Is that right?"

"Sure is," he said, a toothless grin spreading across his craggy face, "I'm her husband."

With the sound of his cackling ringing throughout the tiny office, the stranger stepped outside.

He crossed the yard, pausing at the gate to notice, despite the growing darkness, the tall, angular-looking tough standing across the street from him, leaning nonchalantly against a hitching rail, smoking a cigarette. There was a tied-down six-gun at his hip, set low on his thigh. His stare never faltered, almost as if he was daring the stranger to stare back. Ignoring him, the stranger turned, closed the gate, and walked down the street to find Miss Bessy's.

The interior was thick with the aroma of pork stew and beans. It hung in the air like a living thing, clinging to every item of tired-looking furniture arranged around the sides of the foyer. The stranger dragged off his hat and wiped his brow with his neckerchief. The heat was stifling. Several large oil lamps belched out a dreary light and contributed to the oppressive atmosphere.

He crossed to the reception desk, picked up the tiny brass bell sitting there, and shook it. He doubted the tiny peal was loud enough to be heard, but within less than a minute, a blonde woman emerged, face glistening with sweat, eyes alight with surprise. She came forward, and the stranger found himself relaxing as she smiled.

"Evening," she said.

She was a handsome-looking woman, he had to admit. Wrapped in a tight-fitting apron that barely contained her ample bosom. She reached under the desk and produced a large ledger. She opened it and leaned closer, allowing the stranger an undisturbed view of the soft flesh straining against her bodice. She ran her tongue across her full lips as she studied the pages. Her cologne was sweet-smelling.

"You looking for a single room?"

"I am," he said, placing his hat on the desk. He caught her gaze falling on the dust-covered, battered headgear, the slight down turning of her mouth, her accompanying look of disgust and he swiftly took it back. "Two nights. With dinner."

"And a bath?" She sniffed but at least the smile returned.

"That would be wonderful. Thank you." He watched as she produced a stubby pencil and lowered it towards the ledger. "I met your husband." She stopped. "He said to tell you I might—"

"Get a discount?" She raised a single eyebrow. He waited. Her smile increased. "Why, that's just fine, Mister ...?"

"The name's Reece."

She recorded it in the ledger. "It's a dollar a night. So, for you, two nights will be one dollar fifty."

"That's mighty generous, ma'am."

"I know it is."

Her eyes danced as she held his gaze. He felt his stomach lurch and a thrill ran through his scrotum. He couldn't

3

remember the last time he'd conversed with a female and certainly not one this alluring. How in the name of sanity had that old goat at the livery managed to marry someone so lovely? No wonder he was so worn out. A woman such as she could wear out any man.

"Where you from, Mr Reece?"

"You need that for the register?"

A slight flush appeared around her jawline. "Why no, not exactly. But times being what they are and all ..."

"Missouri."

"Miss ...?" Her expression changed, a sudden veil of suspicion descending over her face. "You ain't ...?"

"What? A Redleg on the run? Bushwhacker?" Reece smiled. "No, ma'am, I ain't either. But I did serve and I'm on my way home if that's what you're asking."

"Honestly speaking, I wasn't, but seeing as you have been so gracious, I shall defer from asking you any more personal questions."

He went to respond but stopped when a large shadow blocked out the dismal light from the lamps. The woman stepped back, her eyes wide with alarm. Reece knew what this meant. It was the look of fear, one he'd seen all too often. Slowly, he turned around.

There were three of them, the man in the center large and angry looking, jacket pulled back to reveal a sagging paunch, hands on his hips close to the twin guns holstered there. One of the others Reece recognized as the man who had watched him emerging from the livery.

The big man cleared his throat. "Miss Bessy may not have asked you your business here, mister, but I will."

Reece, leaning against the desk, scanned the three of them. The third, smaller but as mean-looking as a coyote on the hunt, held a rare Gibbs carbine in his hands. Impressed, Reece pressed his lips together. When he spoke, his gaze never left the breech loader. "I'm resting up."

4

"Resting up from what?" The lean one asked this, his eyes narrowing, his shoulders tensing.

"Travelling."

"What the fu—"

"Hold it, Frank," said the large one, raising a hand to cut the other off, "let's just see what our visitor has to say for himself."

Reece didn't feel as if he wanted to say anything, except telling these three bullies to back off before he bounced them down the street...but he didn't. Instead, he drew in a breath, forced a smile. "I'm going home," said Reece. "I got my discharge papers. You wanna read 'em?"

The big man tilted his head. "Discharge papers? Mister, we get all sorts coming through here and most ain't welcome. You have the look of someone who looks for trouble. You can leave tomorrow. First thing."

"Henry, he's but just paid for two night's bed and board." Bessy's voice came to Reece as if borne on the wings of angels.

"Refund him the diff," said Henry.

Reece pushed himself from the edge of the desk and looked from one man to the next. "You got any authority to put your weight around the way you do?"

"This is the only authority we need," said the one holding the Gibbs. He waved it in Reece's general direction.

"I hope that's loaded," said Reece.

"It is."

"Good. I wouldn't want you to embarrass yourself by squeezing the trigger on an empty breech."

"Mister," breathed Henry, "I don't much like your tone."

"And I don't like yours. Now, who in the hell are you to confront me like this, all tied-down guns and cavalry carbines?"

Behind him, Bessy's voice sounded smooth and friendly when she said, "Henry, why not just go back to Mister Quince and tell him Mr Reece here is only passing through. We can then all take our supper, get a good night's sleep, and get ready for another day in paradise."

The little weasel snorted, Frank guffawed, and Henry blew out his cheeks.

For a long time, nobody said anything until Henry, at last, let his coattails fall across his gut and, with a nod towards Reece, growled. "Just you keep that Remington in its holster until you leave, mister."

Reece nodded and watched them go.

From behind, Miss Bessy released a long sigh. "Why don't I run you that bath, Mr Reece? Then we can all relax a little. What d'you say?"

Reece turned. "I'd say that sounds just perfect, Miss Bessy."

"Bessy is just fine, Mr Reece."

And with that, he followed her through the rear door which led to the narrow staircase and the waiting guestrooms.

CHAPTER TWO

Q uince was in his study, poring over a collection of
papers strewn over the top of his large desk. He did not
look up as someone rapped gently on the door before
putting their head around and saying, "Excuse the interruption,
Mr Quince."

"Come in Henry. Take a seat. Take some coffee if you wish."

Henry stepped inside. He stood still, eyed the coffee pot
holding down some of the papers, and declined.

Eventually, after studying a large map for some time, Quince
looked up. "Well, what is it?"

"A stranger, Mr Quince. Frank saw him coming out of the
livery late last evening. Frank said he was wearing a Remington
Army and looked as mean as a rattler. We confronted him at
Miss Bessy's."

Quince, leaning forward across the desk, considered Henry
for a while. Henry grew uncomfortable under his employer's
gaze and shifted his weight from one foot to the next. He had
settled his hat in front of his ample belly, gripping it with both
hands. He now ran the brim through his fingers. Quince
continued to stare. Henry coughed, ran a trembling hand

through his hair, and got away from those damned eyes by looking at a large painting on the wall beside him.

"Who was he?"

Henry turned, drew in a breath. "He struck me as being—"

"A lawman?"

"Well, I couldn't exactly say for sure, Mr Quince. He was covered in dust and looked as though he'd been riding for days, if not weeks. I didn't notice any—"

"Badge? He didn't wear a badge?"

"No, sir."

"And his clothes? Dusty you say, but a suit? Dark grey, formal?"

"No, sir. Range clothes. Shirt, rough pants, leather gloves in his belt. Gun belt that is. Like I said, Remington Army. Cavalryman's gun. Federal cavalry, sir."

"There'll be plenty of them moving through right enough. From both sides. We need to be watchful, Henry. And marshals. Pinkertons maybe. I don't want no lawman poking his nose in, you understand?"

"Indeed, I do, sir, which is why I followed him to Miss Bessy's. Confronted him."

"And what were your impressions?"

"I did not take him to be with the law, Mr Quince. He seemed too … I don't know, just a feeling I got."

"You fought in the War, Henry. You witnessed a lot of bad things. You must have some idea of who he might be."

"A man not easily spooked, Mr Quince. As if he were used to it. Threats, I mean."

"You threatened him? Henry, that's not the best course to take with men like that. If he is ex-army, he could be as tough as Hell."

"So is we, Mr Quince."

"I know that Henry, but Frank is a hothead, miffed that he didn't get a chance to fight before Appomattox put an end to it."

"As are a lot of the boys, sir."

"That's as maybe but we have to maintain a modicum of control, Henry. I don't want my plans compromised by any gunplay. You understand me?"

"Yes, sir, indeed I do, sir."

"Good." Quince pulled himself up straight. "You think this stranger is gonna be trouble?"

"Not sure, sir. He certainly did not take kindly to being asked questions."

"Well, that's his right, I reckon. No need to push, Henry."

"No, sir."

"But if he pushes back perhaps you could put him straight."

A tiny frown creased Henry's forehead. "Run him out of town, you mean?"

"With a fly in his ear, yes. But if he's a lawman ..." He turned, stood up, and crossed the room to the large bay window that looked out across his manicured lawn. He watched Radcliffe, one of his servants, trimming the grass. He liked that. It gave him a sense of comfort knowing that life continued unabated despite the uncertainties that peace had brought to his land, his business. "We have to be careful, Henry. If he is the law, he may only be a vanguard. We have to make sure he doesn't stumble upon anything. Suspicions must not be raised."

"But how would he know anything, Mr Quince?"

"Easily. A misplaced word in a crowded saloon, a drunken lout's revelations about what we are doing here ... Keep an eye on him, Henry. But from a distance." He turned. "Be wary, Henry. Cautious. Patient. And tell Frank to keep that waggling tongue of his in his head."

"Yes, sir, Mr Quince."

"Now go get yourself something to eat. Me, I still have to work out if there's another way into those old mines."

Henry gave a slight bow, turned, and left.

Quince stared at the closed door. He hoped, no, *prayed* that the stranger, whoever he was, proved not to be anything more than a passer-by. Anything else would need to be met with consequences. If the War had taught Quince anything it was that violence always paid.

CHAPTER THREE

Reece ate his breakfast in a small, cramped, and smoke-filled room in which three tiny tables were crammed together. Each was covered with an intricately woven lace cloth of the most startling white. Miss Bessy certainly took great pride in her establishment, no matter how minuscule it may be.

Running a piece of bread around the edge of his plate, Reece sat back and felt more relaxed than he had for many long months.

The man in the corner, a travelling salesman by the cut of his tweed suit and Derby-hat placed next to his elbow, puffed on a fat cigar, his fat cheeks glowing with grease from his morning bacon. He beamed across to Reece. "Gonna be a beautiful day once again," he said.

"I suspect so."

"My name's Bourne. You here on business?" Without waiting for a reply, the man plunged on. "Mine takes me everywhere now that the West is opening up like never before. Thank the Lord the War did not cause as much deprivation out here as it may have done."

"I reckon it caused enough elsewhere."

"Ah, yes, yes of course, but what I'm referring to, forgive me, is the excesses of violence visited upon the likes of Fredericksburg and Atlanta. And now, with Johnson's so-called Reconstruction plans, I can see any peaceful designs for reconciliation causing nothing but more trouble. Don't you think?"

Reece didn't think. He'd fought for too long to think about much else but his own survival.

Rolling his cigar between finger and thumb, the man's eyes narrowed. "Are you a southern gentleman, may I ask?"

"I ain't ever considered myself as anything but a *man*, mister. Southern or otherwise. It's all the same to me."

"Is it really?"

"Yes, it is. I've met enough mean-minded gentlemen from both sides to know that such a word don't mean diddly if it ain't accompanied by actions."

The other's cheery face grew dark. "I see." He turned his head slightly as he picked up his coffee cup and drank in silence for a moment. He smacked his lips when he finished and settled the cup back on its saucer. "If you're from the North, my advice would be to refrain from being too critical of our ways."

"*Our* ways?"

"The ways of the South, sir."

"Ah, yes. What exactly might those ways be?"

"Hospitality, good manners. Good breeding."

"Like keeping good men confined, you mean? Working long hours on plantations underneath the burning sun, not paying them a single cent? Is *that* what you mean?"

Bourne clenched his jaw and was about to speak when Miss Bessy breezed in, smoothing down the front of her apron, her smile as bright as the morning itself. She reacted to the chilly atmosphere instantly, stopped, and looked with some concern towards Reece. "I hope you and Mr Bourne are getting on famously, Mr Reece."

"As if we'd known one another all our lives."

She gave him a quizzical look as if she didn't quite believe him, crossed towards Bourne, and busied herself tidying away the detritus of his breakfast. "Will you be checking out early, Mr Bourne."

"I have a couple of appointments further west, so yes I shall be leaving in under an hour or so."

"Well, it's been a real pleasure having you stay. Perhaps you will call in again on your return journey. To Saint Louis was it?"

He glanced across to Reece. "Louis*ville,* Miss Bessy."

"Ah yes, how silly of me." She straightened up, her arms full of plates. "I'll make up your bill."

As she passed Reece, she flashed him a smile. "And you, Mr Reece?"

"Another night, I reckon."

"That would be grand."

"Your husband, Miss Bessy? Is he around?"

Appalled, her face lost all of its color. "My husband?"

"Yes, I was wondering if I might have a word with him that is all. My bridle, it's showing signs of wear and I was wondering if he could point me in the way of a reliable blacksmith."

"Oh yes, I see." Her smile returned. "Let me just get rid of these dishes and I'll be right with you."

She left and Reece returned to contemplating his coffee cup. He sensed Bourne stand up but did not bother looking. Until that is, the man paused beside him. He tilted back his head and held the man's icy stare. "You got a problem, Mr Bourne?"

"Seems like you is the one with the problem." He pulled back his coat. In his belt was stuffed a pearly-handled revolver. "I was making polite conversation, but you took it upon yourself to be offensive. I do not respond kindly to such a tone."

"Is that so? Well, let me say, in my defense of course, that I did not find your conversation particularly welcoming. I chose, therefore, to ignore it. As indeed I'd like to ignore you."

"I don't expect to be seeing you again, mister, and I can say it won't be a moment too soon."

"You might consider closing your coat when you speak to me, Bourne. I surely hope you know how to use that thing."

"I do, sir. I served for the Confederacy during the hostilities and saw action many times."

Nodding, Reece lowered his gaze. "Still, I do not react kindly to intimidation, so I'll ask you to close your coat and say 'good morning' to you."

"I've seen your like before, mister whatever your name is. Northern trash, marching through our land as if you own it. Let me tell you, there'll be a reckoning soon enough. Then you won't be so cocky."

"A reckoning? Like at Gettysburg, you mean?" Reece gave a wry smile. "Good morning, Mr Bourne."

Bourne snorted, turned, and strode out. Reece listened to Miss Bessy greeting him in her usual cheery tones, then to his stomping up the stairs to his room, the sound receding until Reece could hear it no more. He blew out a long sigh, took his coat from the back of the chair and stood up.

He found Miss Bessy busy at work behind the reception desk. No doubt she was preparing Bourne's bill. She looked up as he approached. "Off somewhere, Mr Reece? You never did tell me what your business was here in Whitewater."

"Is that what this place is called?"

"Comes from the name the Cheyenne give to the river some two miles from here. A stream runs off it, feeds the old mine. It runs white in the winter. Some believe it is named after the man who found the town. His name was White, you see. But that isn't so." She smiled. "You won't be needing your coat, Mr Reece. It's going to be another scorcher. If you leave it behind, I can clean and press it for you."

"That's very kind."

"It's no trouble."

Before handing it across to her, Reece delved inside and pulled out a folded, tattered piece of paper. "Your husband, Miss Bessy? Is he around?"

Again, that slightly startled look as she took his coat and

draped it over one arm. "He ... truth is, Mr Reece, he didn't come home last night."

"Oh. I was hoping to talk to him about that bridle."

"I can point you in the direction of Noah Barton's smithy, that's no trouble."

"Thank you."

They went to the door of the little guesthouse and stood together for a moment, under the porch. She was right. It was already oppressively hot. Even so, there were people in the street. Groups of men were dotted around the main thoroughfare, which was nothing more than a rutted track with most of the town's buildings set along one side, with a bank and timber yard opposite. On both sides were rolling, low-lying hills topped with towering pines. Loitering in front of a small lumber agent's office were three men, roughly dressed in filthy work clothes. They wore dark expressions and were passing around a stone jug. Clearly business was slow given the heat and they no doubt filled their day with drinking and idle talk. Beyond them, a dilapidated building sporting an impressive sign informing the world this was a baker's shop, with a general store attached. Next to that a saloon of sorts and a cluster of smaller wooden buildings, more shacks than anything else, which seemed to supply the small town with everything it would ever need. At the far end, the blacksmith's, black smoke belching out from a stone chimney at the side.

"I guess it wouldn't be amiss of me to say this town has seen better days."

She gave a short laugh. "Mister Reece, this town never had better days! It's always been a place you didn't want to stay in."

"So why are you here?"

She shrugged. "That's a long story."

They looked at one another. This close, breathing in her perfume, Reece could see how attractive she was, her face youthful, her skin unblemished, those eyes so inviting. He breathed through his mouth and turned away feeling the heat rising to his cheeks. "Maybe you could tell it to me?"

"Maybe I could. After supper perhaps?"

He snapped his head around. "And your husband?"

"Oh, don't worry about him, Mr Reece. I doubt I'll be seeing him for a few days." Her eyes wrinkled up mischievously, "My life is somewhat predictable, Mr Reece, and the most predictable thing of all is my husband's regular insobriety. Well," she patted Reece's coat, "I'll go and sponge this clean for you. You have a pleasant day, Mr Reece."

He tipped his hat and watched her disappear inside.

An after-supper chat with such a fine-looking woman was just what he needed, he thought to himself. Smiling, he stepped down into the street and strolled towards the blacksmith.

CHAPTER FOUR

B efore pulling on his boots, Henry checked the inside, tapping out anything that may have been lurking in the snug darkness. This was an old habit he'd picked up on the range when he was not much more than a boy. Scorpions loved to curl up in the safety of a boot's interior and when he'd witnessed a man called Mitchel screaming after one of the little devils had pierced the sole of his foot, Henry always went through his morning ritual. Mitchel had died in agony some days later, consumed with pain, not even aware of who he was. Old Bill Spade, the wise cook who could rustle up anything from nothing, told everyone that some folk simply reacted badly to certain bites and stings. Whereas some could laugh them off, the poor unfortunate ones, like Mitchel, took it bad and died. "I seen it more than once," old Spade told them as they sat around the campfire one evening, slurping up spoonsful of hot slurry the cook had made for supper. "I'm telling ye, check yer boots in the mornin'. That way one of them evil critters won't nip you in the toe!"

They laughed but Henry took the advice. He was glad he did. There had been several mornings when he'd knocked out a scorpion. This morning, thankfully, there wasn't one and he stood and finished dressing.

Downstairs, Eva, the cook Quince employed from a place called Poland, put down a plate of eggs, fried tomatoes, thick-sliced ham, and hot bread. Henry stood and smiled, licking his lips. "I got to say, Eva, you're the best-darned cook I've ever met."

She smiled, wiping away an errant strand of hair from her face. "Ah, Mr Henry, you are a kind man."

"I wish you'd come visit me in my room, Eva. I'd then show you just how kind I can be."

He winked, she blushed and fled. Laughing, he settled himself down and attacked his breakfast.

He'd barely swallowed down the first mouthful when Manchester, the butler came in. He saw Henry and stopped. "Glad you're here, sir."

"Oh?" Henry raised his coffee cup to his lips and took a sip. He pulled a face. It needed sugar. "Why is that?"

"I did not wish to waken Mr Quince."

"He can be as nasty as a rattler in the morning, I'll give you that. What did you want to say?"

"There's a caller, sir."

"A caller? At this hour?"

The butler nodded. "Shall I ask him to come in, sir?"

"Who is he?"

"He presented himself as a Mister Bourne, from Kansas City."

"Kansas? That's one helluva way. Did he say what he wanted?"

"Only that he had some important news for Mr Quince."

Henry put down his knife and fork, finished his coffee and stood up. "Let's go take a look."

The 'look' he discovered was a short, stout-looking man sporting a brown Derby hat and dark-grey suit pulled back revealing a pearl-handled six-gun at his hip. Frowning, Henry also noted a curious sagging on the left-hand side of the man's coat. Nothing seemed to be in the right place with the man, a hotchpotch of styles randomly thrown together as if, for whatever reason, he struggled to find his identity.

Smiling broadly, the man took off his hat and gave a little bow. "Good day, sir. My name is Bourne."

Something stirred inside Henry. A suspicion born from years of keeping company with vagabonds and confidence tricksters. The end of the War gave every good-for-nothing any number of opportunities to indulge in wrongdoing. There was nothing in this man's demeanor to persuade Henry that he was anything different.

"What can I do for you?" Henry asked, forcing himself to sound relaxed, friendly even. He already felt disadvantaged due to his own gun hanging in its gun belt on the back of the dining room chair he'd just vacated.

"I'd like to talk to Mr Quince, if I may."

"Mr Quince has yet to rise, sir. Can I ask what this is about?"

"Indeed." Bourne, in a deep conversation with himself, chewed away worryingly at his bottom lip. He replaced the Derby. "If I could come inside, I'll reveal my purpose."

On his left, a shadow crossed Henry's line of sight. He turned and was relieved to see Manchester standing in the corner, a Sharps carbine in his arms. He nodded towards the butler before turning once again to the visitor. "You may. Just unbuckle your gun belt before doing so."

Bourne stiffened. For a moment it seemed to Henry that his request would not be adhered to. Looking around, as if half-expecting to see others moving up close, Bourne sighed, shrugged, then obediently took off the belt and placed it gently on the ground next to him.

Henry stepped aside and allowed the visitor to enter.

Standing in the entrance hall, Bourne took in his surroundings before noticing Manchester stepping out of the shadows. "Hey," said Bourne, raising his hands, "ain't no need to put the drop on me."

"We have to be careful," said Henry, dipping his hand inside the man's jacket to relieve him of the so-called Wells Fargo pocket pistol concealed there.

Bourne gasped. "Mister, I meant to—"

"Sure you did," said Henry, hefting the gun in his palm. "I noticed you had this inside your jacket, mister. Just a tad curious as to why you'd need a concealed weapon."

Bourne looked nervously towards Manchester who was now pointing the Sharps directly at him. "Now look, I ain't—"

"Just tell me what you want before I come to the end of my patience."

They all looked up as a stair creaked and Quince appeared, dressed in a silk dressing-gown of chocolate brown.

"It's all right, Henry, I'll take it from here. Mr Bourne, if you'll step this way."

Bourne's face lit up. He deftly retrieved the Wells Fargo, gave Manchester a leer, and swung around to follow Quince into the rear drawing-room.

Henry blew out a long sigh, gave Manchester a quick salute, and went back to finish his breakfast.

CHAPTER FIVE

A warm wind blew up dust eddies from the hard-baked street as Reece sauntered along, glancing across the shop fronts, tipping his hat to the occasional bystander. No one returned the gesture and, before long, he ceased giving welcome to anyone.

At the end of the street, a small, squat clapboard blacksmith's shop appeared in imminent danger of collapse. With its sagging roof and warped walls, Reece wasn't sure whether or not to go inside. The sound of a hammer smashing down on an anvil rang out, heat pulsed from a brazier, smoke rose. Reece took a breath.

Crouching over his anvil, the man's bulk seemed to fill the workshop. He wore a tattered, sweat-stained vest, his bare arms bulging with muscle, and Reece doubted he would need the old cavalry carbine propped up in the corner to help defend himself with. Even so, it was a curious addition to the sweltering heat of the shop. As the blacksmith raised his hammer arm to strike down upon the metal again, Reece cleared his throat.

The man turned. His eyes blazed from a face slathered with perspiration. "Can I help you?"

Reece dipped his head and stepped through the entrance. Reece was tall, but not as tall as the blacksmith. This close,

Reece could feel the man's strength. Impressed, he'd known men as big as this from before. He smiled. "I need my bridle fixing."

"Well, you come to the right place." He straightened up his back and, scanning Reece from head to toe, nodded. "You'll be the stranger staying at Miss Bessy's."

Reece gave a short laugh. "News travels fast."

"It's a small town. Things don't stay secret for long." He carefully placed the heavy, solid hammer on top of the anvil. "You planning on staying long?"

"Not really. Once my horse is rested, I'll be moving on, I reckon."

"I'll have the bridle done by tomorrow if you bring it to me before the day is done ..."

Both of them swung around to look at a commotion breaking out in the street. A gaggle of men spilled out of the merchandise store in an agitated state, shouting, flapping their arms around. From the corner another man appeared, a large light grey Stetson shielding his features.

"That's Sheriff Fieyn. Something must have happened. You wait here." The big blacksmith shouldered his way past Reece and strode across the street to the assembled men. Other townsfolk were joining them. One woman gave a high-pitched scream, her hand coming to her mouth almost instantly. Fieyn stood amongst them, gesturing for them all to calm down. "Quiet, the lot of you," he was saying, but Reece could not make out much else.

Shaking his head as if in disbelief, the blacksmith returned to his shop, muttering, "Seems like old Destry is missing."

"Destry?" He watched the blacksmith take off his leather apron and hang it from a hook in the far wall.

"Miss Bessy's husband." His eyes narrowed. "The livery owner? You must have spoken to him."

"I did. Yesterday."

"Well, he's not been seen since."

"Bessy said he often goes missing."

22

"She told you that?"

"Last night, during supper."

"You got your feet under that table quick enough!"

Reece, who had been leaning in the door well, stood upright, "Hey, now just a goddamned minute—"

"A mite tetchy ain't you, mister?" The blacksmith picked up the carbine. "Supposin' you tell me where you're from?"

Reece eyed the carbine. In such close confinement, Reece doubted he could draw his pistol fast enough to cause the blacksmith to reconsider any hasty action. "Why not put the gun down first."

"Why don't you just answer the question?"

"I'll take it from here, Hanson," said a voice.

Reece turned his head to see the sheriff standing there, thumbs in his belt, eyes levelled towards him.

"Sheriff, I was only—"

"I know you 'was only', Hanson. Just put down the gun before someone gets hurt."

The big blacksmith blew out a sigh but did as he was asked, albeit reluctantly.

"So," said Fieyn, moving inside, studying Reece intensely, "why don't you answer the question, mister. Where you from?"

"If you must know ..."

"That's why I'm asking."

"Kansas. I've been making my way west, taking it easy. Minding my own business."

"Sensible, I'd say. Especially in these difficult times. You stabled your horse with Destry?"

"Last night, after I rode in. I then took a room at Miss Bessy's."

"And you haven't seen Destry since then?"

"No. Why, what's happened?"

"We don't know. He's disappeared. I know he often gets drunk and wanders off, but this is different. One of the men found his horse. No sign of Destry ... but there was blood and that makes me concerned."

"If you're looking at me, I can tell you, I was in my room all night and this morning took breakfast at the guesthouse. You can verify what I say with Miss Bessy."

"I intend to, mister."

"The name's Reece. I'm ex-army, making my way to California to visit my sister."

"Start a new life?"

"In a way. I've had a belly-full of war and fighting, that's for sure. Don't know why you need to know all this but—"

"It's my job to know, mister. This is a small town, but it has a history. A none too pleasant one at that. Let's take a walk back to the guesthouse and on the way, we'll have a cup of coffee at Clapham's." He caught Hanson's glare. "There'll be a search party leaving shortly, Hanson. You can bring along your gun."

"We go to the mine?"

Fieyn shrugged. "It'll be a good place to start if any are willing to go there."

"Most won't."

"True. What about you?"

"If needs be."

"All right. After Mr Reece and I have had a little parlay, we can go up there together. Are you ready, Mr Reece?"

Nodding, Reece shot a glance towards Hanson. "I'll drop off the bridle later on."

"You do that."

They moved down the street, Reece ignoring the looks of the townsfolk milling around, noting that the sheriff walked with a pronounced limp. Mounting the steps up to the little coffee-house, Fieyn winced as he put pressure on his knee. He noticed Reece's questioning stare. "Shot at Shiloh. Damn ball is still in there. Some fancy British doctor said it may well kill me, even now, if I don't get it out."

"Why don't you?"

24

"I don't trust doctors much, Mister. Saw enough butchery during the War. Especially at Shiloh."

"That was one bloody day, Sheriff."

"Indeed, it was. You were there?"

"Not there. But plenty of other places."

They stood, regarding one another with a kind of grudging respect for a few moments before Fieyn turned away and pushed open the door, a tiny bell tinkling above it. There was nobody else inside. Six tables were arranged randomly around the interior, lace tablecloths covering each one. From behind the small counter, there was a bead curtain, and it was through this that a short, grey-haired woman appeared. Setting eyes on Fieyn, she grew agitated. "Oh Lordy, Sheriff, I do hope this man is not—"

"Don't you concern yourself none, Mrs Clapham. This gentleman and I are only here for a coffee and a little powwow."

Without a word, the woman went behind the counter to prepare the coffee. Meanwhile, Fieyn stretched back in his chair. He took out a silver pocket-watch from his waistcoat, the chain stretching across his midriff, and looked at it. "Got this from a Swiss fella as I lay in the field-dressing station. With his dying breath, he said, 'It'll never lose its time'. You know what," he snapped the lid shut and put it away, "it never has."

"A powwow you said," said Reece, not in the least impressed. "About what?"

"Name. That's first off. What is it?"

"Reece."

"Well, *Mister* Reece, how did Destry appear when you spoke with him? I mean, was he agitated, frightened, what?"

"None of those things. I'd only just met him, of course, but as far as I could see, there wasn't anything out of the ordinary about his demeanor."

"His demeanor," Fieyn repeated and nodded his head. "You're an educated man, Mr Reece. Kansas you said you're from. Not sure if I've ever met anyone from Kansas. Are people usually educated from that great city?"

"I ain't from Kansas City," said Reece. "I'm from the *state*. A little settlement not far from the Cimarron river is where I was born. In the middle of a great storm so my ma was always happy to tell me."

"Never heard of it."

"No reason why you should as it ain't got no name as yet. I guess it might have once more people settle there."

"You never go back?"

Reece shook his head then folded his arms as Mrs Clapham arrived with the coffee. She placed the cups and pot in the center of the small table. "Cream?"

"You betcha," said Fieyn, rubbing his hands with expectation. "Mrs Clapham here makes the finest coffee for many a long mile."

Slightly reddening along her jawline, Mrs Clapham gave a suppressed giggle, turned, and flounced away, returning in a few seconds with a tiny pot of cream. She turned to Reece. "You planning on staying another night at Bessy's?"

"Seems like every soul in this place knows my business," said Reece, leaning forward to take up the coffee that Fieyn had poured for him.

"I'll take it that's a no then," said the little white-haired woman before she turned and went through the bead curtain to the rear.

"People are naturally curious here, Reece," said Fieyn. "We don't get many people passing through."

"I'm not surprised. Not exactly the most welcoming of folk. No one gave me a welcome as I went to the blacksmith. Miss Bessy told me it was run by a man called Noah Barton but that wasn't the one who—"

"Barton died some years ago. The business name just stuck is all. Hanson took it over when he arrived here from Sweden."

Reece nodded. "He nigh-on accused me of trying to settle in with Miss Bessy." He sipped his coffee and pulled a face. "The

26

best you say? You clearly ain't been to many other places, Sheriff."

Fieyn chuckled. "I settled here about five years ago." He frowned, lapsing into silence for a moment, "Maybe more. Damn it, I don't know where the years go. I do not need to go anyplace else. It's a good town, with good people. You shouldn't take notice of Hanson. He's gruff, unpleasant at times, but he has a good soul. People here are easily spooked, Reece. Best to remember that."

"No need to remember anything, Sheriff. Once my bridle is fixed, I'll be moving on."

"I'd prefer if you stayed around," he watched Reece over the brim of his coffee cup as he drank. "Until we find out what's happened to Destry."

Reece shrugged. "Why do you place so much importance on him if you don't mind me asking?"

"He's an important figure in our community, Reece. He's virtually bankrolled every small business there is around here. This town wouldn't be what it is if it weren't for Brownlow Destry."

"So, he's rich?"

"Richest man in these parts."

"Then why does he work at the livery?"

"He loves horses," said Fieyn before his face split into a wide grin, "and it keeps him away from Miss Bessy."

"I find that hard to believe. She's a mighty fine-looking woman."

"That she is but Destry is a drunk and she's been known to lock him out of the house for nights on end. True, they were once sweet for each other, but you know how things can get ... tarnished, let's say." He finished his coffee and poured himself another cup. "He's had his share of liaisons with pretty girls, Reece. There's Saint Francine's a little ways out of town. It's what could be loosely termed a place of ill-repute. He frequents it three or four nights a week. A little while ago, he got himself

STUART G YATES

mixed up with a little vixen called Lizzie Coombs. She took his
money, rode off into the night, and ..." He drank again and stared
into his cup. "We found her, about a mile or so out of town.
She'd had her head caved in. There was no evidence to point to
Destry, but folks knew it was him. Miss Bessy threw him out and
he took to sleeping at the livery. That's where he spends most of
his time now, drinking himself to death."

"He sounds like an idiot. Turning away from a woman like
Miss Bessy ... He must be either blind or stupid."

"He's sick," said Fieyn. "That's what he is."

"Sick?"

"Could be the drink, I guess. He mixes his whisky with water
from the local stream. It's as white as milk. Maybe that has
something to do with it, who knows?"

"And now he's missing. Could it be revenge? For Lizzie, I
mean?"

"Maybe. She had a lot of admirers, that's for sure. But it more
than likely has something to do with the mine."

"The mine? I don't get you. A gold mine?"

Fieyn nodded. "That's how some folks think the town got its
name. Man name of White came here back in the forties, found
gold close to the river. It's dried up now, but once I guess it must
have flowed through these parts. All that's left is a trickling little
stream. White, he employed some local Indians and they dug
out a mine. They found something other than gold."

Reece frowned. "Silver? Lead maybe?"

Fieyn shook his head and grew more serious than Reece had
noted before now. "Nope. Nothing metal. Nothing mineral.
Nothing *natural*. The Indians got spooked and ran. *Ran*. White,
he settled here. Others came along as it was the main trail to the
West and the Territories. No mention was ever made of the
mine and it fell into disrepair. Then, recently, things took a turn
for the worse."

The air grew chill. Fieyn turned to look towards the small
window next to the main entrance of the coffee-house. Behind

28

the counter, Mrs Clapham stopped what she was doing, folded up a tea cloth, and came to join the two men. She drew up a chair and sat. "Mr Reece, is that your name?"

"I prefer just Reece, ma'am."

She gave him a withering look. "I guess that's your prerogative, although I don't like it. The incident the sheriff refers to occurred during the War. You know much about the War, *Mister Reece?*"

"More than I care to remember."

"I see. Well then, you'd have heard the term renegades? Bushwhackers?"

"Jayhawkers?" put in Fieyn, his icy gaze settling unblinkingly on Reece.

"I have heard all those terms, yes." Reece did not flinch. He sat, waited, face set hard. "What of them?"

"A bunch of them came riding in here," continued Mrs Clapham. "They shot up the town before Mr Destry took it upon himself to fight it out with them."

"This was before my time, Reece," said Fieyn. "Story goes that Destry rounded up a bunch of local toughs, drove the bushwhackers out of town and cornered them near the mine."

"There was a gunfight," said Mrs Clapham. Her voice held no emotion, but Reece noted how her hands shook as she brought one to her mouth. She saw his look, quickly put her hands on the table and clamped them together. "From that point on, the story gets a little fuzzy."

Frowning, Reece looked from one to the other. "I don't quite get your drift, ma'am. Fuzzy in what way?"

"They disappeared," said Fieyn.

"The bushwhackers?"

"All of 'em. Except of course Destry. He took to his bed and was not seen for almost a week."

"The drink," said Mrs Clapham. "It became his master from then on."

"So, what you're saying is, in the gunfight, everyone was

killed, save for Destry?"

"No," said the old woman, "what I'm saying is *nobody knows* what happened, Mister Reece. And Destry, he ain't ever said."

"And nobody has gone to check?"

She leaned forward, so close Reece could count the pores on her nose. "Mr Reece, we don't go up there. We don't even talk about it."

"But we have to now," said Fieyn solemnly, "to check on Destry. See if he might be up there."

Mrs Clapham released a sharp sigh. "If you want my opinion, Sheriff, you'll steer well clear of that place. You know why."

"I do. But his horse was found close by. It stands to reason he's there."

"I don't get any of this," said Reece, picking up the pot to pour himself more coffee. Finding it empty, he put it down again and turned it around. "Seems to me all of this is old suspicion, probably Indian in nature that keeps people away. Might it not be more accurate to consider it's because of the gold that's still in there?"

Mrs Clapham nodded. "That's how Destry got rich, so the story goes. Maybe he's found another lode and has kept it secret? Someone got to him, forced him to show them where it is, and then they murdered him."

"Could be," said Fieyn.

"Or it could be a whole lot more sinister than any of that," said Mrs Clapham and stood up. "I've said my bit and that's that. Sheriff, don't go there." She turned and left.

The two men sat in silence, the old lady's words sinking deep.

"We'll go to the livery first," said Fieyn at last, "then you can ride up to the mine with me and the others."

"This ain't got nothing to do with me, Sheriff."

"It's got *everything* to do with you, Reece. I think you've got a lot more explaining to do before this whole sorry mess is sorted out. Like, why you're here."

"I told you, I'm—"

"*Passing through* ... Yeah, you said. What I need to know is the *true* reason."

He stood and stared. Reece stared back before blowing out a loud sigh. He moved in step behind the sheriff and together they walked through the town towards the livery.

CHAPTER SIX

The door creaked open, the rusted hinges making such a screech it set your teeth on edge. Destry, huddled up in the corner, turned and squinted towards the daylight framing the figure standing there. It was cold in that old, dilapidated shack but Destry was not trembling because of that. It was fear that took him in its much colder grip.

"So," said the man stepping inside, "feel much like talking yet?"

Destry struggled to sit up. His wrists and ankles were tightly bound with leather thongs which bit ever deeper into his flesh every time he moved. "Only to tell you to go to Hell."

"Ah, that's unfortunate." The man moved across the room. There was a rickety table leaning against the far wall. Precariously balanced on three legs, the fourth corner propped up with a stack of wood pieces, it appeared to be in imminent danger of collapse. Nevertheless, the man placed a small canvas bag on its surface and opened it. Smiling, he rummaged inside and produced a hunk of bread, a small hip flask, and a few slices of cold meat. "You see, if you were nice to me, I might share some of this food with you." He tore off a piece of bread and popped it into his mouth. "Mmmm, fresh and delicious." He turned, smiling as he munched, and took a slug of whatever the flask contained. Smacking his lips, he crammed a slice of meat between his teeth. "Sure you won't join me?"

Destry, unable to prevent his stomach from rumbling or his mouth from salivating, turned away, snarling, "Damn your hide."

"All you need do is sign this," said the man, bringing out a folded piece of paper. He opened it, sucked grease from his fingers, and smoothed the paper out on the table. "You can write, I assume?"

"I ain't signing anything," Destry said without looking at his tormentor.

"Oh, deary me," said the man. He moved with the grace of a big cat and landed a tremendous right punch across Destry's jaw, hurling the old man against the wall with such power that the entire shack shuddered.

Taking him by the throat, the man lifted Destry off his feet, jutted his face forward, and slammed his left fist into the old man's midriff. Gushing out a blast of air, Destry buckled and went limp, retching for breath. The man stepped back and shoved Destry away with a booted foot.

"I'll continue with my breakfast," said the man, slightly out of breath, "so as to give you a little moment to reflect on what your correct response oughtta be."

Moaning, Destry rolled over onto his side and sucked in rasping breaths with a great deal of difficulty, coughing hoarsely with each one.

"Don't you go dying on me, old man. My employer wants the rights to your mine. Make it all legal like. After you've signed, you can go back home to your lovely wife." He chuckled to himself. "She really is a fine woman. Skin as smooth as porcelain, thighs so strong." He took a longer drink from the hipflask. "If you understand my meaning."

"I'll kill you, you bastard," wheezed Destry.

"Oh? And when are you proposing on doing that?" He stepped closer and got down on his haunches, taking another sip from the flask. "Listen, this is how it's gonna be. I'll go back into town, reacquaint myself with Miss Bessy, then come back with more food. By then I reckon you'll be a little more amenable to my demands." He sniggered. "Just like she is."

"I'll die before I sign that paper."

"Well," the man closed the flask and dropped it into his pocket. From inside his coat, he brought out a Wells Fargo revolver and pressed the barrel against Destry's head, "I assure you, you *will* die if you don't put your name on that document. The only thing you need to consider is the nature of your death. I can make it slow and painful, so bad that you'll be begging me to put a bullet in your brain." He pushed the old man's head away with the gun. "But I won't. I'll just keep going. Death of a thousand-cuts is what the Chinese call it."

Destry brought his head up and gaped. "What?"

The man's grin broadened and put away the gun. "Yeah, that's right. Heard about it from a Chinese coolie when I was working in New York. Pieces of your skin is sliced off, one by one. Legs, arms, body. Never enough to kill you outright, but as the pain increases and the blood rushes out of you, you'll eventually die. Real slow. Real painful." Laughing, he stood up, returned to the table, and crammed his mouth with more bread and meat. "That's what I'll do to you, old man, *if* you don't sign. I'll be back later on. Enjoy the smell of this food." He turned away from the table and stepped towards the entrance.

Destry's voice trembled when he managed, "I'll not do it."

"Oh, I think you will."

The man turned and took out the flask. Raising it, he drained its contents in a series of loud gulps before stepping outside and closing the door firmly behind him.

Destry slumped forward, hopelessness engulfing him, and broke down in despair.

CHAPTER SEVEN

"Who was that man?" asked Henry as he emerged from the kitchen. His employer, Richard Quince, was helping himself to a cup of coffee from the pot on the large table.

"His name's Bourne. He's here to do me a little job."

"Hell, Mr Quince, anything you need doing me and the boys can—"

"No, Henry. That's just it. I don't want you or the boys getting involved. You've already introduced yourself to that stranger and that was unfortunate. I don't want any of us – you, me, the boys – being associated with anything that might happen."

"What does that mean?"

"It means, you keep out of it. I don't want you going back to town and talking to that stranger again, you understand?"

"Sure I do, but—"

"There ain't no 'buts' about it, Henry." Smiling, he pointed towards Henry's crotch. "You should tidy yourself up before you speak to me, Henry."

"Wha—?" He looked down, saw his flies were undone, and hastily buttoned them up, his face growing crimson.

"She's a pretty little thing that Eva," said Quince, finishing his coffee, "so I don't blame you."

"Mr Quince, I—"

"Don't concern yourself with it, Henry. My advice would be to take her to your room and enjoy her for the next few days."

Henry, ruffled and unsure where to put his face, looked at the floor and kicked his feet together. "Darn it, Mr Quince, I'm sorry if I have—"

"Henry, I said forget about it. Things might get somewhat heated over in town. I don't want any suspicions falling on anyone from here. That's why I don't want you or any of the men leaving the ranch. Not until Mr Bourne returns with his job accomplished."

"Job?"

"The less you know, the less you can tell. That's the way it's gonna be, Henry, so you might as well get used to it. For the time being at least."

"That's not the problem, Mr Quince."

Quince stopped in the process of lifting his coffee cup. His face froze. Something in Henry's tone caused a prickling of the skin around the nape of his neck. "What does that mean, Henry?"

"Frank. I don't think he took too kindly to the stranger's way of speaking. He rode out this morning to have a few words with him himself."

Quince stared, not quite able to believe what Henry was saying. "Let us hope and pray that he doesn't get up to any mischief that involves Bourne, that's all I can say."

"I'm sure he won't." He readjusted his belt. "Maybe I could go and bring him back?"

"No. You do as I say. Make sure none of the men goes to town, you get me."

Henry hesitated a moment before speaking. "I get you."

"Good." He carefully put the cup onto the table. "Something in your voices tells me you have something else to say, Henry."

"Yeah, I do." Henry swallowed hard and looked askance towards the kitchen door. Eva stood there, watching. She looked worried. Despite this, she gave him a nod of encouragement.

"Well spit it out why don't you!"

"I don't rightly know how to say this, Mr Quince ..." Henry turned again towards Quince. "None of us knew what your plans were, Mr Quince. If you'd only told us, then perhaps ..."

"Just say what you gotta say, Henry."

Henry took a deep breath to steady himself. "The Weasel and Otis went with him."

Groaning, Quince, sinking within himself, slid down the chair and turned a ghastly shade of grey.

CHAPTER EIGHT

L eading his old nag by foot through the woods running along the base of the mountain range, Ezra Soames wished, not for the first time, that he was not alone. But then again, he thought, sniffing the air loudly, he stank like a rotting clam, rank enough to push any companions far away. The urge to stop, change his shirt, perhaps wash in the river was strong. However, the river, he reminded himself, was all dried up now. No rain had fallen for a good few years. The last time he was here, with the rest of them, on a jaunt to shoot up the town and feast upon the flesh of its women, it had been not much bigger than a trickle. Not even a stream. He'd washed himself after his horse had thrown him when it stumbled over a hidden tree root. He'd landed so hard he'd busted his arm. The others laughed and went on their way, leaving him with powder and ball but no food. He hated them at that moment. Now, looking at the ground as he led his old mare by the reins, he wasn't about to make the same mistake twice. Half a dozen years had elapsed since that fateful day. The day he'd managed to make his way to the next town and a doctor who knew what he was doing. His erstwhile friends continued on their way. He heard the gunshots. The screams. He didn't look back. A bad feeling gnawed away at him and had continued all these years. But then, times being so hard, Jesse James taking the right road, he'd decided to try his luck once more in this little town. He knew of the mine. He knew about the gold. What he didn't know, had *never* known, was what had befallen his companions. Now, so close again, he felt he was within an ace of discovering the truth.

He did not feel good about that.

Coming out of the tree line, he saw the man in the Derby hat pulling the door to a broken-down old shack closed with unnecessary force. The entire building appeared to shake. Ezra, dropping to his knees, watched. The old shack, perhaps a small bunkhouse for the mineworkers, might contain something other than tools. Clues, perhaps. A map. Weighing scales. Evidence of gold...

Licking his lips, Ezra waited until the man in the Derby mounted up and rode away. He waited until he was certain the man was not coming back and led his horse cautiously down the slight incline towards the shack. He tied up the nag. Rolling his shoulders, he drew his revolver. He eased back the hammer, scanning the surroundings. The area was open, the ground nothing but scrub, topsoil long blown away. Already so very dry, this would be desert given another decade or so. He looked to the sky. If he knew about such things, he might have seen the distant gathering of black clouds and estimated that rain was coming. Perhaps the idea of the area transforming into desert was to be some way off.

Turning his thoughts away from such notions, he wondered if the gang had stopped this way. Perhaps they knew about the mine even back then. That Nathan, their elected leader, already had wind of what lay on the other side of the gulch. Was his plan to get the gang to shoot up the town, ride up to this cruel, desolate place and help himself to the gold before killing off the rest of them? Could he be so calculating? The man was a vicious killer, that was for sure, but did he have the intelligence to come up with such a scheme? Ezra doubted it. But then, having no word from any of them, that was strange. Given that the Federal government was tracking down and eliminating any vestiges of renegade gangs, Ezra felt sure he would have heard something. Anything. Not even a whisper, however, came his way. All the news centered on Jesse and that wastrel Cole Younger. Ezra knew them both. Had ridden with them in the old days. Despised them back then, despised them now.

A groan trickled from within the shack and Ezra started, jumped back, alert, tense, gun ready.

It came again, sounding like an animal in pain, he thought. Or a man. Taking his time, he looked around him before putting his ear to the thin, warped door. He closed his eyes. Listened.

It was not an animal. As clear as day, the strangulated sound was that of a man.

CHAPTER NINE

B efore reaching the livery, Reece made a short detour to the guesthouse. Fieyn gave him a look but didn't attempt to stop him. Instead, he waited outside whilst Reece went through the door.

It was cool in the tiny reception room. The slight aroma of home cooking wafted from the rear of the building. Moving directly to the small desk, he picked up the tiny brass bell and rang it.

He waited.

Nothing stirred and Reece went through the door that led, he believed, to the kitchen area.

Here, the smell of home-cooking filled a compact room. A well-scrubbed table, laden with plates, cups, and bowls, dominated the middle part whilst against the far wall a solid farmhouse range stood. There was a large pot on the stovetop, bubbling loudly away. Reece lifted the lid and chanced a peek inside. Potatoes and carrots fought for control within the simmering stew, an occasional piece of celery making it to the top before slipping down into the depths once more. It smelled delicious and Reece fought down the urge to take a spoon and taste a mouthful of the stew.

A soft footfall caused him to spin around in a half-crouch, hand instinctively going for his handgun.

"Goodness, Mr Reece, you're jumpy!"

It was Miss Bessy, standing with her hands in front of her, clenching a tattered dishtowel, face glistening with perspiration, an errant lock of hair falling across her face. She was stunningly beautiful. Catching his breath, for a moment, Reece could hardly breathe.

Her eyes were huge, drinking him in, and her soft mouth parted, the words trickling out like warm honey, "Are you all right?"

She stepped closer. Her perfume overpowered even the homely smell of cooking and Reece closed his eyes for a moment, heart-swelling, tongue growing thick in his mouth. "Yes," he managed to say at last.

Her hand brushed along his arm. "Are you sure?"

He stared at her fingers, lingering there against his bicep, and he wanted the moment to last forever.

Gradually, he summoned the strength to reveal to her the news about her husband. His fingers curled around hers. "I have some bad news, Miss Bessy."

Her face did not reveal any change in expression, subtle or otherwise. "Is it Destry?"

"Perhaps we could step inside your parlor? Somewhere a little more ... comfortable?"

Without a word, she led him through the door into an even smaller, chintz dominated room. Soft flower-patterned fabric covered not only the sofa and armchair but the walls as well. A small French window led into a square, high-walled yard where washing, moving gently in the breeze, hung from a clothesline. If it wasn't for the heavy news he had to convey, Reece felt this was a place to relax, to wallow in comfort and contentment.

"So, tell me what has happened, Mr Reece," she said, sitting down on the sofa. She gestured for him to settle beside her. He did so. Her close proximity stirred a myriad of emotions, some of which he'd come to believe were no longer available to him. She reached over and squeezed his hand. "I promise you, I will not overreact or become hysterical, whatever it is you have to tell me."

He stared at her hand covering his own, felt the press of her thigh against his and wished for another life, one in which he and Bessy would share endless days and loving nights, wrapped around one another.

"He's disappeared," he said without raising his eyes.

"That's nothing new," she said. "He often goes off on a drunk, sometimes for days."

"No, this is different. They found his horse." His face came up at last and he held her stare. "They found blood too."

She paled at that, took back her hand and stared into the distance, perhaps a trace of a tear developing in the corner of the eye closest to him. "Where?" She turned to him again. "Where did they find the horse?"

"On the road to the old mine."

Her mouth parted. A tiny shiver ran through her. "The mine?"

Nodding, Reece resisted the urge to take her in his arms, to hold her close, reassuring her. His heart thumped in his chest. He could not remember being this close to a woman who was so delicious.

"But he *never* goes to the mine. Never. At least ..." She forced a smile. "It's not a place people like to go anywhere near, Mr Reece."

Reece shrugged. "I don't think anyone knows exactly where he has gone, just that the horse was on the road to the mine." He shifted position, trying hard to keep the concern out of his voice. "Why wouldn't he go there, Bessy?"

Producing a small, silk handkerchief from her sleeve, she dabbed her eyes with it, sniffing loudly. "Don't you already know?"

"No. how could I? I've only just arrived in town."

"I know. But *why*, Mr Reece? Why are you here?"

"Passing through. That's all. I have a sister, over in California. That's where I'm heading."

"Are you sure there's no other reason?"

"Of course there isn't. Why? Should there be?"

He wiped her nose with the handkerchief. "I'd like to believe you, I truly would. Mr Bourne said much the same thing."

"Bourne? What's he got to do with this?"

"Nothing, as far as I know. He was kind to me, that is all. Destry … he often fails to come home, spending his time at the livery, avoiding me."

Reece stared but remained silent. He suspected Bourne's act of kindness was very much physical in nature. "Why would he want to avoid you, Bessy? I …" He wanted to tell her that if any man who avoided her was either because he was blind, or mad. But he didn't. Instead, he wrung his hands and waited for her to answer.

"You know about the men who came here, no doubt? During the war? Renegades they were, not soldiers. Desperate men, violent, full of hate. Confederate bushwhackers."

"Yes, the sheriff told me some of the background …"

"Yes. I'm sure he did. And you'll also know that my husband drove them out of town. They made a last stand at the mine. A gunfight… When Destry came back from that he was not the same. He was changed. You understand me?"

"He took to drinking."

"More than that. He was a different person, Mr Reece. He was not the man I knew, the man I loved. He would drink and rage, his words like knives driving deep into my heart. Such hateful, terrible words."

"He hit you?"

Her head came around. "No. Never that. But he may as well have. He'd disappear for days on end. I knew where he was. He would visit that damned woman and he'd come back stinking of drink … and her cheap perfume. He'd clamber into bed next to me, his hands all over me and I'd scream at him and ..." She broke down, the tears coming hard and fast. Bent double, the handkerchief covering her eyes, she wailed and spluttered. "Damn him for what he did, for what he'd become."

Reece sat and waited, struggling to keep his impatience at bay.

Perhaps catching his mood, she sat up, recovering something of her natural composure. "Apologies, Mr Reece. I do not weep for my husband, but for the promise my life once held. One of happiness, despite the absence of children." A darkness fell over her features. "I cannot have children, Mr Reece. Even though I have never had any control over that, it is my one big regret. When Destry changed into the man I no longer recognized, it seemed to amplify those regrets and a wedge was driven between us."

"But why did he change? What had happened to make him into somebody so different?"

She shrugged. "Something happened in that mine, Mr Reece. Something dark, something terrifying. Destry knew old man White, had met him years before we were married. I do not know what passed between them but Destry ingratiated himself with White and the old man repaid him with a map of the mine and gold. Enough gold, Mr Reece to enable him to purchase this little guesthouse, to make our lives comfortable. Even when war broke out, we kept the business moving. And now, now it simply ticks over. Just about."

"And Destry has the livery."

She gave a short, scoffing laugh. "Yes. He has his bolt hole. A place where he can drink and debauch himself with women like Lizzie Coombs."

Reece stared into the open fireplace. It looked as if it been dead for a long time, not unlike Bessy's marriage, he mused. A sham. A performance.

"If you must go up there," she said, squeezing his hand again, "promise me you will not go inside."

"What if he's in there?"

"He won't be. When White died, Destry went to the mine to see if he could find more gold. He had the map, you see. White's map. But the only thing he came back with were nightmares. After those bushwhackers made their last stand there, he boarded up the entrance and made it impenetrable."

"What, he buried them inside? All of them?"

"I doubt their demise had much to do with Destry and the others." Her eyes closed. "It had to do with what was in there, Mr Reece, and whilst he still had his wits about him, he made sure that what was in there stayed in there. Deep in the ground."

"It's haunted, is that it? Ghosts and spirits and the like?"

"Not ghosts, Mr Reece. Something far worse." She gave his hand a last squeeze before she stood up. "Demons."

CHAPTER TEN

G athering himself, Ezra drew his pistol and eased back the hammer. He held his breath, counted to three, and, putting his shoulder against the flimsy entrance, smashed through the door.

There came a frightened yelp from the far corner. Taking a moment to allow his eyes to adjust to the gloom, Ezra picked out the shape of a man cowering against the wall.

"It's all right," he said, putting his gun away. He took a step forward. The man yelped again. "I ain't gonna hurt you."

"It's too late," the man said, his voice like that of a terrified child, high-pitched, brittle at the edges. "You can't make me. You can't ..."

"Can't make you what?"

The light coming through the door made little impression on the gloom, but it was sufficient enough for Ezra to see an oil lamp set upon a sideboard, ancient and warped. He went to it, searched for matches, and found some in one of the cabinet's drawers. He was surprised when one readily flared up. He set the flame to the lamp's wick and adjusted it as the glass bowl glowed with a reassuring red warmth. Turning, he raised the lamp in his hand and moved it from side to side in a slow, wide arc, illuminating the darker recesses of the broken-down old shack.

"What is this place," he mumbled to himself. There were broken pieces of furniture littering the floor, but other items as well. A rusted cash register, sets of scales, the weights of varying sizes, strewn at every angle. There were broken-backed ledgers too. Empty, dark encrusted ink bottles, withered quills. The desk upon which all of this once stood, was a shattered mess, pushed into the opposite corner.

"It's an assayer's office," he said, shaking his head. "Or what once was."

The man groaned.

Ezra stepped closer, raising the lamp, bathing the huddled figure in its light. Black, frightened eyes turned towards the glow and Ezra got down on his haunches. "Who left you in here?"

"Please," said the man, a horrible rattle coming from his throat, "I need water. Please."

Ezra shot a glance towards the door. His water canteen hung from his saddle and he went to move when the man groaned, "Under the table. There's a gourd. Please."

Ezra quickly delved under the old table and found the goatskin gourd there. He pulled out the stopper, took a sniff and wrinkled up his nose. "What the hell ..."

"Just give me some."

Ezra obliged, tipping the gourd to the man's lips. He took long gulps, gasping when he'd finished. Ezra sniffed at the contents again.

"Take some," said the man, "it'll do you a power of good."

Tentatively, Ezra took a mouthful. Surprised at how sweet it tasted, he took a longer draught.

"You must leave this place," said the man urgently. "He'll be back and then ..."

Ezra nodded. "I saw him ride off. Who is he?"

"He's ..." He turned his body, bringing up his tied hands. "Cut me loose, please. I beg you. Then we can get out of here before ... Before it's too late."

"He won't be back for a while, I shouldn't reckon."

The man shook his hands. "It's not only him we need to be wary of ... We're close. Close to the mine. We can't stay here. We must go, please. Please." The shaking of his hands grew more desperate.

Ezra rocked back on his heels. "There's gold, ain't there. In the mine. I know it. That fella, with the Derby, that's where he's gone, I reckon. And you? Who are you?"

"It doesn't matter. Untie me, please."

"When you tell me what I want to know. Not before."

The man collapsed within himself, arms dropping, chin falling to his chest. "Damn you. You don't know anything. Just like him, just like him. Fools. All of you, fools." His face came up, suddenly alert, energised. "There ain't no gold, don't you get it? White, he found a little, but not so much. The rest is legend. Nothing to do with riches at all, only death. You understand? Death awaits us all in that mine. I knows it, I've seen it. I've faced what it is that lies in there, buried deep. Those injuns, they knew it and they ran. Ran for their lives. And so should we. I promise you. Run." He sat up, thrusting out his hands again. "Cut me loose, for the love of God, before it's too late ..."

"Mister, I don't know in the name of all that's holy what you is talking about but it all sounds crazy to me." He stood up and stepped away.

"No! Please, cut me loose. We can go back to town, tell the sheriff, end all of this once and for all."

"There'll be no end to it until I get my hands on that gold, mister. I knows you is lying, lying to keep me away."

"Dear Christ, that isn't it! Please, just untie me and we'll ride out of here. I'll tell you everything. The truth. The reality."

"Reality? Mister, I don't think you know the meaning of the word."

"But I do! Listen, please, just cut me loose and I'll tell you everything. We led 'em up here, you see. Those renegades, those bushwhackers. We cornered 'em here and they ran into the mine. It's nothing more than a hole in the ground, you see. Dug out by White all those years ago, but they managed to get inside, and we followed 'em in and that's when the shooting started. And when we—"

"Just wait a goddamned minute," hissed Ezra, drawing his pistol. "Bushwhackers? You fought bushwhackers up here?"

"Years ago. Just as the War was ending, they came here. We drove 'em out of town, and it was here that they—"

"Nathan? Nathan Kelly and his men? That's who you mean, ain't it." He sprang forward, growling, the gun barrel jabbing into the old man's forehead. "It was Nathan you shot up here? In this god-forsaken place? That was *you.*"

"Oh, sweet Jesus," the old man blabbed, pushing himself hard against the wall, "we had no choice. They came here, shooting everything up, and we chased 'em out of town, followed 'em up here and ... Oh God, don't you understand, don't you see? They holed themselves up in the mine and then ... Then ..." He broke down, body consumed by violent sobs. His words were now a garbled mess.

Ezra, breathing hard and fast, stepped away. "You murdered 'em, didn't you? Every one of 'em. And now you want it all to stay a secret. What you did. That's it, ain't it? Damn your hide, *answer me!*" He lashed out with his boot, catching the old man under the jawline, smashing him over onto his side. Shaking, consumed by a red wave of anger, Ezra rammed the gun into the man's shattered face. He was barely conscious, skin broken around his chin, blood breaking out as the swelling rapidly engulfed his mouth and lips. "I should kill you now, you bastard."

"All right," the man whimpered, "I'll tell you, just please don't kill me."

"Tell me what, you piece of filth?" He pressed the gun harder still and pulled back the hammer. "I'll shoot you dead like the dog that you are!"

"*Please!*" The man rolled away, tied hands covering his head as best he could. "I'll tell you. The truth." He drew a deep, rattling breath, and turned his face towards Ezra. "The truth is there's gold there. Freshly dug."

"Gold? I knew it – I just knew it! How much gold is in there?"

"Lots. There's tools up there, tools I was using before that sonofabitch, the one you saw, ambushed me. I didn't tell him about the gold, not a word."

"So why has he left you here?"

"I told him of the map I made, you see. I have it back in town and he's gone to fetch it."

"Is there a map?"

"Yes, of course there is ... but you don't need it because the gold I extracted, it's just there, a little way into the entrance. I didn't tell him that. I thought I could get myself free while he was away, get ready for him. Kill him."

"Jeez," said Ezra, stepping away again. "You really are a piece of work, ain't yeh."

"I don't wanna die, mister. Please, just set me free, I'm begging you."

Shaking his head, Ezra scooped up the lamp and placed it once more upon the sideboard. "To hell with you," he said and took another drink before throwing the now empty gourd into the corner. He turned towards the door.

"No! No, you can't leave me in here. For the love of God!"

"I'll leave you with the light, but that's all. When your friend comes back you can tell him who was here, but by then I'll be well on my way. With the gold."

Releasing a bout of harsh, forced, and mocking laughter, Ezra returned outside, the sound of the old man's desperate wailing ringing out across the open countryside.

Going to his horse, Ezra mused that the man's sobbing was the only sound to be heard. There were no birds here. Nothing. As if the very life had been sucked out of everything. Despite the lure of the gold, Ezra shivered, mounted up, and headed deeper into the mountainside.

CHAPTER ELEVEN

Reece found Sheriff Fieyn leaning against the wall of the town drug store, rolling himself a cigarette. He blew out a loud sigh as Reece approached. "Thought you'd skedaddled the time it's taken you. Where the hell you been?"

Reece shrugged. "Talking."

It was clear in Fieyn's expression that he was not best pleased. "It ain't none of my business, Reece, but—"

"Yeah, you said it, Sheriff, so let's just leave it right there, all right?"

"Fair enough."

With a brief nod, Fieyn moved away towards the livery stables, with Reece falling in alongside.

There was little sign of a break-in as the two men searched through the small office. Nothing they discovered suggested that Destry had left either abruptly or against his will. Indeed, the opposite seemed to be the case, with ledgers and other paperwork neatly put away. Trying the safe, Reece discovered it to be locked.

"What is it you're hoping to find?" asked the sheriff from the other side of the room. He was in the process of opening a bottle and smelling its contents.

Reece got down on his knees and tried turning the solid lock handle a few times. "Bessy said something about a map."

"As far as I know," said Fieyn, finding a glass, blowing into it, then filling it with the dark liquid from inside the bottle, "Old Man White made a sketch map of the mine out of which he dug some gold." He sampled the drink, closed his eyes, and sighed. "My, that has a fine taste. Bourbon." He turned, raising the glass slightly. "Want some?"

"Not right now," said Reece standing up. Hands on hips, he studied the safe intensely. "Why would he need such a safe as this? It's English. Latest model." He reached out and ran his fingers across the embossed makers mark in the center of the steel door. "Chubb, 1841. This would cost a lot of money I think."

"Maybe he has hidden treasure inside." Fieyn chuckled. "Any gold he managed to find or take from White he squandered a long time ago."

"Bessy told me he bought the guesthouse with it."

"Yeah ... but she made no mention of the ranch, I shouldn't wonder. White's ranch. The one Quince now owns. Good land that is, well-watered, fine grazing for his cattle and horses."

"Quince. He owns almost everything around these parts so I hear."

"Almost." Fieyn finished his whisky and put the glass down hard. "Time we went up there, where Destry's horse was found. We might find a clue."

"Why not go straight to the mine?"

Fieyn raised a single eyebrow. "Didn't Bessy tell you about the mine's history, what happened up there?"

"She did but surely you don't believe all that nonsense?"

"Not sure what I believe, Reece. I don't ever go up there. Nor does anyone else."

Nodding, Reece stepped towards the door, gave the safe a final look and went outside. "I'll check on my horse," said Reece as Fieyn came up next to him. "I'd prefer to ride my own, so I need to check she's been well fed and rested."

"I'll meet you in a few moments. Try not to be too long."

Reece tipped his hat and went towards the stables.

———

Fieyn sat in the rocking chair outside the jailhouse. From here he had a good view of the lonely street, a street which seemed strangely unfriendly at that moment. Apart from a group of old men jabbering to one another outside the barbershop, nothing stirred. Trying to shrug off the feeling of impending doom, he failed, the heavy atmosphere pressing in all around, overwhelming him. Perhaps it had to do with that talk of the mine, the wrenching up of memories. He shivered, rolled his shoulders, and went to pull out his tobacco pouch when he realized three toughs were standing in front of him, their faces hard. He recognized them all, shifted position, abandoned his tobacco for now. "Can I help you, boys?

"We're not here to cause trouble, Sheriff," said Frank Trent, one of the ranch hands from the Quince holding.

"It never entered my head to think you were, Frank."

"We're just here to put that stranger in his place," said the one everyone knew as Weasel.

Fieyn groaned. "Now what's that supposed to mean?"

"It means," said Frank, chewing on a good mouthful of tobacco. He ejected a long, brown stream of juice, "we have some unfinished business with that Reece."

"Sod-buster is he," asked Weasel, "a drifter, a good-for-nothing?"

Fieyn raised his eyebrows and allowed his eyes to wander over Weasel's slight frame. "Now, I guess you might know more about that than me, Weasel."

The scrawny little ranch hand made a move for the gun he had stuffed in his waistband. Frank got there first, clamping his hand over Weasels. "Hold on, Weasel. The sheriff don't appear to understand the seriousness of what is occurring here."

"Oh, I understand all right, Frank, I just don't understand what this *unfinished business* you might have with Mr Reece is. I can tell you, what with you all sporting guns, that you is going about this in the wrong way."

"To hell with that, Sheriff," said Frank. "I was affronted. I want an apology at the very least."

"I'm sure if a wrong has been done, Mr Reece will give you that apology. But I know nothing about any of this, boys, and the way you is confronting me here, it ain't good."

"Good or not, you tell us where he is."

"Why? So you can shoot him?"

"We'll shoot you if you don't tell us," said Weasel, shrugging himself free of Frank's restraining hand at last.

The third tough, Otis, gave his companions a frightened look. "Boys, our gripe ain't with the sheriff."

Weasel rounded on his companion. "You shut the hell up, Otis. We is here to settle this matter and that is what will do."

"Seems to me you is blowing this into something much bigger than it needs to be," said Fieyn. "Frank, you don't need to do all this. Back down, return to the ranch, have a few drinks but don't come into my town looking for a fight."

"Your town?" barked Weasel and burst into laughter. "This ain't no more your town than it is mine, you sorry peace of piss. This is Mr Quince's town, and you know it."

"And he sent you, did he?"

"Huh?" Frank stuck his thumbs into his belt and leaned forward a little, "Mr Quince ain't said nothing to anyone of us. You got a hearin' problem, sheriff."

"I ain't deaf if that is what you mean?"

"Maybe I do. You is an old, cranky coot that is for sure, so let me repeat myself — we is here seeking satisfaction from that stranger Reece for the way he spoke to me. I am affronted and I do not take kindly to any man treating me the way he did."

"Like I said, I know nothing about that."

"That don't mean squat. Where is he right now?"

"We'll be going out of town shortly."

"That's not what I asked you, God damn it!"

"It's all I'm gonna give you."

"Like hell." Weasel pulled his gun. "Tell us or I'll splatter your shopfront with your brains."

"*Weasel,*" screeched Otis, "this ain't what we planned."

"Shut up."

Frank stepped forward. "Sheriff, where is he?"

Without taking his eyes from Weasel's gun, Fieyn sighed. "I'll not forget this, Frank."

"Where is he?"

"Livery. Why not meet us there, then we can clear this whole nonsense up? In a *civil* manner."

"I think that's good advice," said Otis quickly.

"Yeah, you would," said Weasel, returning his gun to his waistband. "Why in hell did you come along anyways if you don't have the sand to see it through?"

"Boys," said the sheriff, "let's all just calm down, all right? There ain't no need to make this into something it's not. Let's move on over to the livery and Mr Reece can give you an apology and that'll be that."

"I don't think so," said Frank.

"Oh? You want more? What?"

"I want him to understand he can't talk to me that way."

"So, let's go right back to what I said – what you meanin' to do? Shoot him?"

"Let's leave that for him to decide shall we."

Studying each man with long, lingering looks, the sheriff blew out a breath and slowly stood up. He waggled his finger towards Weasel, "You make sure you keep that gun in your belt, Weasel. I would not advise you to try that trick with Mr Reece."

"Why's that? He some sort of gunfighter?"

The thought, if it had ever crossed any of their minds, now

voiced loud seemed to have a curious effect on them all. Frank, losing some of his former arrogance, went to Weasel, "Just let's see how things go, all right."

Breathing a long sigh, Fieyn stood up, rolled his shoulders, and put away his tobacco pouch. He then led the way to the livery.

It was a short walk. Those few old men stopped what they were doing and watched this curious entourage meandering along the street. The sheriff at the head, with the three toughs a little way behind. They appeared tense, eyes darting this way and that, expectant, alert.

They rounded the corner to find Reece leaning against the timber fencing enclosing the tiny paddock in which his horse stood. He spotted them and weighed up the situation almost immediately, sensing trouble was heading his way.

Sighing, Reece pushed himself from the fence. This was not what he wanted. Since the end of the War, his only wish was to put conflict, anger and hate behind him. Find a new life, a new direction. He'd seen too much death, too much suffering, experienced too much fear. It had dried him out inside, screwed up his emotions, made him hard, grim, indifferent even. He hated what he had become. He hated the look on those men advancing towards him, a look he knew so well. Their hard, brutal faces reminded him of the deprivations he'd endured. The violence he hoped he'd left behind. Resigned, he allowed his right hand to hang loosely by his side and waited.

"Reece," began the sheriff, throwing up his hands, "I'm sorry about this, but—"

"Shut up, you idiot," spat Frank, pushing the sheriff away. "I'm here to clear the air." He widened his stance a little. He wore two guns, tied down at his thighs. As he waited, he chewed furiously on his tobacco.

"What seems to be the problem."

"I don't much like the way you talk, mister. Nor do I like the way you look."

"Not much I can do about that."

"Yeah, well you have a pretty mouth, 'cepting it spews out a lot of nasty sounding words. Like you said to me back at Miss Bessy's. I want you to apologize."

"For what?"

"For what you said."

"Now, that's where you've got me – I don't remember. Tell you what though, why don't I just apologize anyway. How's that." Reece smiled. "I apologize."

"Yeah, yeah," said Otis, growing more nervous with every passing second, "that's it, that's good Mr Reece. Thanks." He went to turn.

"Will you shut up," spat Weasel.

Otis did just that, snapped his head towards Fieyn and said, "Please, Sheriff. Can you tell him?" He looked again at Frank. "Come on Frank, you got what you came for."

Shaking his head, Weasel stepped forward, his hand hovering by his gun. "I don't think so. Ain't that right, Frank."

"Sure is," said Frank. "That ain't no apology."

Reece frowned. "Oh? Then what sort of apology is it you're looking for?"

"The grovelling kind," said Weasel. "The kind where you get down on your knees and beg our forgiveness."

"It won't surprise you boys none if I say ..." And here Reece grinned. Fieyn saw it and recognized, with a jolt, that Reece was actually tempting the toughs to go for their guns. "I won't be doing that."

Perhaps Otis saw it too. He groaned, "Oh my God."

Fieyn went to put his hands out, to ward off some invisible force and try and bring the situation under control.

Frank saw it and frowned.

As for Weasel, he took it for the provocation it undoubtedly was, and he went for his gun.

CHAPTER TWELVE

After coming across the dead horse, he followed the narrow, rutted path into the woods, emerging on the other side to find the air chilly, the sky black with threatening clouds. Before him, a mere hundred paces or so, the mountains soared upwards, their peaks shrouded in grey mist, their sides jagged. Little if any vegetation grew here, the bare rock hard and unforgiving. The entire area hung heavy with foreboding as if the very ground itself formed a natural barrier to further advancement. Beneath him, his horse shied away and, despite his almost constant urging with boots slamming into its side, the animal refused to budge. Dismounting, he looked at it and saw her eyes wide and white with terror. Reluctantly, he led the horse back to the tree line and tied the reins to a low branch. He drew the carbine from its sheath, checked its load, and moved on.

The stony ground crunched beneath his feet, sharp shale unyielding, pressing into the soles of his feet through the leather of his boots. This was an unfriendly place, every rock, every piece of dried, withered tree, every tremble of fleeting breeze seeming to cry out with a warning that he should turn back.

Ezra stopped. A dread feeling of being watched seized him and he scanned his surroundings, senses on high alert.

There was nothing. Even so, he continued to wait and listen until, satisfied, at last, he moved on, but much more cautiously now. Ahead, the remnants of the mine entrance, no longer a tunnel, a landslide of rocks and debris having closed it, possibly forever. As he drew closer, he noted how the rocks here were black, mirroring the darkness beyond perhaps. They glistened with something wet, and he looked to find the source for this but could not. Frowning, he stepped right up to the blocked entrance and ran his hand over the surface of the nearest boulder.

He yelped and sprang back, clutching his hand with his other. It felt as if he'd been burned and he peered at his palm, expecting to see red and blistered skin. He let out a sigh of relief. There were no such blemishes, the flesh unbroken, normal. He looked at the rocks, staring at them with a renewed intensity, almost believing they would erupt into flames at any moment.

But how could that be, he chided himself. They were rocks, nothing more. And yet ...

He took another step closer, much more slowly this time, considering every crevice, every uneven, broken area. Something made these rocks wet, something made them hot. Deep, deep below this mountain, hot, smoldering vents must be spewing out heat from the very bowels of the earth. He'd seen such things before on his journeys west. Geysers, erupting as if by clockwork, sending up huge fountains of vapor, heated from the furnace that raged beneath the surface. Could this be something similar? It had to be.

"Halloo there!"

He sprang round, instinctively bringing up his carbine. It was an ancient, single-shot piece, almost fifty years old, but it could still do its job, especially in his expert hands. He brought the stock to his shoulder and peered down the barrel, moving slowly from left to right, covering the area in a wide arc.

There wasn't anybody there and yet he had heard the voice, he knew that much. Perhaps...

Stepping away from the covered entrance, he turned his gaze to the mountain and there, high on a crest, a figure stood, waving its arms in windmill fashion, rocking from left to right.

Ezra released a strangulated moan and lowered the carbine. The figure was well out of range, but he could tell it was a man. Squat, bow-legged, he must have come from the other side of the mountain and could well be lost.

Turning away, Ezra gave the closed mine entrance one more look. The rocks no longer appeared wet but had become a dull, grey, metal color. He dared not touch them. "Fool, it's your imagination, that's what it is," he said to himself out loud and looked again at the mountain top.

The figure was no longer there. Unease crept up his spine and he screwed up his eyes, pressed his finger and thumb into them, and shook his head. He looked again. Still nothing.

"Halloo there!"

The voice sounded so much closer now. Ezra span around in a half-crouch, the carbine by his waist now. Whoever this was, they were playing games with him.

He gasped.

A man, possibly the same man, stood close to Ezra's horse. He appeared to be shrouded in mist with no facial features discernible despite there being such a short distance between them. The horse appeared unperturbed and continued to munch of grass tufts. That in itself was strange given how spooked the animal was before.

"What do you want, friend?" asked Ezra through gritted teeth. Something wasn't right about any of this. All around him the atmosphere, already chilly, grew perceptively colder, almost as if it were in the grip of winter. He shivered, wishing he'd donned his coat.

Ezra waited. The figure remained silent and unmoving. It no longer moved its arms. It simply stood and watched.

"Friend," said Ezra, unable to keep the rattle from his voice. Fear was slowly rumbling in his guts, icy tendrils spreading upwards and outwards, "I asked you what you want. I'm only here looking and have no designs on anything from these parts. Tell me what you want and I'll—"

A great groaning started up from deep within the ground, like the throaty growl of an enormous dog. Ezra whirred around, terrified that this could be the beginning of an earthquake. He knew such things existed and was well aware of the dangers they possessed.

The sound seemed to be coming from inside the mine. And it was growing as if its owner was advancing from the depths. "What the hell..." Shaking uncontrollably, Ezra decided it was wise to get as far away from this place as he possibly could. He turned.

The figure was no longer there.

And neither was his horse.

CHAPTER THIRTEEN

Moving with an agility that belied his age, Fieyn pistol-whipped Weasel across the back of the head. The scrawny tough screeched and crumpled, releasing his gun which clattered to the ground. At the same time, Reece moved forward with all the grace of one of those Russian dancers who had visited Chicago some years before the War, and landed a swinging left into the side of Frank's neck, just under the ear. He went down like a deflated balloon and lay in the dirt, motionless.

"Dear God Almighty," breathed Fieyn, squatting down to check on Weasel's pulse. The little man was bleeding from a nasty looking gash in his scalp, "where in the hell did you learn to do that?"

Choosing to ignore the question, Reece merely shrugged before turning his attention to Otis who was standing, face deathly white, arms raised, mouth agog. "Don't kill me," he spluttered.

"Son, if I meant to kill you, you'd already be dead."

Stooping down, he relieved the unconscious Frank of his guns.

"Otis," said Fieyn, holstering his own gun, "you can help me take these two to the jailhouse. Then, I'll ask you to ride over to Mr Quince's ranch and tell him what has gone on here today."

Dropping his arms, Otis looked incredulously towards the sheriff. "You mean, you ain't gonna lock me up too?"

"I will if you don't stop blabbering. Now, grab hold of Weasel's feet and help me lift him."

"I'll saddle my horse," said Reece.

———

Sometime later, Reece and Fieyn mounted up and took their mounts out of town. They had something of an audience with assorted townsfolk watching the two men in hushed amazement. Fieyn kept his face turned straight ahead, but Reece couldn't help noticing Bessy who stood outside her guesthouse, drying her hands on a dishtowel as she always seemed to do. She gave him a fleeting smile, which he returned, mouthing, "I won't be long." She answered, "Take care," and then went back inside. Her simple words caused his heart to swell and, not for the first time, he thought that perhaps, if life proved good over the next few days, he might ask her to go for a ride with him, get to know her a little better.

They met up with a handful of men from the town, including the blacksmith Hanson. There was a nervousness about them, their horses too skittish.

"Bormann here found Destry's horse," said Hanson, struggling to keep his own mount under control. Reece eyed them, amazed that the animal could bear the weight of such a big man as Hanson was.

"Lead the way, Matthew," said Fieyn, his tone gentle, perhaps because he'd picked up on the fear running through the tiny group.

Bormann grunted, jutting his chin towards the nearby tree line. "On the other side."

"Near the mine?"

A ripple of murmurs ran through the men. Bormann shook his head, "No," he said with some relief. "Not far from White's shed. Where he counted his gold."

"I thought he didn't find that much," said Reece.

"He found enough," said another.

"Enough to set himself up for life," added Hanson.

"That'll be the ranch," said Fieyn, "the ranch now owned by Richard Quince."

"He bought it?"

Fieyn shrugged, turning his horse slowly towards the trees, "White gifted it to Destry some years back, who then sold it on to Quince." The sheriff blew out a loud sigh, "Let's get this done. We can continue talking after we get back."

They rode in silence, reaching the wood within a few minutes. As they entered the gloom of the over-arching trees, the temperature changed, growing cooler. Bormann led the way, leaning over his horse's neck to stare at the ground as he navigated his way through a narrow, twisting path hyphenated by numerous potholes, exposed roots, and jagged rocks. The going was infuriatingly slow, and, with every step, the sense of foreboding grew. Reece, next in line behind Bormann, stared ahead, the trees a seemingly impenetrable barrier to whatever lay on the other side of the wood. He was not one to suffer from any form of unwarranted phobia but the feeling of being pressed from all sides made him realize just how easy it would be to succumb to claustrophobia. An unlooked-for shiver ran across his shoulders. He turned in his shoulders to see the others, huddled over their mounts, faces downcast, collars of their coats pulled up high. The air tasted strange. The trees hissed and swayed with a light breeze. No birds sang. It was as if they were being sucked deeper and deeper into a grim, threatening tunnel. He turned again to see nothing but trees.

"I don't ever remember this wood being so big," said Fieyn from somewhere in the middle of the group.

"Me neither," said Bormann. He pulled up his horse and stared. "It weren't this deep when we last came across the horse."

Urging his horse forward, Reece came up alongside their guide. "Maybe we took a wrong turning?"

"There ain't no turns," retorted Bormann, sounding vexed. "There ain't but one trail and we're on it."

"You sayin' we is lost?" Fieyn joined them, leaving the rest to gather a little behind, exchanging frightened mutterings.

"No, I ain't," said Bormann, his voice now sharp, close to anger. "I came the same way as last time. It just seems longer, that's all."

"Are you sure?"

Bormann shot Fieyn a dangerous look. "Damn it, Sheriff, you wanna lead this party then go right ahead."

"I was merely—"

"Shoot," spat Bormann, "I wished I'd never seen that damned animal. I say we turn around and go back to town. Destry will turn up when he's good and ready."

"You know we can't do that," said Fieyn. "You found his horse so he can't be much further. We'll keep going."

Shaking his head, Bormann kicked his mount's flanks and pressed on.

"We'll give it another hour," said Fieyn in answer to Reece's questioning look. "If we ain't out of this damn wood by then, we'll go back."

"Miss Bessy ain't gonna like that."

"Shoot, Reece, seems to me you've become mighty fond of that woman."

Shrugging, Reece looked at Bormann's back. "He couldn't have made a mistake so let's just keep going."

"Yeah, and then, at Miss Bessy's guesthouse, we can discuss what exactly you is doing here, Reece."

"I'm getting a little tired with all this suspicion, Sheriff."

"Call it instinct, but you arriving when you did seems a tad fortuitous if you ask me. And now Destry is missing and you is cozying up to Miss Bessy."

"Sheriff, I'd ease on back a little if I were you."

Fieyn twisted his mouth and gnawed for a moment at his bottom lip. "Seems like I've hit a nerve."

"I ain't gonna ask you again."

"Okey-dokey. I seen how you put that lanky streak of cow-piss Frank on his skinny ass, so I'll not press my point. But we will talk when this over, make no mistake."

"Talking is free, Sheriff," Reece kicked his horse forward, "but insinuations I can do without."

It was within the hour when the strung-out band emerged from the wood, brilliant sunshine instantly lifting their spirits.

"There she is, damn it!" said Bormann, waggling his finger towards a dead horse lying on its side amongst a clump of coarse grass.

"Check it out Hanson," said Fieyn, "but be wary."

The big blacksmith grunted and dismounted. Light-footed, he moved with surprising grace towards the dead animal, checking each side as he did so. The clearing was wide and open with little vegetation to give much cover. The ground was hard and broken, littered with sharp shards of what looked like flint.

"There are tracks," shouted Hanson, brushing the flat of his hand across the ground next to the horse. "I reckon Destry must have run off from here. The horse," he stood up and pushed his hat towards the back of his head, "it's been shot."

"Shot?" Fieyn dismounted and made his way across the ground, with Reece a little way behind, to join the blacksmith.

"That's a big-bored rifle," said Reece, peering towards the dried wound in the horse's throat. He turned and scanned the distant mountain range. "Whoever shot it could have positioned himself somewhere amongst the rocks."

"Those mountains are unscalable," said Fieyn. "My bet is, he took his shot from one of those knolls," he pointed towards a cluster of small hillocks which pressed against the foot of the mountain.

"That's fairly open."

"True, but I doubt he was much concerned with Destry returning fire. Destry was no marksman."

"That means the rifleman knew just that."

"I reckon."

"And also, that he knew Destry was coming this way."

Grunting, Fieyn slowly took out some tobacco and paper and took to rolling himself a cigarette. "Thing is, why would Destry come all the way up here?"

"To visit the mine?"

Fieyn stopped and held Reece's gaze. "No one visits the mine, Reece. No one dares."

"So where would he run off to?"

"Only one place he can run to from here," said Hanson. "Old White's work shack."

Stopping in the act of lighting his smoke, Fieyn looked aghast at the big blacksmith. "Jesus."

"Why?" asked Reece, looking from one man to the next, "what's the problem with that shack?"

"Plenty," said Fieyn grimly and slowly returned to his horse, leaving Reece standing perplexed and troubled.

"It's where we think those bushwhackers, chased out of town by Destry all those years ago, rested before they ran to the mine. Where they were cornered and killed," said Hanson. He blew out a loud breath. "But nobody knows for sure."

"Why's that?"

Bormann walked up, serious and skittish, eyes forever darting this way and that. "Because we never found the bodies," he said.

"Destry is the only one who knows the truth, and he ain't ever said," added Hanson.

"But the shack," pressed Reece, "why are you so fearful of it?"

"There's something inside it," said Bormann quickly. He

shifted his gaze around the others. "Stories tell of people changing after they've been inside."

"Changing? In what way?"

The big blacksmith placed a heavy hand on Bormann's shoulder, and the man grew silent.

Reece wanted to ask more but from the dark look on Hanson's face, he decided any further questions could wait. He watched Bormann and the big blacksmith return to their horses before allowing his eyes to follow the clear signs of where Destry made his escape. Something was waiting for them all not so very far away up ahead. Whatever it was caused a stirring deep inside Reece's core, a feeling he had not experienced for many years, not since that dark day when he'd brought another set of bushwhackers to justice.

CHAPTER FOURTEEN

A little time before, having watched Reece ride out of town, Miss Bessy returned to her kitchen. She was preparing the evening meal, chicken stew with dumplings, and had a dozen buns already rolled and primed for the oven. She enjoyed cooking. If pushed, she'd have to admit that it was the only thing she had in a life run dry. Years before, when Destry was so fine and his attentions so sincere, she believed she had found her niche. This place, her simple yet happy existence, all was well. How quickly everything had been swept away. She had no doubts what had allowed the rot to set in – it was that damned mine.

The War, of course, was the root of it. If the country hadn't split and did its best to murder itself, those terrible men, bushwhackers or whatever the moniker was, none of them would have ridden into town with their guns drawn.

Standing, leaning over her preparation table, the rolls well-floured, she cast her mind back to that dreadful day and, as she remembered, her eyes clouded over with the tears of so much lost.

. . .

She recalled it was a morning much like any other that chill April in 1865 when the riders came. The evening before, her few guests, huddled around the dining table, helping themselves with gusto to their meal, gossiped about the War and the recent developments. News rarely came so far west but these events were so momentous that everyone talked about it. "Seems that as long as Mahone can hold Grant back at Petersburg, then the South has a chance," a tall, thin man of tender years said. The murmurings grew in volume amongst the guests. It appeared that nobody quite believed the South could ever hold out in the face of such overwhelming odds. "There's talk of a ceasefire," said one, portly gentleman, "perhaps even a surrender." The assembly settled into an uneasy silence. Miss Bessy, who always kept herself aloof from such talk, later spoke to her husband about what the news might mean. Destry had a dark look about him. "If the South is defeated, we can expect a whole lot of stragglers coming this way."

His words proved prophetic.

The town was slowly waking up, several gangs of men trudging downcast towards the hillside where they would work through the day cutting down the trees that were the lifeblood of the town. There had been some hope that the goldmine, discovered by old man White all those years before, might prove the start of something big but in the end, there wasn't much there. Enough, however, for White to buy his ranch and start up the little town that still bore his name.

This day, the town woke up to something a whole lot worse. Riders, perhaps half a dozen of them, rough-looking men dressed in filthy rags, their dark eyes and sallow faces grim reminders to anyone who dared stare long enough that the shadow of death hung heavy around their shoulders.

Shooting their handguns in the air, whooping and hollering with that infamous 'Rebel yell', they caracoled their horses in the center of Main Street, kicking up clouds of dirt and dust.

Mr Burrows was the first to die. Such a good man, coming

down the steps of his lumber merchant's shop to see what all the noise was about. They shot him dead, the heavy slugs hitting him in the chest, blowing him back through the open door of his establishment. From within came a horrible scream and his wife appeared, wringing her hands, distraught, wondering what evil had befallen her world. She soon discovered how evil this entire world could be as two of the riders jumped from their saddles, manhandled her inside and had their way with her.

The others continued in their feast of depravity and violence, shooting anyone who dared venture outside, riding their horses along the boardwalks, setting fire to the haberdashery store before crashing into the saloon to fill their guts with drink and anything else they could find.

Bessy, peering from an upstairs window, reeled away in horror and ran down to find her husband. She went through the back, not daring to go into the street, and ran to the livery. There she found Destry and told him what was happening. Destry, a man well-used to violence, instantly took charge. Going to the rear entrances, he gathered together several townsfolk, armed them, and came up with a simple plan. Lure the riders from the saloon then attack from the flanks with enfilading fire. It was an effective tactic, one he'd witnessed many times during the Mexican War. He had no doubts it would work again.

The firefight, when it came, was short and swift. The two riders rolling out of Burrows' store were the first to die. Cackling to themselves, sated with their physical excesses, they had little idea what was waiting for them. The first notion they had that doomsday had arrived was when their bodies were perforated by a fusillade of well-aimed bullets from the waiting townsfolk. The eruption of gunfire brought the others bursting from the saloon, guns drawn, firing wildly in every direction. Destry, marching behind his hurriedly assembled band, coolly gave his commands, "Steady boys, pick your mark, fire when ready."

Caught unawares, the riders continued to shoot as they ran for their horses tied at the hitching post. One of them screamed and fell, blood spewing from his throat and head. The man who appeared to be their leader blasted away and managed to hit two or three opponents. Screaming for his men to mount up, he was already galloping off before he was fully in the saddle.

Destry shouted for the townsfolk to cease fire and watched with a kind of grim satisfaction as the riders charged towards the nearby woods. He knew that on the far side the men would emerge into a wide, shattered plain enclosed by the soaring mountains. There was no way out. They would have to stand and fight.

Unless they made for the mine entrance.

A good place from which to make a stand.

At least, that is what they would believe.

The townsfolk saddled up and set off in pursuit. Bessy watched from the door of the guesthouse as Destry led them towards the woods and she couldn't help but be filled with pride that her husband showed such enterprise, such courage. She stood and waited for almost an hour, straining to listen for the sound of distant gunfire and when Destry finally returned, he rode alone. His face, awash with grime, was taut with fear. Tears ran down his cheeks, making tiny rivulets in the dirt. His eyes, wide with horror, would not turn to her. He did not speak, ignoring his wife's pleas for explanation, and stomped into the saloon. She followed him, pulling up short when she saw the body of Owen Tusk, the barkeep, sprawled out across the floor, eyes staring sightlessly, dried blood enveloping his head like some ghastly crimson halo. She emitted a low moan. "Who were those men? What has happened to them?"

Destry stood behind the counter, draining glass after glass of whisky. He never answered her, leaving the saloon in silence. He visited Lizzie Coombs for the first time that day. The husband Bessy knew, had shared her life with, left her in spirit if not in body. He still had not returned.

Allowing her mind to return to that dreadful day, she realized it was not the War that had changed her life completely, it was the mine. The mine, which Old Man White had dug out all those years ago, would have remained forgotten if Destry hadn't forced those men there to fight and die. She didn't know the whole story of what happened, nor did she want to. Not now, not with the promise of a new page turning at long last.

Reece.

He seemed a good man. Dependable. Strong, honest. Not like the others who had come to her, comforting her for fleeting, brutish moments during her lonely hours. Yes, however infrequently, she'd enjoyed their company, the feel of them, their strong arms, their urgency. She was thankful for the rush of lust, the breathlessness, the surrender but when they were done, they dressed and left. And she, feeling empty, would throw herself into her cooking and her baking. No point in lingering on any of it, no point in believing it was anything more than a physical release of pent-up desire. Just as it had been the night before Reece came into her guesthouse and looked at her with those eyes. My God, did he have any idea the effect those eyes had on a woman?

A sharp cough brought her out of her reverie with a start. She jumped back to find Bourne standing in the doorway to her kitchen, his Derby in his hands, moustache recently waxed, his eyes dancing with a curious light.

"Why, Mr Bourne, you startled me."

"It was not my intention, gracious lady," he said with a slight bow. "I was merely returning to pick up my meagre belongings before I continue on my way."

"I thought perhaps you had already left. I heard you—"

"Ah no, that was nothing more than an early morning ride across the prairie, to clear the mind, so to speak."

"Oh, yes, yes I understand." She dried her hands on a nearby dishcloth, "I'll go and fetch your clothes for you and then—"

She was about to make her way out of the room but Bourne stepped across and barred her way. He was grinning. Bessy, drawn to his mustachioed mouth, was unsettled by his almost maniacal grin. "Gracious lady, if I may…"

Mesmerized, she watched as his hand reached out to stroke her hair.

"I watched you last evening," he said, his voice low, a tiny tremble accompanying every word, "and I noticed how you returned my stare."

"Mr Bourne, I never—"

"Please do not fight against what is in your heart," he said, his hand moving more firmly down the side of her face to stroke her neck. "Your life here is so hard, and you, dear lady, strive endlessly to make this place something of a success. It must be so arduous to have to work through every day on your own."

"Oh, Mr Bourne, no, you must remember, my husband …"

"I know full well he has no time for you." He moved closer, dipping his head to her throat, his lips brushing against her soft flesh. "I have enquired, you see. He is a drunkard and you, so alone, have sometimes sought out affection from other quarters. There is no shame in it, no shame at all."

"Mr Bourne, please …" She wanted so much to step away but there was no denying the press of his mouth sent such a wave of sensation through her that it caused her heartbeat to pound.

His kisses, so light, fluttering across her face, her lips, were sweet, soft, punctuating each sentence. "Allow me to ease your burden for a short while, gracious lady. To give you some more of that affection you so clearly yearn for."

"Mr Bourne…"

Her voice, barely a whisper now, spurred him on. "You will not be disappointed, dear lady." He threw his Derby across the room before curling his arms around her waist, his mouth enveloping her own. She buckled under the intensity of his advance. "You will be well satisfied, I assure you."

She gasped as his hardness pressed against her. "Oh my…"

His mouth moved from her face down to the front of her blouse, the swell of her breasts straining beneath the material.

As one of his hand settled on her buttocks, the other delved beneath the folds of her dress and as he sought out the softness of her sex, she at last found the strength to push herself away, hastily rearranging her clothing as her breathing came in short gasps. "Mr Bourne, you are mistaken if you believe this is what I need. I am sorry if I have led to think I might be receptive to your advances, but I must ask you not to—"

"Sweet lady, do not deny your own desires," he said, taking a step forward again. Pulling off his jacket, he pushed his arms through the braces holding up his trousers and smiled, "I shall take you to heaven." He lunged.

"Mr Bourne," she gasped, throwing up her arms to ward him off, "please, I have no desire to—"

"But I have the desire," he said, voice thick with lust, "and it is my intention to give you what you so obviously need."

His trousers dropped to his ankles and there he stood for her to take in every inch of him, his confidence overwhelming.

"Come," he said, taking a shuffling step, "we'll do it first in here, on this very table and then, later, in your bed. The bed you have shared with your husband but from now on will always think of as ours."

Quickly, she looked around, spotted the heavy cast-iron frying pan, and seized it by its handle. She swung this makeshift weapon with all her might and smacked it into the side of his head with a tremendous, dull clonk.

Taken by surprise, Bourne staggered sideways, eyes blinking, unable to comprehend what had happened. A second or two passed before the pain hit home. He cried out, hands clutching his head, and teetered on the brink of collapse.

Unwinding herself as if being released from a mangonel, Bessy struck him a second time, an enormous blow directly under his jaw, sending him spiraling backwards, jarring the small of his back against the edge of the table. He cried out and landed with a tremendous crash to the ground.

Bessy stood, body shaking, mouth trembling, unable to

believe what she had done. True, his advances were perhaps unwanted, but to have caused him such pain, to have hit him so hard to have ...

She got down on her knees beside him.

He wasn't breathing.

His eyes were open and fixed, and she remembered poor Owen Tusk and how he'd looked after those riders had shot him. Poor Mr Bourne looked exactly the same.

She clamped a hand over her mouth to prevent herself from screaming. He was dead.

CHAPTER FIFTEEN

He came stumbling towards where he believed the crumpled, sagging hut to be. He couldn't be sure as his eyes were bleary and he had difficulty focusing. Moving at speed, weaving drunkenly from side to side, close to exhaustion, he'd run like he hadn't run for years, not since he was a small boy when his body was new, his limbs hard and fast. Now, all those years of drinking, smoking and other, questionable practices, had taken their toll. Wheezing, eyes watering, the cramps in his thighs like the Devil's own pronged fork, he pitched over and landed heavily on his knees. Sucking in air, he stared at the building where he'd left Destry, not quite remembering it looking the way it did right now. Certainly not with smoke pouring out of the chimney. Someone was there. The man who had taken his horse perhaps? Tugging out his pistol, Ezra wiped his nose with the back of his free hand and moved closer.

Somebody was singing inside. A woman, her voice melodic, sweet, as if she were used to it. A professional. If not, then someone who could hold a tune. Something prevented him from bursting straight inside. He took a look around him. There was no one there. Not even horses. Could this be another place, a cottage rather than a miner's hut?

Before he could formulate any answers or make sense of what was happening, the door was torn open and a woman stood there, wiping her hands on her apron, her face flushed with the heat from within. The smell of home cooking invaded his nostrils and Ezra stared in disbelief.

"Mom?"

The woman's face cracked into a broad smile and she stepped aside, "Why, Ezra! Where have you been?"

Ezra stood swaying on the step, not sure what the make of the vision before him. His mother, alive again? No, how was this possible? And not how he remembered her the last time he'd set eyes upon her. Then she was laid out in her sweat-soaked bed, the diphtheria well and truly victorious, grey skin sagging loosely over her shrunken frame. He'd reached out and touched her, immediately yanking his hand away from her burning brow. As red as a deep boiled lobster, her body consumed by heat. Her feverish eyes settled on him, her thin mouth cracking open, "My baby boy ..." Those were her last words.

Or were they? For here she was, brimful with health. Alive. Very much alive.

"Come on inside," she said, voice cheery, full of vitality. "You've had a shock. I have some rye whisky, which I know you like, and some beef with dumplings. Come on," she gripped his shirt sleeve and yanked him inside.

The place was not as it was before. There was a range belching out heat, filling the cramped room, and pots bubbled on the stove top. Curled up beneath it, luxuriating in the warmth, was a cat in deep sleep. Ezra thought he recognized it but, shaking his head in an attempt to dispel the images all around him, he scanned the walls. This was not the hut he'd left Destry in, that much was certain. This was homely, clean, and ordered. A small, well-scrubbed table, set for dinner, with wooden bowls awaiting the soup, cutlery neatly arranged. An oil lamp in the center sent out a comforting orange glow.

"Mom," said Ezra, swallowing hard. "What's happening?"

"Happening?" She poured him a generous measure of whisky into a small, stubby glass and thrust it towards him. "Drink that, it'll make you feel better."

He stared at the glass for a long moment before he took it. It looked like whisky and, breathing in its aroma, it certainly smelled like whisky. He took a tentative sip and gasped. "What the hell ...?"

"Drink it down, baby boy. There's plenty more where that came from."

He studied her with wide, disbelieving eyes. She was a strong-looking woman in her late forties, maybe early fifties, the woman he knew as his mother when he was not yet a teenager. "How ...?"

"Don't ask, baby boy, just accept it. Now sit, drink your drink, and I'll bring you some stew. You look famished."

She eased past him and went to the stove, stirring through the stew with a wooden spoon. Ezra stared again at his whisky, shrugged, and drank it down. It burned in his throat and all the way down to his stomach, where it rumbled and growled. "Jeez," he said, "that's the best-goddamned whisky I ever tasted."

"Don't cuss, Ezra," she said, with her back to him as she stirred, "you know I can't abide cussing."

"Sorry, Mom." He flopped down into one of the three chairs set around the table. "I'm shocked, is all. Mom. What are you doing here? How can you—"

"What. Be alive?" She chuckled. "I got better is all, Babyboy. I got better almost as soon as you left."

"But that can't be. You had the diphtheria. Doc Lawrence said so. He told me I should leave, that if I stayed there any longer, I could catch it myself."

"So, you ran. And you never came back."

"Mom! That's not how it was."

"Oh? Really?" She turned and stepped across to the table. She took the wooden bowl before him and went to return to the stove.

He noted her hands. If her face was that of a middle-aged woman in the prime of health, her hands certainly were not. They were wizened and gnarled, more claws than hands, the nails black, loose white skin mottled, painful looking, puss-filled blisters covering the surface. Gawping in disbelief, Ezra swiveled in his chair as she began to ladle piping hot stew into the bowl.

"Mom, I don't understand this. How can you be here? Miles from home, so close to where...Mom?"

She slowly turned.

Ezra let out a scream, springing from his chair so violently it toppled over and crashed to the floor. Groping away from her, he did his best not to stare, but an invisible, irresistible power forced him to look.

Her face, no longer the mother he knew, now a diseased, shrunken thing, thin greyish skin drawn taut across the skull, transparent, allowing the white bone beneath to shine forth. A living skeleton, a half-decomposed corpse, reeking of sickness, blood and green-tinged phlegm dribbling for her slack, purple lips and shriveled nostrils.

The bowl clattered from her skeletal fingers, one wizened hand reaching out as she took one step, then another. Her jaw fell to her chest and an ear-splitting scream issued from the cavernous, toothless hole that was once her mouth.

Ezra broke and careered out of the room, ripping open the door in his frenzied desire to escape from the horrors he had stumbled upon.

The sunlight hit him full in the face, blinding him momentarily, and a voice he did not know came to him, assertive and composed.

"Boy, you just stay the hell there and do not move!"

The unmistakable sound of a revolver being cocked was the only other command Ezra needed for him to do as he was told.

CHAPTER SIXTEEN

O tis did not believe he was a brave man and rarely if ever, thought of himself as such. Now, leading his horse from the town, he made a slight detour on the way to the Quince ranch. He needed time to think, to get his head sorted out. What to say to Quince, to make his boss understand the reasons why Otis was not in the town jail along with Frank and Weasel. Quince had not seen what that stranger Reece could do. If he had, he'd understand. As it was, he'd label Otis a coward, a man not willing to carry out instructions. The Lord only knew what the boss's response would be. Undoubtedly it would be violent. He was a man who detested weakness of any kind and it had been only at Henry's insistence that Otis got the job as cowpuncher. And that only because he was Henry's nephew. Otis doubted any such relationship would save him now from one of Quince's notorious outbursts. So, nervous and concerned, he wandered away from the direction of the ranch and crossed the expanse of broken ground towards an area of scrub punctuated with wooded glades. This was not a place he knew nor had heard of.

Reining in his horse, he took a slug from his water canteen. He'd filled it from the nearby stream, and it tasted sweet and refreshing. He took a long drink and paused a moment to look around. Was it the water making his senses more alert he wondered? He had felt tired but now everything was invigorated, refreshed. Head clear, he found concentrating easier. Even so, nothing stirred in that place, not even a bird. The atmosphere grew eerie, the air colder, and a chill wind developed. The rustling of the trees threw up an unfriendly sound. Amongst these, dark shadows stirred, drawing his gaze ever deeper into the gloom. An involuntary shudder ran through him and he took another drink before moving on. He soon spotted a clearing. It was here he came across the long-deserted camp.

Set in a slight depression, surrounded by those tall, dark trees, the remnants of a hastily abandoned homestead clung to the parched grass as if desperate to hold on to what had once been a happy place, a place to grow, live. Now, little sense of those moments remained. The dark imprints of where several wikiups once stood were a poignant reminder of the people who once lived here, together with the burned ground in the center where they would have gathered around campfires, roasting game, conversing. Otis took it all in and wondered what had happened to cause them to flee. He put his water canteen away, dismounted and edged forward, dropping to his knees to study the brown-tinged grass. Whoever had lived here made these fires long ago.

Something rustled in the trees and Otis stood up and froze, waiting. A strong urge to break for cover took hold of him but his legs refused to work, his guts turning to jelly. Despite the pistol in his waistband offering some protection, his hands could not reach for it. Nothing worked anymore. He was petrified.

A man stood some way off watching. Dressed in animal skins, head adorned with a buffalo headdress, its horns tipped white, he held a lance in his right hand. The weapon, made from finely hewn wood, was as tall as he, and its blade, fashioned from flint, glistened in what remained of the sun.

Otis watched mesmerized as the man moved out from

among the trees, his stride assured, triumphant almost, his free hand rising. But not in a greeting. He seemed to be urging others, unseen, to appear. And, inevitably, they did. Around a dozen of them emerged from the gloom, unformed, almost transparent shapes at first gradually becoming more substantial as they advanced. Thin, emaciated semi-naked warriors, armed with ancient weapons – stone axes, wooden clubs, the occasional bone bow strung with sinew, arrows already nocked.

Encircling him, within ten paces or so, they stopped, fiery eyes blazing from those gaunt, skull-like faces. Coming to a halt, swaying slightly as if ruffled by the breeze, they studied him. The longer Otis stared back the more he came to realize they were not so much moving as drifting between solid form and unde-fined vapor.

The shock that what he witnessed was not reality but closer to something from a dream returned life to his senses in a rush. Screaming, he wheeled around and dashed towards his horse, which seemed as unaffected as if it were munching grass in a sunlit meadow.

Leaping into the saddle, he kicked the horse into a mad gallop and, keeping himself low, burst through the trees into open prairie, driving forward and not stopping until the reas-suring sight of the Quince ranch came into view.

CHAPTER SEVENTEEN

Bessy stood for a long time, staring down at the inert mass lying on her kitchen floor. A hope, temporary, as fleeting as a summer breeze drifted into her mind – this was all a horrible dream, that all she needed to do was close her eyes, turn around and life would return to how it was. Clean, dull, predictable. But no, when she finally steeled herself to force her eyes open again, he remained as he was after she'd hit him. Bourne. Dead.

Her first instinct was to run. To bundle together a few items, saddle up one of Destry's little ponies from the livery, and beat a retreat east, to her old home in Ohio. Her parents were long gone but her cousin Rosa continued to live there and now that the War between the States was over, travelling would be so much safer and she could ...

No, none of that was going to happen.

Clawing for the table edge to stop herself from collapse, she wept at the futility of it all, the hopelessness. There was a dead man in her kitchen, and she had killed him. If she ran now, they would come after her, catch her before she crossed the state line, and haul her back for trial. The shame of it. The ignominy.

She was guilty, there was no getting away from that fact, despite the killing not being premeditated in any way – she was defending herself. They'd believe her, she convinced herself, biting down on a fist. Of course, they would.

She turned away, pulling out a handkerchief from her sleeve, and pressed it into her eyes. Murder it may not be, but it was a killing, and she was responsible. What to do, how to get through this?

Confused, distraught, torn between the host of alternatives that flew into her mind, only for all of them to be instantly dismissed. Which one to choose. What to do for the best?

She froze, rigid as a noise reverberated through the guest-house, sounding so much louder than it usually would. Her senses, grated and on edge, seemed to amplify everything. Rooted to the spot, she heard the main door opening with a jerk. She'd been meaning to do something about those fallen hinges, to stop the door from scraping noisily across the floor, but right now she was grateful she hadn't. It gave a moment. Rushing to the kitchen entrance, she stepped into the reception area in time to see Nathan Hoffstedder coming in. He was peering at the ceiling with an expression of deep concentration on his craggy, life-worn face. Noticing Bessy, his eyes lit up. "Well, howdy-doody, Miss Bessy! I'm here to measure up."

Blinking a few times, she had to stop herself from reeling backwards. It was as if she'd stepped into another world, an outsider looking in, viewing everything from a detached distance. She shook her head, bewildered. "Measure up?"

"Sure, don't you remember?" He came closer, looking all around him, eyes moving up and down, side to side. He was an athletic-looking man, square-shouldered and granite-jawed. Bessy didn't know that much about him, save he was known to be a good worker *and,* of course, a close friend of her husband Destry. Rumour had it that it was he who introduced Destry to that whore Lizzie Coombs. "We spoke about it, you wanting the foyer all redecorated. I'm here to make some estimates for you, give you a price." His frown deepened and the light went out of his features. "You don't remember, do you."

"Why sure I do," she said, even though she didn't recall anything, not one word. Nothing existed for her except those few dreadful moments when Bourne stood before her and she'd hit him and he fell, dead. Other than the memory of that, her mind was a blank.

"Are you all right? You don't seem so—"

"No, no, I'm fine." She forced a tiny chuckle, swept back a lock of hair, and smiled thinly. "Well, to be absolutely honest, I'm not feeling so good. I was just about to lock up and go to bed to try and get myself better for this evening."

"Oh my, miss Bessy, I beg your pardon! You should have said and I'd—"

"It's fine. *I'm* fine. At least I will be after a little nap. Hope you understand."

"Of course. But I'll just measure up and then I'll be on my way."

She stared at him in horror, her stomach flipping completely over. The thought of Bourne lying there, the blood leaking from his head. No, she had to dispose of the body, clean up, rearrange everything. Time was pressing and she couldn't take the risk of Hoffstedder peeking into the kitchen. "No!" she blurted out in a panic. She saw his shocked look and immediately threw out her arms, her voice gushing with forced friendliness. "Please, it's all right, Mr Hoffstedder, perhaps you can come back when I'm feeling up to it. Shall we say tomorrow?"

"It'll take but a few moments, Miss Bessy."

"I'd like to be here as you work."

She waited, holding her breath, giving him her best puppy-dog eyes. He gnawed away at his mouth, not quite convinced.

"*Please ...*"

She saw him falter, about to speak, then a sudden decision and he clapped his hands together, "Well, yes, sure, why not. I'll call around same time tomorra." He tipped his hat, "Sure hope you'll be feeling better."

"Oh, I am sure I will be." Beaming, she went with him to the door and showed him out. At the foot of the steps, he turned, doffed his hat once again, and trudged off down the street. She watched him and, when she was sure he wouldn't be coming back, hastily jumped back inside, drew the bolt across the bottom of the door, and rushed into the kitchen.

The body lay stretched out as before.

This was a nightmare that wasn't about to go away.

CHAPTER EIGHTEEN

From the corner came a whimper, so tiny Reece may have missed if he had not turned up the flame of the oil lamp and shined it into the inky darkness. He gasped at what he saw. Destry, huddled in a tight ball, trembled under a torn and tattered sheet, his eyes red-rimmed, skin the pallor of chalk, lips blue. "Help me," came the voice. "I need water." Instantly, Reece thrust the lamp into Fieyn's hand and went to the stricken Destry. He called out for someone to fetch a canteen and when one of the others returned with one, Reece put the tip to Destry's cracked lips. Coughing and gasping as the water hit the back of his parched throat, Destry bent forward, retching. Reece held him around the shoulders, despite the stench which invaded his nostrils. The man was awash with the sour smell of sweat, piss, and feces.

"Dear God," said Fieyn, appalled, "who in hell would leave him like this?"

"I don't know," said Reece, putting the canteen to Destry's mouth again. This time, Destry took his time to drink. "Let's get him outside, warm him up a little."

Several men took Destry out into the sunlight. It was diffi-cult. Destry seemed to have no strength in his legs, and he was not a small man. After a good deal of cursing and grunting, they eventually managed to put him down among a cluster of rocks and propped him up against a small boulder. The sun bathed him in its warm glow and almost immediately the color returned to the man's skin.

From the opening of the shack, Reece looked towards the other man who had greeted them on their arrival and who now sat on the broken boards of the veranda. He appeared to be in some sort of trance, murmuring under his breath, holding himself as he rocked backwards and forwards. The only word Reece caught was the repeated, "Mama," but whatever else accompanied this was almost impossible to pick out.

"Something terrible happened here," said Fieyn with feeling. He nodded towards the bunch of riders who had accompanied them. "Look at them, they're spooked real bad."

Reece grunted. He too had noticed the atmosphere of the shack, the penetrating cold, the threat of something awful lurking in the very marrow of the building. "At least we've found him and can take him back. No need to go through the woods."

Nodding, Fieyn turned towards the dark screen of trees that formed a natural barrier to whatever lay beyond. "None of us will be going through there."

"I'll talk with Destry, see if I can get him to make some sense of what happened here."

"I appreciate all that you're doing, Reece. Helping, I mean. I want you to know that."

Without answering, Reece turned and went over to where Destry sat. He got down on his haunches and forced a smile. "How you feeling, Destry?"

The livery stable owner's head came up. He seemed slightly more at ease. His eyes, however, continued to betray a haunted look. "I have been better."

"Feel like telling me what went on here?" He twisted and pointed towards where the other stricken man continued to rock himself. "That fella. Why is he here?"

"I don't know. He came into the shack, almost as if he were expecting to find something. I was so weak I couldn't speak, only managed to raise my hand, and give him a sign. I had no idea who he was or what he wanted but I was hoping he might help. He drank some water. And then, he took to acting real strange, as if he were talking to someone."

"Who?"

"I don't know. There was no one else there."

"He wasn't the one who tied you up in there?"

"No. That was the other fella. Listen, before I gets into any of that, I want you to promise me you won't go to the mine. There ain't nothing there worth looking and if you were thinking you might--"

Picking up on the mounting desperation in Destry's voice, Reece frowned and nodded. "I think we've already decided none of us wants to go through those woods."

Destry released a long, slow sigh. "Thank God."

"Why? What's there, Destry?"

Those black eyes, so recently filled with terror, grew wider, the fear returning. "Just promise me..."

"I already did that. Tell me what's there."

"I can't. I daren't."

"You're gonna have to if I'm to convince the others not to continue." Reece hoped his lie would work. His curiosity was building. He had to force himself not to reach out and shake the terrified man before him. "They is awful keen to go and dig for more gold."

"What?" Destry sat forward, more animated than Reece had ever seen him. "No. You must stop them, Reece! You must."

"Then tell me what the hell is going on because my patience, if not those of the others, is close to breaking."

"All right, all right." Destry pressed a hand over his face and dragged it downwards, wiping away the thin film of grease and grime covering his flesh. "You've got to listen well, Reece. This ain't something I ever want to repeat. I ain't even told Bessy."

Reece repositioned himself on the ground. "Go ahead and just take your time."

Nodding, Destry gathered himself, settled his gaze upon the ground between himself and Reece, and quietly began.

"It was after the bushwhackers started shooting up the town. They set fire to some of the buildings, and I just knew we had to do something. The War was almost over, although we didn't know that then, we knew something was happening. We'd had strangers coming and going, telling us about the defeats the Rebs were suffering ..." His face came up. "I was never a secessionist, you understand. I never believed anything good would come of a war. We'd been lucky here. We hardly got any wind of what was happening, and no soldiers ever came this way. Until those bush-whackers, of course. They was desperate, and I knew they would burn the town to the ground if we didn't do something. Anyways, that's what we did. We shot two of 'em outside the saloon and the rest, they high-tailed it out, straight up here. We were after 'em, shouting and hollerin'. I had the idea of forcing 'em towards the mine because ..." He shuddered. "I knew what was there, you see. After Old Man White had taken his gold, he used the money to buy his ranch. I visited him, looking for work. We grew close and when I asked him how he'd managed to find the money to set himself up, he took me aside, told me about the mine and how I was to never go there. I thought he was just trying to stop me from finding my own lode. I ignored him, of course, spent my nights planning on what I could do. He'd told me he'd blocked the entrance up, so I had to get help. Problem was, who was I to trust?"

"So, what you do? Come up here on your own?"

"Nah, as I said, I'd made a plan. I got to talking and went up there with some young bucks I made acquaintance with. Arapaho they were. They'd been working cutting down trees for the lumber company. In those days there were so many trees that the company could never get enough men to work up there. Those Indians, they had no idea they was supplying wood for the railway companies that would cut through their land and rob 'em of everything they knew ..." Shaking his head, he took Reece's proffered canteen and took a long drink. "I told 'em they could make a bundle of money if they went with me to the other side of the valley. They didn't seem to know much about anything so one Sunday afternoon when everything was as dead as the grave, we went through the woods to the other side."

He rocked backwards, his eyes staring at something far away, the memories taking hold of him, changing him. As he spoke, his voice sounded hollow, as if it were not his own, but someone else's telling the story, someone deeply affected by what stirred in his brain. "It was like stepping into something unknown. Unnatural. The air, as soon as we came out from the trees, was different. Colder and unfriendly. I never thought air could be like that, but it was as if that place was telling us to keep away. The Indians, they were paralyzed by it."

"By the air?"

"By fear. That is what was in the air, Reece. I didn't pick up on it at first, just noticed the strangeness, but slowly I got to realizing it, like waking up out of a dream. Fear, as real as the mountains that towered over us. I couldn't figure it but when I pushed 'em, ordering 'em to go to the mine, to start digging through what old White had used to block up the entrance, they made but one strike with a pick and they screamed. All of 'em, at once. One smack into that earth and I saw 'em all give a little jump back as if an invisible fist had punched 'em all right between the eyes, and they threw down those tools and ran. I called after 'em, begging 'em, but no power was ever gonna bring 'em back. I watched 'em disappear into those woods and that was the last I ever saw of 'em."

He stopped and the silence fell. Deep, penetrating. Reece couldn't stop himself from shivering. He turned to check that Fieyn was still there and saw the sheriff talking to the man sat on the veranda. If they were talking about the same things, then fairly soon everyone would be running back to town.

"What did you do?" asked Reece at last.

Destry took a deep breath. "I picked up that pick and I drove it deep into those rocks. I knew I had to break through, find more gold. I was possessed, I guess. Greed, it's a mighty powerful emotion. I attacked those rocks with everything I had and then I heard it ..." His mouth slowly opened. "Like a growl. So deep, so far away. I thought it might have been a bear but ...Something else. Moving. Coming closer."

Again he paused. "I don't know what it was but when the smoke trickled out from the hole I'd made, I knew I had to get away, so I did."

"Smoke? What, from inside the mine?"

"Not much, you understand, more like the size of a snake. But it smelled kinda weird. Not nasty or bad, sweet it was. Even so, I knew it weren't something I wanted to take into my lungs. I reckons that's what them Arapaho saw when they started working. Anyways, I rode back into town and did my best to forget. But when those bushwhackers came and we chased 'em away, I knew there was gonna be a reckoning. Not just for them, but for me too."

"They ended up at the mine?"

"They had no choice. There was no other way out. They didn't know, how could they, that it was a dead-end, that the only hope they had was to shoot it out with us. So, they made some sort of defense in the mine entrance." He nodded his head, feverishly. "Yes, that's right. They used tools and broke through, using the rocks to hide behind. As soon as we came out of the woods, they set up shooting at us. We broke for whatever cover we could but caught in the open, we were sitting ducks. I think three of us went down, shot dead. We was all but ready to flee when we heard it." His hands flew to his face, slapping hard against his cheeks. "We all heard it. They did too - the bushwhackers. A horrible, shrill type sound, like an eagle makes as it flies across the sky but so much louder, so much more ... terrible. We all stopped and waited. Within just a few seconds, the ground moved. It buckled and reared up and those bush-whackers took up screaming." His eyes opened wider, staring into the depths of his memory. "They screamed, begging for mercy. Mercy from what I don't know. None of us knew. We just lay there, unable to move."

Reece, the strain of listening to every word with such inten-sity, blew out his cheeks in exasperation. "Destry, are you telling me that something attacked them? From within the mine?"

"I suppose I am, yes." A shadow fell over his face as he continued. "Maybe it was that damned smoke, I don't know. It was coming out of the cracks in the ground. Not like before, when the Injuns saw it. This time it was like what comes out of chimneys in a factory. We watched it and the silence came down heavy as lead, so total we could hear our own hearts thumping inside our chests. Them bushwhackers, they were no longer shouting or firing their guns. It was as if they'd never existed. I motioned for everyone to move forward. We split into two groups, fanning out on either side of the entrance, just in case it was a ruse. The closer we got the more it became evident it was no ruse." Shaking his head, he closed his eyes briefly. "I crept forward, listening for a sign they were in there, waiting to pounce, but there was nothing, except for the smoke. I got down on my knees, put my head against the side of the entrance where the rocks were smoother, listening for some clue as to what might have become of them. I sat up and peered into the dark-ness stretching before me. It was a tunnel, hewn out of the rock, no doubt by White all those years before. I couldn't pick anything out. It was too dark, darker than night, darker than ... Reece, it was like I was looking into the very gates of hell."

Reece blinked. "Hell? Destry, what are you..."

"Listen to me." He shot forward, grabbing Reece by both arms, his fingers like claws, digging into Reece's flesh. "It *was* hell, Reece. It *is*, you understand? As I looked, I could sense it. Something. A huge, horrible something. I saw it, Reece, its outline, so black, blacker than the mine itself. It filled the entrance with its size. And even though I could not see its eyes I felt it looking at me, inspecting me, looking deep, deep inside. Then it spoke."

With an effort, Reece managed to prise Destry's hands away from his arms. "It spoke to you? Destry, what the hell are you saying? That someone was trapped down there? An old miner? What?"

"Not a goddamned miner, Reece! Jesus, ain't you been listening to me - it was a thing of evil, not of this world, not of any world."

"Ah hell, Destry," he stood up, angry, disappointed in himself for allowing the rantings of a depraved old idiot to waste his time like this. "We came up here to find you and find you we have. I don't want to listen to any more of this nonsense. If you killed those men well, from where I'm standing, I reckon they deserved it. You ain't going to jail for what happened up there, Destry, so just say it!"

"No, no, Reece, you don't understand. Those men, they disappeared, left no sign. It was as if they'd never existed. And that's why I'll never go back there because the others, they went inside. They went searching. Maybe it was curiosity, maybe the lure of gold, I don't know what it was, but the blackness swallowed them up - that *thing*, whatever it was, it devoured them, Reece. Every single one of 'em. I heard it, rumbling and groaning, like it was enjoying what it was doing!"

"I've heard enough of this, Destry. You hear me? Enough!"

"I had some sticks of dynamite and I put them against the entrance, to blow it down, seal 'em all in there forever. But, before I could do it, that thing, it said my name. 'Destry,' it said, 'Destry.' That was it, nothing more, but it chilled me to the very core of my soul, Reece. I lit the fuse and ran, straight back here to the shack." He stretched out a single, trembling digit towards where Fieyn stood. "I stayed there, not believing what had happened, not believing I could have done what I'd done. I'd trapped them, don't you see? I'd made a grave for 'em, for all of 'em. I buried them and whatever it was that lived in that damned mine."

"Well, that's it, then. Once we get back to town, Fieyn will make out some sort of report and then you can face the descendants of those poor bastards you buried alive up there."

"No," gasped Destry, "no, it wasn't them I buried. Don't you see, haven't you worked it out? They were already dead. That *thing*, it killed 'em but me, I sealed it inside. It's in there still and it's hungry, Reece, it's hungry!"

CHAPTER NINETEEN

B ourne was not a big man but he was a man, nevertheless. And he was dead. His body, still limp, refused to budge as Bessy struggled and strained to drag him out of the kitchen. Barely able to pull him over the stone-flagged floor, she collapsed on a nearby chair, exhaustion, and despair almost getting the better of her. Until that is, an outrageous thought came to her.

She deliberated for a long time over what she believed could be the perfect solution to her crime. For crime it was. Of that, there could be no doubt. She had struck him with tremendous force, far more than what Bourne's advances warranted. They'd imprison her and she'd lose everything. Burying her face in her hands, she battled down the tears, but the hopelessness remained.

Outside, at this time of day, she knew a few people would be wandering along the main street, most visiting the mercantile store. Beyond it, the town jail with the sheriff's office attached. Fieyn was gone, along with Reece, searching for Bessy's reckless husband. She had no idea how long they would be, so she needed to act quickly. With a resolute stride, she left the guesthouse, locked the main door – which was something she never did – and marched towards the jail.

"Why, hello again, Miss Bessy!"

Her heart leapt up into her mouth and she whirled around to find Hoffstedder standing, leaning against a hitching rail on the opposite side of the street, grinning like the great oaf he was.

Before she could react, he rattled on, "Now that you're rested, I'll call around and get started on the measuring up, if that's all right with you?"

She gaped at him. Measuring up? Oh God, she'd forgotten, hadn't figured this intrusion into her plans. She reeled backwards, hand coming to her forehead, the feeling of the world conspiring against her growing with every rasping breath issuing from her throat. "Oh my ...No, no that won't do."

Frowning, Hoffstedder tilted his head and wandered towards her, a frown of concern cutting into his features. "Say, are you all right, Miss Bessy? You look kinda peaky."

"What? Oh, no, that's just ... Listen, Mr Hoffstedder, now isn't really a good time, I have to go to the sheriff and—"

"He's gone, Miss Bessy. Went off with that stranger and a few others, to find your husband. Surely you knew that?"

"What? Oh, yes, yes, of course. No, I..."

"Is anything wrong? Something I can help you with? I don't think there's anyone in Fieyn's office 'cepting for those two wild boys locked up in the jail. Maybe if you tell me what the problem is I could help you out?"

Hand falling to her face, she unconsciously squeezed her cheeks with finger and thumb. Why wouldn't this awful man leave her alone? Every moment wasted talking with him brought Fieyn's return ever closer. "Mr Hoffstedder," Bessy said, a new strength coming into her voice, "I need to get on. Thank you for your concern but there really isn't anything you can do."

"Like I said, if you..."

"Please, Mr Hoffstedder – I have to get on. Thank you and good morning."

She swung away, eyes closed, hoping against hope he'd disappear. Not daring to breathe, she continued on her way to the jailhouse and mounted the steps. She knew he was still there; she could feel his eyes boring into her but, steeling herself not to face him, she went through the door and pushed it closed behind her. Only then did she release her breath.

Inside the cramped, dreary office, it took a few moments before her eyes adjusted to the gloom. A man, tall and gaunt, stood inside the tiny cell, his skeletal hands gripping the bars, huge black eyes glaring out from the chalk whiteness of his face. Somewhere close behind him the shape of another lay stretched out on the narrow bunk.

"Well, good morning, ma'am," said the thin one, licking his lips as his eyes travelled over Bessy's body.

She recoiled at his stare, at his lewd expression, his tongue running across those wet, slack lips.

"You come to serve us breakfast ... Or maybe something else?"

He chuckled to himself. Bessy wavered, reconsidering her initial thought. To get these men to help her. To take Bourne out to the rear of the guesthouse, cover him in her flat wagon, take him out of town, dump the body, return, and ...

Groping for the nearby chair, she collapsed into it and sat, staring at the floor, overcome with despair.

"Hey now," said the thin one, his voice sounding genuinely concerned, "if you've got a problem, Miss, we can help. I promise you."

"Frank?" The other man sat up from the bunk and joined his partner. "Who is it?"

"It's Miss Bessy," said Frank. "She needs our help. Ain't that right, Miss Bessy?"

She forced her head up. "I'll pay you."

"You'll pay ... Missy, you have to get us out of here first."

"I will," she said, breathlessly, "I will, I just need you ... I need your help and I'm willing to pay you. A lot."

Frowning, Frank turned to his partner. "A lot? You hear that, Weasel?"

"How much is 'a lot', lady?"

Bessy shifted her gaze towards the wall behind Fieyn's desk. On a wooden rack hung the jail keys, dangling from a hook. Propped next to this were two repeating carbines and a scatter-gun. Without hesitation, she went to the shotgun and picked it up.

"Hey now," said Frank, some of his former cockiness deserting him, "what you fixing on doing, Miss Bessy?"

She cracked open the gun, pulled out a drawer in the desk, and fished out a bunch of cartridges. She fed two into the shotgun and closed it with a resounding snap. Pulling down the keys she turned and hurled them through the bars of the jail-house cage in which the two men were ensnared. "Let yourselves out and then step outside. I'm not much good with a rifle but I reckon even I could put a hole in you with this thing."

"What's this about, lady?" asked Weasel, watching Frank retrieve the keys and rattle one of them into the lock.

"I'm willing to give you fifty dollars if you help me and keep your mouths shut."

"Fifty dollars?" Frank grinned as the lock clunked. He pushed the heavy iron door open. "Sounds like whatever trouble you've gotten yourself into is kinda big."

"Move," she said, surprising herself at the ferocity of her voice.

Frank shrugged. "Sure thing, Miss Bessy. For fifty dollars we'll do whatever it is you need us to do."

Hands raised, the two men edged slowly towards the main door, both of them keeping their eyes glued to the shotgun in Miss Bessy's shaking hands.

"You be careful with that thing," said Weasel.

"You be careful and do as you're told. Now, outside, and check no one is watching. I want this done quick and easy."

"Whatever you say," said Frank and stepped out into the daylight.

CHAPTER TWENTY

Reece sat in silence, using an old, twisted twig he'd found to scratch random patterns in the dirt. Beside him, Fieyn quietly rolled himself a cigarette. "That drifter told me his story," said the sheriff, lighting his smoke and puffing on it for a few quiet moments.

"What did you make of it?"

"Not sure if I can make sense of any of it. He seemed sincere enough although he couldn't offer up any kind of explanation."

"What happened to him?"

Fieyn gave a quick resume before he sat down on the steps next to Reece.

"Does sound weird," said Reece.

"He refuses to go back inside, keeps saying it's Destry's fault."

"Destry has his own nightmares to come to terms with. None of this makes sense, not to me at least."

"He told you everything?"

"I guess. He broke down towards the end. I'd say he was terrified."

"I know Destry's story well enough – it's been all around the town and back a hundred times. How he chased those bush-

MILKY TRAIL TO DEATH

whackers up here and that they're still locked up inside that damn mine."

"Bushwhackers." Reece pressed the twig into the ground with considerable force. It snapped under the pressure. "I've had my fill of those."

Fieyn studied his companion. Without a word, he rolled Reece a cigarette and handed it over. Reece took it with a slight nod of thanks and leaned forward, cupping his hands around the flame of Fieyn's struck match. "I tend not to think about it too much," said Reece, blowing out a stream of smoke. "I ain't never spoken about it."

"No reason why you should," said Fieyn, looking out towards the mountains.

"That damned Partisan Ranger Act meant any bunch of dumb-assed murderers could group together and do what the hell they wanted. They were mean, violent, and Godless. Dressed up to impress with their gaudy embroidered shirts, some of 'em wearing six or even more pistols. They thought themselves blessed – invincible."

"I'm guessing you're gonna tell me you proved 'em wrong?"

Nodding, Reece studied the burning end of his cigarette. "You're damned right, Sheriff. They came into my hometown – no more than a few houses thrown together along with a tiny church and a schoolhouse." He laughed. "Penny taught half-a-dozen kids their letters and numbers. She was well-loved was Penny."

"Penny? Your wife?"

"Sister. Youngest of our family. The eldest, that's Rachel, she's over in California."

"So, you were the middle one. Always the toughest."

"No, that was Nathaniel, but he got himself killed at Chicka-mauga. Dumb-ass stupid thing to do. Jordan, my other brother, got his at Wyse Fork, which was *really* dumb as he was in the artillery, and ..." He shook his head again and, after giving his cigarette a final pull, threw it away. "What happened with them bushwhackers was before all that. I was serving with a frontier force when I got news of what they did. A bunch of 'em led by John Nichols rode in and shot up the town. Killed a lot of towns-folk, including three of the kids and the old parson, who was the only one who tried to stop 'em...apart from Penny."

"They murdered her too?"

"Yeah ... after they done what they done."

"You mean ...?"

"You want a picture?" Reece's eyes raged and Fieyn turned away. "Damn, I'm sorry," Reece said urgently, "I didn't mean to ..." He stifled something, swallowed hard, blew out a sigh. "You heard of John Nichols?"

"Can't say I have."

"They strung him up, eventually, for all the things he done. So, I guess a kind of justice was made." He shook his head. "Perhaps ..."

Fieyn waited but Reece said nothing more for a few moments. He took his time, gathering himself. It was difficult bringing it all back. He'd kept it buried for so long, believing that was the best way to deal with it all. Now, with it all welling up from deep within, although he dreaded how he felt, he knew this was a vital moment. The demons had to be expunged.

"We was operating close to Sedalia," he began, voice low, reluc-tant almost, but gathering in assuredness as he continued. "We were all tired, exhausted. The killings, from both sides, had got to us all, sucked the marrow from our bones. Sometime in the late winter, a young scout joined us, bringing fresh eyes to our search. I don't reckon I've ever met anyone so skilled, before or since. His name was Cole, and, despite his tender years, he had a maturity about him that gave us all confidence in his abilities. He also renewed our desire to get the job done. We'd shot on sight whole bands of bushwhackers operating throughout Missouri and the governors of Sedalia were happy enough to grant us immunity as attacks on isolated farmsteads and unwary travelers continued. The one placed at the top of their list was John Nichols.

"Cole picked up the trail easily enough and set us on our way. He left us then, having been assigned to other duties, and we were grateful for his service. But then, a diversion meant our hunt for Nichols took something of an interruption."

He rubbed his face with both hands as if he were washing away the grime that the retelling brought to his skin. After blowing out his cheeks, he returned to his story. "We fell upon a bunch of renegades who were concentrating so much on their excesses that they did not notice us until we were upon them.

"It was only as we drew close that we saw what was happening. A small homestead, a few animals, a tiny patch of struggling vegetables, and a field of corn. A small barn, ablaze, the horses already tethered, awaiting removal. A steer, butchered, and the menfolk, stripped naked and lashed to fencing. Not so far, close enough for them to be in full view, three women pegged on the ground, a young girl held firm by a brute and forced to witness, together with the men, what occurred. Each woman feasted upon, in turn, by those devils."

"Feasted?"

Reece stared deep into Fieyn's. "That is the only way I can put it. Their mouths were clamped around necks and breasts. Blood spewed from torn open veins, even as those men drove into those helpless women, soaking them all in red gore. Violence and bestiality melded into one. Their screams, they will live with me forever."

"Dear Christ. So ... what did you do?"

"Several others were milling about. We shot them, showing no mercy, even as they fell to their knees and begged us to stop. Dismounting, we set about the others. I killed the one holding the girl whilst the others pulled the rapists away from their victims, dragged them across the yard and bundled them in the center. They were wild. Writhing, kicking, shrieking, all desperate to return to their ..." He shook his head. "We tied 'em up, back-to-back and set them in a tight circle. The women, they were past caring for. I cut free the men and they ran to their women, throwing their arms around them. But they were already dead.

"Those men, they didn't hesitate. Without any encouragement from us, they gathered wood and straw bales, bundled them around those monsters and stepped away to gather their wits, preparing themselves for what they planned to do."

"Burn 'em?"

Reece nodded. "We stood back and did nothing to stop 'em. I don't think any of us wanted to anyways, after what those monsters had done. I remember the look on the faces of the menfolk, as if possessed, as they set upon their purpose, and those bushwhackers, struggling hopelessly, teeth-gnashing, spitting out blood from their gaping mouths, skin unearthly white ... almost as if they was already dead."

"Like corpses, you mean?"

"They already had that horrible green tinge you see in corpses. How, or why, I cannot begin to comprehend, but I saw it. I saw it all. 'They came from hell,' one of the menfolk shouted out, his face turned skywards, 'dear God forgive us. Forgive us all!'

"What in creation did he mean by that?"

"I don't know. The ones tethered together? They were not like the others we'd killed. And when the straw was set alight and the flames licked at their limbs, their screams ... Screeches wrenched from their throats, loud, chilling, so high-pitched my ears almost burst, forcing me to clamp my hands over them. These were not natural sounds. Not of this world anyway.

"I could not turn away. I had to witness it all, compelled by something so powerful, so strong I could not resist. It all seemed endless and perhaps that was how it should be. As punishment, retribution, nothing could surpass this. I watched as those flames engulfed them, saw them helplessly buck and kick until, at last, their struggles ceased, and they died, burned alive until they were nothing but a twisted, charred mess.

"We buried the women, the eldest of the men, maybe the father, said some words. We stood a little way off in silence. None of us had anything to say. What could we say? We'd witnessed something so *unholy* it had struck us all dumb.

"Maybe an hour, maybe two, I can't recall, we slowly drifted away. The gunshots rang out not long after. There were three, evenly placed. We reigned in, exchanging looks but nothing else. When a fourth shot shattered the silence, we rode on, no need to return and confirm what we all knew – the father had killed 'em all before turning his pistol on himself.

"I didn't know it then, didn't know it until I returned here only days ago."

"Didn't know what?"

"Those killings, that burning of those *things* ...it was close to here, Fieyn. A mile or so from the town of Whitewater." He released a long sigh. "I think it's all connected somehow. Don't ask me how I know, it's only a feeling but a mighty strong one. The mine, what Destry spoke about, there's something here. I didn't want to believe it but now, having heard the story from the drifter about seeing his mother and all ... there is something here. A presence."

Fieyn stared. "If that is true ... If what you saw is linked with what Destry spoke of, then his sealing of the mine has to be the finest thing he's ever done."

"Yeah." Reece stood up and stretched out his back. He readjusted his gun belt and gestured towards where the drifter remained sitting as if in a trance. "But perhaps what happened to him means that whatever it is that Destry trapped inside has somehow found a way out."

CHAPTER TWENTY-ONE

Henry lay on the big double-bed, arms behind his head, staring up at the ceiling. Next to him, one slim leg draped over his, Eva stared up into his chiseled face while her fingers absently played at the thick mat of hair covering his chest.

"Do you think we will ever have our own place?" she said wistfully.

He slowly lowered one hand from its position and stroked her hair. "Is that what you'd like? A little spread, breed horses perhaps? Grow beans?"

"Make love," she said, "without having to forever worry about getting caught."

"Yeah," said Henry with feeling, "that would be something."

"It is nothing but a dream, I know, but I so long for us to be together."

"It could come true. If Quince rewards me when all of this is done."

"You think he will?"

"I'm hopeful. If the rumors are true, there's gold in that mine. A lot of gold. I've been with him for a long time, right through the War, and kept him safe. He owes me, I reckon."

She grunted before she rolled over onto her back. "That mine is a bad place. They say it is haunted."

"Pfff, that's just nonsense."

"I listen to the cleaners, the two Shoshone girls, and they talk about it. When that man came ..."

"Who? Bourne?"

"Yes. When he came to talk to Senor Quince about finding a map of the mine, they wanted to run away. I had to convince them nothing bad would happen to us here."

"Indians are always full of fairytales, Eva. Mexicans too."

She propped herself up on her elbow and glared. "You should take notice of those fairytales, Henry. Those girls, they told me things."

"What sort of things?"

"About what happened in the mine, to those riders who came to the town at the end of the War.? They disappeared, Henry."

"You don't know that. No one knows." He blew out a loud sigh. "That's what Bourne was supposed to find out from that wastrel Destry. As soon as he gets back then we'll know more."

"And you will go there, to the mine?"

"It's what the boss wants. Destry has a map, we know that much, and it'll show where we can best extract the gold. It'll take some time but once we hit the seam, we will be rich, Eva. Rich beyond our dreams. And *your* dream will come true."

"It's a simple dream, my love. You and me and a small spread. We can live out our lives in peace, together."

"Making love, you said." He grinned at her then sucked in a breath as her hands drifted to the warmth between his legs and his heaviness lying across his thigh.

"Yes. Like now, only more.'

She moaned as she traced the outline of his hardening manhood. He gasped as she rolled on top of him, her soft hands guiding him once more to satisfy her endless desire for his lovemaking.

. . .

The slam of the front door crashing against the inside wall rever-berated throughout the house. Henry sat bolt upright, instinc-tively reaching for his gun as the voice came, shouting loud and urgent, "*Mr Quince? Mr Quince, you've gotta come quick!*"

Hastily pulling on some clothes, Henry took the stairs two at a time. With his gun drawn, he careened into Manchester who had Otis in an embrace. But not a welcoming one. The young cowpuncher, his eyes wide with terror, sprayed spit as he strug-gled to free himself. "Get Mr Quince! Henry, oh Christ, Henry, call Mr Quince!"

Twisting his head around, Manchester shot Henry a pleading look. "Get the boss, Mr Henry. I don' think I can hold him much longer."

"Otis," snapped Henry, stepping up close, "you calm down now, you hear, and tell me what the hell is going on!"

For a moment it seemed Henry's sharp tones worked. Otis abruptly stopped, his frantic breathing the one remaining indica-tion he was distressed beyond words.

"All right," he said, voice a virtual whisper.

Manchester relaxed his grip. That was his first mistake. His second was not swiveling his body. He screamed as Otis rammed his knee into the butler's groin. Gathering himself, he drew back his fist to finish the much older man but stopped as Henry pressed the muzzle of his Colt against Otis' head and cocked the hammer. "You cease, Otis, or I'll kill you where you stand."

"What in the name of the Almighty is going on here?"

Henry didn't turn. He didn't need to. Quince's booming voice was unmistakable.

His employer came up alongside Henry. He was breathing almost as hard as Otis. Dressed in a silk dressing-gown, feet pushed into plush slippers, with his voice thick with sleep, Quince boiled with barely controlled rage. He wrenched the gun from Henry's hand and aimed it directly towards Otis. "Tell me."

Something changed in Otis's expression. Perhaps the memory of what he'd witnessed, perhaps the enormity of the situation he now found himself in. Whatever it was, the light went out of his eyes, his shoulders slumped, and he dropped heavily to his knees and broke down in tears, hands clamped over his face, wailing like an infant.

"Richard, Richard don't do it."

Perhaps the only one in the entire household to have any control over Quince, Jennifer, his current lover, appeared from upstairs, leaning over the balcony, face awash with horror.

"Richard put the damn gun down and let him speak."

Quince appeared to falter. Henry took the chance and relieved his boss of the gun. At his feet, Manchester was moaning a little less loudly now, mumbling, "I'm sorry, sir, I'm sorry."

"Shut the hell up, Manchester," spat Quince, stumbling to the large dining table which dominated the room. He swept up a decanter half-full of amber liquid and poured himself a healthy measure into a cut-glass tumbler.

Ignoring Otis, Henry stooped down and helped the stricken Manchester to his feet. Appearing next to him, Jennifer took his place and helped the butler across to the table where Eva was already pouring him a drink. Henry watched them all and it struck him how orderly they all seemed as if nothing out of the ordinary had happened. He wanted to laugh but then Otis croaked and once again all of his attention was drawn to the young cowpuncher.

"We gotta get ready," said Otis between sobs. "They ain't far and there's plenty of 'em. Henry, we gotta get—"

"What the hell are you babbling about, boy?"

"Injuns, Mr Henry. I seen 'em on my way back from town. Lots of 'em, more than there should be."

"Indians?" It was Quince and, throat now lubricated with whisky, he sounded more in control of his emotions. "You saw Indians?"

Nodding vigorously, Otis climbed to his feet. "Oh yes, Mr Quince, I seen 'em. In their camp, naked as the day they was born, weapons ready, dancing and chanting the way they do and—"

"Dancin'?" Quince strode forward, gripped Otis by the chin and marched him directly into the far wall, slamming him up against it. "There ain't no Indians around here, boy. Hasn't been since before the War. You get me?"

Blinking rapidly, Otis squirmed beneath the strength of his employer's grip. He struggled to remember exactly what it was he'd seen. "I'm certain I saw 'em, Mr Quince."

"Damn your hide, boy, if you've been drinking and I find you're lying to me, I'll..." He took in a huge breath. "Where is Frank and Weasel? Did you leave them in town? What happened?"

. "The drifter, he put Frank down as if he were a wet rag. Fieyn did for Weasel, clubbing him on the back of the head and—"

"Fieyn? That miserable cur, I'll grind him to dust!"

"They put 'em in the jail and told me, *ordered me*, to come and tell you what they'd done."

"Why?" said Henry, coming up close, "Why would Fieyn say that to you?"

"I don't know, Mr Henry, I just know he did. They was planning on going to the mine, you see, and they wanted you to know that that was their plan."

Quince relaxed his grip and Otis sagged against the wall.

"The *mine*?" Quince looked at his trail boss. "Why would they go to the mine?"

Henry shrugged and was about to speak but Otis got there first, "They were after Destry, boss. He's gone missing and someone had found his horse. So, they went there to look for him."

"So, they've all gone to the mine?" Quince released the young cowpuncher and stepped away, leaving Otis sucking in breath, bent double, barely able to believe he was still alive by the look on his red face.

"Where was Bourne, Otis? Did you see him anywhere?"

"No, Mr Henry. Not a sign."

Quince was staring into space, lost in thought, "And the drifter ... what is his name?"

"According to Bourne, his name is Reece," said Henry, at last holstering his pistol. "He's not a drifter, Mr Quince. He's some sort of lawman."

Quince's eyes glowered. "A lawman?"

"Or a bounty hunter. Bourne wasn't sure, but that's what he said this Reece is. Good with his gun, he reckoned."

"And his fists, by golly," said Otis quickly. "I never thought I'd see Frank dumped like that. One blow."

"And what did you do?"

"*Me?* Damn it, Mr Henry, I got out. And as I rode away, I came across that camp, with them injuns, and they looked as if they were getting ready for a raid. Maybe here."

"There ain't no Indian camp," said Quince and returned to the table. He sat down heavily in one of the chairs arranged there. Jennifer, without instruction, set to massaging Quince's shoulders. "Any Indians were rounded up and sent to the reservation."

"They must have got out."

"No." Quince reached over for the decanter and poured himself another drink. "We'd have heard."

"This camp," said Henry, holding Otis' stare. "Describe it."

"Well, it was ... To be honest, Mr Henry, that's the weird part. It seemed to have been abandoned, a long time ago for sure. But those savages, they came upon me like ghosts, moving as quiet as the breeze. Surrounded me they did. I only just managed to get away."

"Like ghosts ... Otis, you're sure they were Indians? What I'm saying is, they weren't drifting soldiers, returning from the War?"

"No, Mr Henry, they was savages. Naked they was, armed with axes and knives."

115

"No firearms?"

"Not that I could see."

"What are you getting at, Henry?" asked Quince.

"There used to be a camp not so far from here, in the old days. I remember a band of riders attacking it, butchering the women and children there. During the War that was, when those Indians were about to be rounded up and taken north to one of the reservations. As far as I recall, those riders, they burned the settlement to the ground."

"They've come back," said Otis, moving as if in a dream towards the open door. He looked out across the sprawling ranch. "I reckon they've been waiting for the War to end and now they're set to reap their revenge."

"For what?" asked Quince from the table. "It wasn't any of us who burned down their camp. Why come here?"

"Boss ..."

All eyes turned towards Henry, whose expression had grown drawn, haunted. "I was there together with Fieyn, Brad Swail, Destry too. And Old Man White. There was a rumour that a bunch of savages had rustled some steers. Times were hard, people starving all over, but those savages, they were suffering worse than most. We got news that they were to be moved, made safe in the reservation and White, he said he couldn't abide that seeing as they were murdering dogs. He had some history with 'em and, with the rustling in everyone's mind, we went there."

"History? What are you talking about Henry?"

"The mine, boss. The gold White found there. Those Indians, they said the land was sacred to them, that it was the resting place for ancestors. Ancestors from before the age of man, so they said."

"Are you kidding me?" Quince got to his feet, a little more unsteadily now as the drink took hold.

"Hell, I don't know if any of it is true, but those Indians sure believed it and they were not happy with White going there. I reckon that was why he was so anxious for us to attack their camp." Closing his eyes, he took a deep breath. "Which we did. We burned it to the ground and ..." His eyes opened and they were wet. "We butchered them all. Men, women ... children."

"Sweet Jesus," gasped Otis, turning from the door. "And now they're coming. Coming for all of us."

Eva cried out, making the sign of the cross before collapsing onto a chair.

Everyone else stood and stared.

CHAPTER TWENTY-TWO

A cross the rutted yard, the two men sweated, struggled, and cursed as they dragged Bourne's inert form towards the small outhouse, beside which Bessy stood waiting, the scattergun in her hands.

"Put him under a pile of old timber and tarpaulins," she instructed. "No one ever comes in here."

"They will once he starts to ripen," said Frank, putting his hands into the small of his back and arching backwards.

"When that happens, we'll move him."

"We?" scoffed Weasel. "Lady, our involvement in this sorry mess ends after we cover him over."

"That's right," joined in Frank. "You're on your own from now on."

"Check his pockets," Bessy said, motioning with the scattergun. "You can keep any money but any papers, letters, plans and such, you give to me."

"Plans?" Weasel got down on his knees and rifled through the man's jacket. "What sort of plans?"

"Never mind, just look."

Weasel grunted and continued with his search.

"Quince won't have paid him yet," said Frank, "so I doubt he'll have much money."

"Quince?" Bessy reeled backwards, slamming herself into the jamb of the door. "He works for Quince?"

"You didn't know?" Giggling, Frank stepped in front of her. "I reckon once Mr Quince gets wind of what you've done, he'll be paying you a visit."

"Fifteen dollars," said Weasel with a whistle and stood up. He waved the bills in his hand. "A tasty sum, but not enough to ensure our silence."

"What the hell do you mean by that?"

Frank tutted, took a glance towards his friend and laughed. "How much do you think that'll take, Weasel?"

"She said fifty for moving the body, I'm thinking another fifty to keep our mouths shut."

Nodding his agreement, Frank turned once again to Bessy. "I think that's just about fair. A hundred dollars...*each*."

"*A hundred*... Are you out of your mind? I don't have that sort of money lying around."

"Then you need to run over to the bank to get it, otherwise the next person you'll be talking to will be Mr Quince himself."

His laughter filled the space, a horrible, malicious sound causing Bessy to become light-headed. Nauseous and confused, her knees buckled beneath her, threatening to give way. Frank took his chance and struck as quick as a rattler, his hand streaking out to seize the scattergun and wrest it from Bessy's hands. She gasped and froze, disbelief etched into every line of her face. And then, he slapped her hard. With a yelp, she crumpled and slid down the wall. Towering over her, Frank pressed the twin barrels hard into her head.

Late afternoon, the sun already dipping below the mountainside. Soon, the chill evening air would bite, fires would be lit as people prepared for the night. Out here, in the bleakness of the still-

119

developing Territories, the weather was cruel. In the summer, the daytime heat unrelenting, the nights as cold as the freezing wastes of the far north. Weasel knew all about the far north. He'd labored there for years, digging for gold amongst cruel rock sides, panning in freezing rivers. This was nothing for him but for Bessy, it was as if she were tramping through huge snowdrifts. She trembled uncontrollably, hugging herself, nothing but a thin shawl to protect her from the elements. Ignored tears ran unchecked down her face. Someone calls out to her. She ignores that also. Weasel's hand grips her around the bicep. He is hurting her, and she steels herself to bear it, to get through, to do as ordered. There is no choice. She murdered Bourne and these horrible men are helping her, at a dreadful price.

Stumbling up the steps to the bank, inside old Morrison is lighting an oil lamp. He lifts his head and frowns as Bessy steps inside with her agitated companion. Penny Minister is in the corner, filling out a form. She goes to speak but checks herself when Bessy flashes her a warning look.

"Why, good afternoon Miss Bessy," Morrison said and slipped behind the counter. He fits the bolt under the levered hatch and delicately settled a pair of pince-nez on his face. "How can I help you?"

Bessy, breathing raggedly through her mouth, shoots a glance at Penny then back to Morrison. "I want to withdraw two hundred dollars."

Morrison goes to speak then stops, mouth agog, eyes flickering, not quite sure he has understood. It takes him a moment to recover his wits. "Two ... two-*hundred* dollars?"

"That's right, you old goat," hisses Weasel, leaning ominously forward. He continued to hold Bessy by the arm but now his free hand creeps menacingly towards the gun in his waistband. "Is there a problem?"

Morrison, the frown cutting deep into his features, shook his head. With his eyes lashed to Weasel's gun, he swallowed loudly and forced a strangulated laugh. "No, no. Of course not, but—"

"Ain't got time for buts," said Weasel, fingers drumming the revolver, "so get the Goddamned money."

"It's not that I can't," spluttered Morrison, destressed, noticeably confused about what to do. To take some comfort, he turned his pleading eyes on Bessy. "It's just that, for such a large amount, I'll need Destry's signature on the application as well as your own."

Bessy watched the man's Adam's apple wobbling as he gulped loudly. Next to her, Weasel blew out a loud sigh. Penny, from the corner, stood up and briskly left.

"Where the hell you goin'?" said Weasel, turning so fast his hand came free from Bessy's arm. Instantly, with the sound of Penny's heals clunking across the wooden floor so loud it filled the whole bank, Bessy leaned over the counter and mouthed towards Morrison, 'Help me.'

Either because of Morrison's shocked expression or the fact that Bessy leaned close towards the diminutive bank-teller, Weasel reacted with lightning speed, drawing his pistol and pointing it directly towards Morrison. He cackled, "Get Miss Bessy her money, pip-squeak, or I'll blow a hole in your head so big you could run steers through it!"

Instinctively, Morrison shot his hands upwards, "I can't – not without her husband's say-so."

"Do it," spat Weasel and he cocked his pistol with exaggerated slowness, "or I'll end your miserable life right here and now."

Frank sat at the large kitchen table, his feet propped on its surface, and opened the paper Weasel had surreptitiously taken from Bourne's pocket.

It was a sketch map, crudely drawn but easy enough to follow. It showed a route, taken from the town to the mine. A scratchy, snaking line trailed through the woods but then, instead of making towards the shack and the mountains beyond, it veered off to the right, cutting a path through the woods. Unless it was sign-posted, mused Frank, it would be difficult to follow with certainty. The handwriting, which picked out certain places, the town, the shack, the woods, was difficult to decipher but he thought he could pick out the words 'cut down tree and stones' but wondered what that might mean. Only a visit would make everything clear. He frowned, peering closer. The trail twisted through the wood in a wide detour and eventually ended way behind where the mine was situated. A large X marked the termination of the path. But what might be there, Frank could not tell. There was nothing in the writing to indicate what it could be. Simply an abrupt end.

Folding the map, he leaned further back in his chair. It creaked underneath his weight, but he ignored it, tapping his mouth with the map, deep in thought.

The chair creaked again but he did not think anything of it. The furniture throughout the guesthouse struck him as being old and close to collapse. Bessy and her husband were struggling for money, that much was clear. Travelers rarely visited the town and, what with the war now ended, people's ambitions were centered on California, not washed-up, tired and remote old places like Whitewater. Perhaps though, with this intriguing map and the promise of something advantageous, fortunes might change.

Again, the creak. Frank sat up, angered by what he believed to be the imminent collapse of the chair. He twisted around to inspect the joint closest to where the seat joined the legs and caught sight of the figure standing in the doorway. A figure that Frank thought he recognized but couldn't be sure due to the bandana worn across the man's mouth and jaw. Might it be Bourne? But Bourne was dead, wasn't he?

Frank screamed, throwing himself backwards, hand scrambling for the gun at his hip as the chair crashed to the floor.

"Oh, sweet Jesus," he said and clawed at his Colt revolver.

The gun in the figure's hand fired once, blowing a hole as

large as a grapefruit in Frank's chest, sending him spiraling backwards across the kitchen to smash into a collection of pots and pans, which set up a tremendous noise. But Frank didn't hear any of that. He wouldn't hear anything ever again.

The figure stepped over to Frank's bloody body and retrieved the map. He studied it carefully, laughed once, and threw it into the far corner.

He no longer needed it.

Whitewater was a small town, a cluster of barely a dozen buildings set along a narrow main street. Several narrow passageways led to rear yards but essentially the town was one street. Small, compact, rundown and depressing. So, the gunshot, when it came, could be heard anywhere and everywhere in that small place. And Weasel, who was debating whether or not to put a bullet into Morrison's head or not, froze senses on full alert and cocked his head to listen.

"What the hell ...?"

Snapping his head around to face Miss Bessy once more, he gasped, "Shit ... Who might that be?"

Bessy shrugged. She expressed little concern in her features. Dismissing her, Weasel strode through the bank entrance and into the street, calling as he went, "Don't move. I'll be back."

Pulling back the various pieces of debris that disguised the body, he gasped when Bourne's eyes sprang open. Raising a hand to calm him, the man continued to throw the wooden slats aside.

Groaning, Bourne tried to sit up.

"You rest easy," said the man through gritted teeth.

"What ..." Pressing a hand against the side of his head, Bourne winced and immediately withdrew his hand and saw the blood there. "Who..."

"You've had a knock is all," said the man and helped Bourne to his feet.

"But ... Who...Who are you?"

"I shot the one who did it to you, sitting there like he owns the place. He ain't owning anything more, I can tell you."

"Yes, yes, but ..." Putting the back of his hand to his forehead, Bourne swayed to his right and would have collapsed if the stranger had not held onto him.

"Take it easy. You wait here for a while, get your strength back. Here," he produced a canteen of water. Bourne took it and drank greedily from it.

"What ... I don't understand any of this. Who are you?"

"I'm a friend. I saw what Bessy did, letting them Frank and that skinny one out of the jail. I followed 'em and waited outside until Bessy and Skinny went down to the bank. I reckon that was for a payment of sorts. I went through the back of the guesthouse, saw the blood in the kitchen, together with Frank and put two and two together. It was easy enough to follow the blood trail to here. You're lucky to be alive."

"Yeah ..." Bourne studied the blood on his fingers. "It was Bessy. She hit me, damn her."

"Hit you? What with, a sledgehammer?"

"As good as." He took another long drink from the canteen and handed it back. "Thank you."

The man lifted the badly folded map. "You know what this is?"

"Yes!" Bourne made a grab for it but the stranger snapped it away. "That's mine!"

"It could well be, but I think I'll be taking care of it for the time being. Maybe we can come to an arrangement. What do you think?"

"All depends on what that arrangement is."

The stranger smiled as he carefully put the map inside his coat pocket. "Let me explain it to you then."

. . .

124

For himself, Weasel couldn't explain the awful sense of fore-boding creeping through his guts as he approached the guest-house. A man of limited imagination, he took life as he found it without looking for reasons why things happened the way they did. Not in the least religious, his belief system was based on how much he could drink before he fell down, deciding argu-ments with either his gun or his knife. In his twenty-two years on this planet, he had killed three men. Not a large total by any means, nevertheless one of which he was immensely proud. It made him feel more of a man, sent shivers of fear through his opponents, gave him a certain aura of respectability amongst his peers. Especially men such as Frank. Now there was someone who knew how to end an argument. He'd seen Frank gun down four men and knew, for certain, there were more. Frank had come out of Missouri after the Civil War's end and rumour had it he'd rode with 'Bloody Bill'. Whether or not that was true, Weasel didn't care. He knew Frank as a stone-cold killer, capable with both gun and fist. Which was why, given everything that had happened, the way the stranger put Frank down with such ease was a matter which caused Weasel a good deal of concern. There'd be a reckoning, he reassured himself as he marched along the street, eyes fixed straight ahead. And when they next met that stranger, they'd put him in the ground, Frank and him.

This idea perked him up a little. He had no idea if the gunshot had come from Bessy's, but he wasn't taking any chances. The stranger may already have returned and, on finding Frank at the guesthouse, had tried to get the better of him. Again. Well, if that was the case the reckoning was closer than anyone thought possible and Weasel, he'd be the one who ...

His thoughts came to an abrupt halt, as did he. A man was coming down the steps of the guesthouse. A man who shouldn't be there.

Bourne.

Weasel forced himself to wait. Consider his options. The man was Bourne all right, standing there, large as life. But surely, he was dead, wasn't he? The way they'd dragged him into the little outhouse, put all sorts of rubbish over his body. No man could have continued to sleep through that. Miss Bessy had told them she'd hit him, hard and, truth be known, one look at him lying there was proof enough that Bourne was no longer of this world. There could be no chance he was faking it. And yet, there he was.

Rubbing his chin, Weasel took a few deep breaths before he slowly pulled his gun from his waistband. He moved forward carefully, not wishing to cause Bourne any alarm that may spurt him into action. Weasel knew of the man's reputation. What was it Henry had said, 'The man is an assassin? Cold, heartless, willing to do anything he needs to. Don't upset him any, either of you.' That was back at the ranch before they came into town to face the stranger. How long ago was that? A day? It felt like a month, maybe longer. If Bourne had recovered and got up, gone back into the guest house, came across Frank ... Weasel swallowed hard and eased back the hammer of his gun.

Perhaps the reckoning was right here and right now.

"Bourne," he shouted, stopping again some twelve or so paces from where Bourne stood, deep thought, staring fixedly at something in the distance. He didn't react to Weasel's voice. "Bourne, you sonofabitch, what you done with Frank?"

Bourne, despite Weasel screaming his name loud enough to catch the attention of every inhabitant of Whitewater, did not flinch. Readjusting his jacket, he turned on his heels and moved in the opposite direction and headed towards Destry's livery stable.

With an almost uncontrollable urge to put a bullet in the man's back, Weasel stood heaving in breaths until he felt able to walk. To his left was Miss Bessy's guesthouse. Frank would tell him what was going on so, with renewed determination, Weasel strode across the street, heading towards the main door without another look in Bourne's direction.

So intent was he that he failed to notice the tall figure of

Nathan Hoffstedder approaching him from the opposite direction. "She's not well," he hollered, pulling Weasel up short.

Turning, Weasel gave the man a withering look. "What did you say?"

"Miss Bessy," said Hoffstedder, coming up close. "I just spoke to that other gentleman outside the livery. I believe he is staying here in the guesthouse but when I asked him about Miss Bessy's condition, he blanked me. He appeared to be in some sort of a daze. Perhaps he is a man on a mission. A little like yourself."

Weasel blew out a breath and turned to face this distraction. "Who in the hell are you, pipsqueak?"

Hoffstedder blinked and reeled backwards slightly. "I'm the decorator ..." He paused, putting his fists on his hips, "and I don't take too kindly to your tone, mister."

"Tell you what," fumed Weasel, drawing his revolver, "let's just say you turn around and go back to your mama before I plug you."

There was no reply save for a tiny whimper leaking from Hoffstedder's throat. Grunting, Weasel went through the main door.

The utter silence brought him up sharp. It was not a natural thing and caused the skin around his scrotum to tighten, the sweat to sprout from his forehead. The hand holding the gun shook and it took him some effort to ease back the hammer. "Frank?" He gave a little start, his own voice sounding almost unnatural, certainly unwanted in that stark, cold hallway. He went to the small reception desk. The ledger was open, and he turned it around. There was Bourne's name below that of another guest. Reece is all it said. That had to be the stranger, the one who'd put Frank's lights out.

Frank. The thought of his friend reminded him of why he was here. He waited, mouth open. Gradually, his senses picked out tiny, insignificant details. In the distance the steady, hollow thud of the grandfather clock coming from the lounge, a cart driven down the street, a horse galloping away, birds singing as they nested amongst the branches of the apple tree in the back yard. Normal, everyday sounds. Nothing sinister or unnatural about any of them and yet an atmosphere of terror seemed to emanate from every corner of the guesthouse. He cast a look to the staircase. Despite the day, the top stairs were cloaked in darkness. Anything could be lurking up there. Then, to the lounge, where guests might sit and relax before dinner, or in the evening, sip drinks. It was not a large room, a card table, three armchairs and a small sofa. The fire was prepared for the night when the temperature would drop. Other than these features of normality, there was nothing to cause him alarm. He drew in a deep breath. This time, when he spoke, his voice was little more than a croak, "Frank?"

At the end of the hallway, next to the dining room, was the kitchen. Here Miss Bessy prepared her numerous, splendid meals. Although Weasel had never stayed here, he was well aware of its reputation. He suddenly realized he was hungry. He should help himself to some eggs, he decided and stepped into the small, cluttered kitchen.

He saw the body immediately. Frank, his eyes wide open, body lying at an impossible angle, surrounded by pots, broken crockery, and so much blood Weasel struggled not to throw up there and then. He wheeled away and almost crashed into Hoffstedder who stood before him like a statue, face ashen, lips trembling. "Oh my God," he muttered.

Unwittingly, Weasel leaned into the man, resting his forehead against his chest. "It's Frank," he said.

Hoffstedder placed his hands on the other's scrawny shoulders. "We need to get the sheriff," he managed to say.

Hoffstedder's voice brought life back to Weasel, who sprang backwards, snorting breath through his nostrils, waving the revolver for emphasis as he blurted, "I'll kill him, so help me God. I'll kill him!"

Before Hoffstedder could offer up any reply or questions, Weasel pushed past him, rushing out into the diminishing daylight. He had only one thought now – to find Bourne and kill him. The mystery of how the man had recovered was not something which Weasel wished to consider right now. Such answers would come afterwards. He broke into a run and soon reached the livery.

Bourne, however, was long gone.

CHAPTER TWENTY-THREE

Ezra Soames pricked up his ears as the voice came to him, seemingly from the very air itself. "Come home to me now, my lovely. Come home to me. These men are dangerous. They are dangerous for us all, my lovely. Do what you must then come home to me."

He searched the surroundings for her. His mother. The only one who had ever accepted him loved him. She was here, impossible as it may seem, but she was so close. Her words, soothing despite being full of warning, brought a warmth to his body. But where was she?

He sat, as he had done since the others came upon him, on the broken-down veranda of the old shack, head in hands, until her voice drifted over him, like a soothing balm. Now, sitting up, he checked those others close by. None of them appeared to have noticed the voice. The ones who questioned him, the tall stranger and the sheriff, they were talking to each other. The group of other men were sharing something from a canteen. They laughed. Perhaps it was whisky. The only other, the man he'd found inside the shack, the one called Destry, stood alone, staring into the distance. A broken man, his experiences so terrible Ezra doubted he would ever recover.

Shrugging off these notions, he turned towards the woods. Was she in there, his mother? He frowned. How could she be? What was she doing here? The images of what he'd seen in the shack returned, the quaking in his guts growing. "My lovely," she said again, so quiet yet so insistent. "My lovely, do what you need to do. These men are dangerous, my lovely. Protect me. Protect us both."

Of course, she was right. She always was. She'd steered him through those dark days of his early life, defending himself from a violent, unpredictable father. He remembered how she'd shielded him from the blows, taking the fists meant for him on her own body. Never complaining, always willing to sacrifice. How he'd come home that night when war loomed, blind drunk, blaming everyone for what had happened. Ezra, fifteen years of age, stepping in as the first fist streaked through the air. He caught the wrist, slammed his own punch into his father's guts, dropping him like a stone. "I'll not take this anymore," he'd screeched and hit his father repeatedly until the man moved no more.

"You have to go," she'd said to him, already gathering together a few things, including her husband's old Paterson. "Take Jasper and ride south. They'll not follow you there, not now."

So, he'd kissed her and left, galloping off into the night, keeping himself well away from other folks, sleeping during the day, riding through the night. He sought food from the occasional farmstead. Some gave him hunks of bread without question, others were less generous. In less than a week, he was amongst the gathering armies of the south. It was not long before he fell in with bad company and found himself on the fringes of the Army of Virginia. He rode with men with far blacker hearts than his, ambushing Federal supply wagons, robbing banks, burning down farmsteads. It was only when they broke into one particular home, murdering the menfolk before turning their attentions to the women. Something snapped inside Ezra at that moment and, as his fellows partook of what they deemed were delights, Ezra slinked off and, mounting his horse, rode off never to return.

He persuaded himself his sense of right and wrong was far superior to the men he rode with during those dark days. Nathan Kelly caught up with him, spoke to him about duty, the need to continue the fight no matter what it might cost a man. "Even if it means selling your soul, Ezra," he'd said but riding into the town of Whitewater was something Ezra simply could not do.

The night before, unable to sleep, he'd wandered down to a brook. The water there was little more than a trickle but the Moon, peeping out from between the clouds, cast a silver glint upon the surface and for a moment, Ezra lost himself in dreams of home, his mother, of a life that might have been.

Something moved behind him, a fallen tree branch snapping underfoot. He whirled, gun already in his hand. "Who's there?" he demanded, standing up, struggling to make out any shapes in the darkness as the Moon disappeared behind those black clouds.

"You must not go, Ezra."

His body jerked in a spasm of utter terror. That voice, one he knew so well, the impossibility of it being here. "Ma?"

The figure appeared from the night, a vapid, not wholly formed shape, drifting in and out of reality. That voice, however, as real as life itself. His mother's voice, if not her body, coming to him in a soft, gentle whisper. "Do not follow them, Ezra. Nothing but ill will come of what happens tomorrow."

"Ma? How did you—"

"*Listen to me,*" her voice came, much sharper than before. "Do *not* go with them. Ride away now and do not look back."

"But, Ma, how can you ..."

He stopped, realizing he was talking to nothing but the night air. Whoever it was who had spoken to him, his mother or some imposter, a dream of hallucination, it was gone, mingling with the night, leaving him confused and terrified.

Without understanding, he did as she instructed and rode off. Now, years later, the lure of this place forced him to return and here he was, tramping along a half-concealed track through the woods, leading him to somewhere unknown. Whatever drew him ever deeper into the tangle of trees, it was irresistible. He did not stop to consider what drove him or why. He did not care. His mind, his will, they were no longer his. A force beyond understanding guided him now and there was little if anything he could do to resist.

After barking out orders, Reece went across to Destry who was standing, as if in a trance, gazing into the distance. Reece cleared his throat and slowly Destry came out of his daze and sighed. "You should never have come here."

Reece frowned. "What?"

"I knew from the moment I saw you that you were trouble. That's why I didn't accompany you to the guesthouse. I knew that once Quince's boys set eyes on you, trouble would follow."

"Don't try to be too self-righteous, you ungrateful bastard. You didn't accompany me because you had your own assignation to fulfil, Destry."

"What the hell are you talking about?"

A smile slowly crept across Reece's mouth. "Jesus, it didn't take you long to go back to your own self, did it? Your meetings with Lizzie Coombs, they—"

"Lizzie's dead, you blockhead!"

"I know that. But there are other whores over at Saint Francine's. That's where you were heading that night, so don't make out it was anything else."

"Now who's being self-righteous?"

"Get your things together, Destry. We're going back to town. When we get there, we can talk again."

"*Talk?*" He turned and spat. "I'll not talk to you again. I'm grateful for you finding me but there's gonna be a reckoning with

Quince and that gunfighter. What's his name? Bourne? Only then can you and me settle our differences."

"So Bourne's a gunfighter, is he?"

"Something like that. Gun hand, killer, whatever. He's meaner than a rattler with a toothache, I know that much. He has designs on Bessy, so I'd be mighty careful if I was you."

"Me? She's *your* wife!"

Destry's eyes narrowed. He was about to speak when Fieyn stepped up between them, his face serious. "He's gone."

Reece frowned. "Who?"

"The fella we found – what was his name? Soames?"

"Ezra," put in Destry. "Ezra Soames."

Nodding, Reece looked towards the wood, so deep, so dark. "You think he's gone to the mine?"

"Who knows?" said Fieyn. "Whatever he does is up to him, but the men are getting spooked. They want to head back to town now that we have Destry."

"I think that's probably for the best," said Reece.

Without another word, Reece strode over to where the horses were gathered, signaling to the men to mount up. After a pause, Destry followed with Fieyn close behind. Within ten minutes the band were making their way towards Whitewater.

None of them, not even Reece, noticed the rider on the hillside watching and only once they were all out of sight did he carefully steer his horse down the incline and make his way towards the narrow, hidden path which snaked through the woods.

CHAPTER TWENTY-FOUR

"I don't think he's coming back."

Morrison was stood in the bank doorway, half-crouching, looking down the street. The developing gloom did not make picking out details any easier and he sighed with frustration. "I can't make much out, Miss Daisy, but I think he went into your guesthouse."

"All right," she said, stepping up behind the bank teller. "What we can do is shut up and wait for the sheriff to return. That's the safest thing to do."

"And what if he does come back?"

"We bolt the door from the inside. This is a bank, Mr Morrison. It's built to withstand an assault."

"An assault?" The little man quaked, rushing inside. He turned up the large oil lamp on the table where Penny Minister had sat. This reminder gave Bessy the semblance of hope. "Perhaps Penny told someone?"

"Penny?" Morrison rubbed his hands together. It was growing cold, as it always did once the sun had gone down. Soon he would need his coat. "She might, she might not. Not sure who she can tell as most of the menfolk have gone looking for your husband."

"Word sure gets around fast."

"It's a small town, Miss Bessy. Not much goes unnoticed."

Was that a thinly disguised barb, Bessy thought. If it was, she was not to be drawn and chose to ignore it. Instead, she closed the door and lowered the crossbar. She then stooped and rammed home the bolt. "That should keep him out. Is there a rear entrance?"

"No. As you say, this is a bank. A brick box. One tiny window, which we can shutter, looking out onto the street is the only weak spot."

"We have no fire. No stove."

"Nope. Nothing." He shrugged. "Mrs Clapham brings me coffee and doughnuts for my lunch but that's my only luxury. I open at eight, close up at five."

"Won't your wife be worrying, Mr Morrison?"

"I'm usually home by six." He pulled out a silver pocket watch from his waistcoat and flicked open the silver lid. "She won't be worrying until at least seven. We've got almost two hours."

"Unless Mr Reece and Mr Fieyn return before then. With Destry."

"Let us pray that is the case."

Bessy went to the tiny window adjacent to the door. From here she could not quite make out the far end of the street where her guesthouse stood. Their only warning of Weasel's return would be when he demanded entrance. The thought worried her. What would they do then?

"That other man, the salesman?"

Bessy turned. The oil lamp oozed a weak, sickly yellow glow that seemed to wrap itself around the diminutive bank-teller and gave him a sickly pallor. She forced herself to hold his stare. "Mr Bourne."

"Yeah, that's him. Maybe he'll come a-calling?"

"I shouldn't think so," she said with a shudder and sat down at the small writing desk. "We'll just hope and pray that the sheriff will be here soon."

Nodding, Morrison pulled on his coat and moved behind the counter. "I'll finish the books, if that's all right with you, Miss Bessy. I'll then lock the money inside the safe. No point in not carrying out my duties just as normal."

Nodding, Bessy looked at the door, imagining that horrible Weasel pounding on it, demanding she open up. If she did, what next? She didn't have two hundred dollars, she doubted she barely had one hundred. Her offer came out of desperation, Bourne lying in the kitchen, the blood from his broken head leaking over the floor. Why had it come to this? How was it possible for life to take such a gut-wrenching turn for the worse? She was content enough running her guesthouse, transient guests coming and going, nobody asking anything of her, expecting merely what their payment for bed and board allowed. No complications, no problems. All in all, what she had was a simple life. Occasionally, as she often found herself remembering such liaisons with a certain wistfulness, a man would drift into her life. Nothing permanent, nothing hopeful. Until Reece, of course. There was something about him, which set him apart from any other. A brooding, mysterious individual, the way he looked at her sent a thrill through her heart. There could be no mistaking what that look meant. Perhaps with him, there could be something ...

With a start, she realized how much life had changed since his arrival. Were the two connected, or was that simply her imagination filling in the gaps? Certainly, before he came into her life things had gone seriously downhill, not least being the demise of Bourne.

She sighed, propped her chin on her hand, and closed her eyes. All these issues could be sorted once the sheriff returned. A full, honest explanation of what had happened with Bourne was the only sensible way to deal with it all.

CHAPTER TWENTY-FIVE

They deliberated in their own minds as to what to do next. Ezra Soames had slinked off and the assumption was he'd cut a path through the trees. A search resulted in no sign of him and now, at the edge of the deep, forbidding wood, Reece and Fieyn stood, neither speaking. Until that is, Destry came up behind them. There was a distinct note of mockery in his voice. "He's been summoned and there isn't a damn thing either of you can do about it."

The two others exchanged a look, and both turned to face the diminutive Destry. "Summoned?" Fieyn scoffed. "Who by? His momma?"

Destry sucked in a breath. "You don´t understand, Fieyn. You never have. You know what happened in the mine. Those raiders. Their disappearance. You've never accepted that there were powers at work, invisible powers. Unworldly."

"Unworldly?" Now it was Reece's turn to mock. "What are you talking about, Destry? All that ghost-nonsense again?"

"It's got nothing to do with ghosts. You, Sheriff, you know that, don't you?"

"I don't know anything, Destry. You've spouted this off many times since, but the truth is no closer to being revealed."

"No, not by you at least. You've never involved yourself in any of it, not from the moment those murdering bushwhackers came rushing into town, blazing away with their guns. You did nothing. You didn't come up with the rest of us and, afterwards, you sat in that jailhouse of yours with the doors locked, drinking whisky."

"You shut your mouth."

"You know why you didn´t come out, don´t you. I do. We all do. You was *scared*. Scared of what you knew was up there."

"You don't know anything about me or how I felt."

Reece could sense the sheriff´s body quaking with pent-up rage. He reached out and gently placed his hand on Fieyn's forearm. "Easy, Sheriff. Don't let him get you all riled up."

"And you?" spat Destry, turning his venom on the newcomer. "What are you doing here, Reece? Nobody seems to be able to understand your presence. You've been here before, haven't you?"

The silence roared around them. Fieyn was the first to react, jerking his arm away from Reece as his anger burst forward. "Is that true? You've been here before?"

"What if I have?"

Fieyn gaped. "When?"

Shrugging, Reece sighed and folded his arms. "I was in a troop, hunting down some bushwhackers."

"The ones who came here?"

"I don't know. We lost 'em. We tramped around for a while, but our scout had been relocated to other duties, so we didn't have the necessary skills to read any signs, or tracks. So, we turned back."

Fieyn, face drawn, body shaking, stared at Reece with incredulity. "They were the same men who came to Whitewater, killed poor old Burrows?" Fieyn shook his head. "And you never thought fit to tell me?"

"I didn't think it was all that important, Fieyn."

"Not all that ..." Fieyn swung away, face reddening appreciably. Squeezing his fists, he appeared to be struggling to prevent his anger from overwhelming him. "You knew what went on here, don't you? You've always known."

"Some. But I know a helluva lot more now." He nodded towards Destry, "Thanks to him."

"You should have said something," continued Fieyn. "I understand now why none of this shocks you. You know all about it – the killings, the gold, all of it."

"That´s why he´s here," said Destry. "For the gold."

"That´s not true," said Reece, dropping his hands. This altercation was developing into something unwanted and, he admitted to himself, potentially dangerous. Fieyn, for one, appeared more than agitated, as if he were fit to explode. Destry, on the other hand, had a mischievous air about him, enjoying setting the other two against one another. Was he doing this on purpose, to cause a rift, but for what reason?

"Then why *are* you here?" demanded Fieyn, rounding on his companion.

"I told you – I´m passing through, nothing more. I´m on my way to California to be with my sister. Look, Sheriff, you need to remember the reason I came up here, to this shack, was to help find Destry. Yes, it's true I've been here before, but not to the town itself, nor the mine. Once we realized we were not going to pick up their trail, my troop turned back. Other things took up my time and I did not return."

Fieyn's eyes narrowed. "Until now."

Taken aback, not only by the vehemence of Fieyn's comment but also the developing change in his demeanor, Reece couldn't help but move his hand closer to his gun. There was something strange, unexpected, and alarming in the sheriff's transformation and Reece speculated on whether it might have something to do with either Destry's words or the close proximity of the woods. They certainly seemed to give off an unsettling aura.

"If I'd have wanted the gold," said Reece evenly, "why would I involve myself with this search for him?" He jabbed a finger towards Destry. "I'd have come up here all on my lonesome."

"Perhaps you did," said Destry. "Perhaps you and that Bourne fella, you were in cahoots. Strange you should meet up with him at the guesthouse the way you did."

"It was *you* who told me about the guesthouse," said Reece, struggling now to keep his temper, "and, besides, how do you know about what might have gone on there – you were sleeping off another drunk somewhere."

"Why you—"

Destry rushed forward, teeth snarling, hands stretched out like the paws of a bear, preparing to crush. Reece reacted easily and devastatingly. Like a well-oiled machine, he moved with liquid grace, twisting away from the charge, driving his fist deep into Destry's side. Destry squealed, began to topple. With the same fist, Reece cracked a second blow into the area behind the man's ear and Destry crumpled to the ground.

Aware of Fieyn reacting, Reece drew his gun, snapped back the hammer and pointed it directly towards Fieyn before the sheriff managed to get within a breath of his own handgun.

"Try it, Sheriff, and I'll send you straight to hell."

Some way off, the others stood watching, paralyzed in fear and indecision. None spoke. One of them released a low whistle.

At Reece's feet, Destry groaned loudly but other than that, there was little movement from him.

"We're meant to be working together on this," said Reece quietly. Eager to defuse the situation, he gently disengaged his gun's hammer. "Let's all just calm down and talk this through."

Face distorted with seething rage, Fieyn took several breaths and, eventually, the redness faded from his cheeks and his eyes grew softer. It was almost as if he were emerging from a deep sleep. Or nightmare. "Jesus," he said in a long, heavy sigh. He squeezed the bridge of his nose with finger and thumb, screwing up his eyes, shoulders rising and falling. Suddenly, the strength left his legs, and he was pitching sideways. Reece, holstering his gun, caught him, and gently lowered him to the ground. Despite the sheriff's eyes being open, he seemed unaware of his surroundings or what was happening to him. A strange mist glazed over him and Reece, snapping his head to the audience some paces away, barked, "Water. Get me some water."

During the next few, desperate moments, Reece worked hard to revive the ailing Fieyn. The sheriff lay rigid, as if bones and muscles had calcified, turning him into something akin to a statue. There was little response to Reece's constant urging, not even a blink when he slapped Fieyn across the face.

"What's the matter with him?" asked Hanson, the big black-smith stepping over them.

"I don't know," said Reece, rocking back on his heels. "We should get him to town and let the doctor take a look."

"It's that serious?"

"Maybe. I seen men like this in the War. Not so much as a bullet-graze but falling down after a fight, then dying some hours later." He looked up at the blacksmith looming over him. "Heart problems is what it is, I think. We have to be careful taking him back."

"And Ezra?"

Shrugging, Reece stood up. "To hell with him. If he's gone to the mine then, if what Destry says is true, he won't be coming back."

CHAPTER TWENTY-SIX

Whatever Destry had said did not feature much in Ezra's thinking as he walked through the encroaching trees. A somnambulist, eyes wide open but registering nothing, driven only by the voices running around inside his head, he surged forward. Despite the occasional overhanging branch scraping across his forehead, to break skin, spill blood, he strode on. A hidden or exposed root might cause him to stumble, but nothing more. He did not look for such dangers. The sun, if it was even struggling to shine, barely penetrated the gloom. As if directed by an invisible light, Ezra continued. Nothing would, or could, cause him to deviate.

And then, as if drawing back the blinds, a pinkish light illuminated his surroundings as he emerged into the evening.

To his left, the mountains soared and, in their foothills, the area underneath in which the mine wormed. This was a long way from the entrance shored up by Destry all that time ago. This was an unknown, rarely visited area, the thick woods creating a natural barrier to exploration or discovery. And yet even a cursory glance would reveal a simple wooden door fashioned from roughly hewn planks in the mountainside. Twisted and gnarled, it seemed fit to collapse. The merest touch or slightest push and it would fall away to reveal ... What? Slowly returning from his sleep-like state, Ezra rubbed his eyes and stared. A door, to where?

Eyes growing accustomed to the light, senses reawakening from their strange, dream-like state, Ezra shook himself like a dog emerging from water. He studied the old door, curious to what it led to – was it an entrance or exit? Looking around him, aware of the open grassland stretching on into the distance and gaining from some comfort that he was alone, he approached the doorway.

Something moved. A shadow, racing across his line of vision, disappearing – or more disturbingly, appearing from the old door. He froze, peering forward. Was it open? Had it opened by itself or had someone done so from within? He waited, frayed nerves jangling around inside him. There was something, a difference, a charge in the air. Even though the sun descended, and the temperature changed, the chill felt intense, unnatural. He shuddered as creeping terror engulfed him.

With a jerk, it suddenly occurred to him he did not have his handgun. He checked the holster and found it empty. Why had he not checked it before? Panic rising, he considered going back, retracing his steps through the woods, returning to the old shack where the men from the town would escort him to jail, to a warm bed ... whatever. He didn't care. Gripped with uncertainty he teetered between moving forward or retreat.

In the end, the decision was made for him.

CHAPTER TWENTY-SEVEN

E asing open the shuttered window, Morrison peered out into the street. Roused by the sound of approaching horses, he'd glanced across to Bessy, who had fallen asleep. He delayed waking her. But now, with riders coming down the main street, he called to her. She jerked herself upright, blinking.

"I think it's the sheriff and that other fella, the newcomer."

"They have found Destry?"

She was rushing forward before Morrison managed to say, "I think so, but it's getting dark, and I can't—"

"Let me see," she said impatiently, pushing the bank teller aside. "I can't ... Yes, by golly, there he is!"

She was tearing at the bolt and throwing back the door bar as Morrison shrugged himself into his topcoat, knowing it would be cold outside.

Bessy ran across the street towards the riders. Already Reece was reining in his horse as others moved across to a small, low building, a swinging sign above the door announcing it as a doctor's surgery.

"What's happened?" Bessy asked, gripping hold of Reece's reins. Calming his horse, he slipped from the saddle.

"Destry's fine if that's what you mean. The sheriff is my chief concern – he came over all faint up near the old shack and I'm thinking it could be his heart."

Bessy's hand flew to her mouth, "Oh my!"

Without a pause, Reece reached out and took her hand. "Are you all right? You seem ..."

Morrison came up close. "We have not had a particularly good time of things since you and the sheriff left."

Reece frowned. "What do you mean?"

"That horrible little man, the one called Weasel, he threatened ..." Bessy's breathing shuddered as she recounted what had happened. "He forced me to the bank, demanded I take out two hundred dollars ... Oh, Mr Reece."

She broke down, falling into his arms and he held her, stroking the back of her head as he turned his gaze towards Morrison.

"It's true," said the bank teller. "Not quite a hold-up but as good as."

"Two hundred dollars. That's a lot of money. What did he want it for?"

Bessy brought her tear-streaked face up. "Oh Reece, it was all so horrible. I don't have the words, but I need to explain everything before—"

"It's all right," Reece said gently, "you don't have to explain a thing."

"Yes, I do. Please, just come with me."

They sat on the guesthouse porch. By now the sun was dipping below the horizon but even so, as he studied her features, his tongue grew thick in his mouth, her utter loveliness mesmerising. He didn't think he'd seen a woman so beautiful before, her features perfect, hair lustrous, her mouth drawing him in.

"I'm not sure how to begin," she said.

"Take your time, Miss Bessy."

"Please, I think we can be on first-name terms now, don't you think?" She smiled. "Although after what I have to say, you might think differently."

"Let me be the judge of that, *Bessy*."

Emboldened, she stared into the distance, took several shallow breaths, then one larger one. "Mr Bourne. He arrived here just over a week ago. On business, so he said, but I wasn't sure what type of business it was. There's not much here to interest anyone, apart from the lumber but I couldn't see why he would want to involve himself in something that is dying."

"You suspected he might not have been absolutely honest?"

She shrugged. "Perhaps. Thing is, I didn't particularly care. Ever since Destry took to drinking, spending all of his time either in the saloon or over at Saint Francine's I'd become, how shall I put it, empty. Yes, that's the word. Empty. Mr Bourne, to put it bluntly, he filled a need in me."

Reece had to stop himself from reeling backwards. A tiny whimper escaped from his throat. She quickly rounded on him, taking his hand again and squeezing it firmly. "Please, Reece. You need to understand, he was ...Oh God, there's no point in disguising it. His very arrogance sent a thrill through me. He noticed it of course. We get so few customers now unless there is a cattle drive, and he was so different from the normal type that stays."

"He ..." Reece cleared his throat. "I mean, *you* and he, you ..."

"Yes. I think I wanted it as much as he did. He was rough, arrogant, selfish, but I am alone here, Reece. I run the guesthouse on my own, doing everything while Destry drinks and drinks. It's been like that ever since he returned from that damned mine." She squeezed Reece's hand again. "Don't think of me as a harlot, Reece. I was lonely, longing for some comfort even if it was fleeting."

"You fell in love with him?"

Her mouth fell open at this question, his voice so fragile and tremulous, even fearful of what her response might be. "Oh God,

Reece, *no,*" she blurted. "He was nothing more than a distraction. A break from the utter monotony of my life."

"I'm sorry, I shouldn't have asked you that. Your decisions are your own."

"Often, they are ones I regret, Reece. I certainly regret allowing myself to become involved with him. He seemed to expect me to be always willing to share his bed. Like the desperate fool I was, I did. Many times. But soon, I grew to hate his very presence, the sound of his footfall on the stair, the smell of his whisky breath. All I could do was hope his stay would end, that whatever he'd come here to do would soon finish. I knew he often went over to the Quince ranch. Brad Swail came to tell me he'd seen Bourne riding like someone possessed after one of his meetings."

"Brad Swail?"

"An old friend. He didn't trust Mr Bourne, thought him of being 'up to no good' as he said to me." Shaking her head, she turned away. "Oh Reece, I wish I'd never laid eyes on him. I wish ..."

"It's all right, Bessy. I understand."

"Do you? I'm not sure that you do. I'm lonely, unfulfilled, and now, after Bourne, I feel so *dirty*. I've let myself down, Reece, made myself a laughing stock and now you, you must think so terribly of me."

"I don't," he said, leaning closer. "I'm not much for philosophizing or reading meaning into things but a woman like you, Bessy, you ain't got nothing to rebuke yourself for. This is a damnable place, what with its history and that mine casting a shadow over everything, and I can fully understand why you'd want to find some sort of escape. So, please, try, if you can, to put it behind you. I'm not here to judge."

She reached out a touched his cheek. "What are you here for?"

He flinched as he became aware of approaching footsteps.

Destry, with several others, guns drawn, grim determination

in each of their features. Reece stood up, body coiled like a spring.

"You've got some explaining to do, Reece," said one of the men, stepping up onto the porch.

"You're damned right," spat Destry. The gun in his hand looked huge.

"You be careful with that Dragoon, Destry. Back off," hissed Reece.

"No, *you* back off!" Destry gestured for the others to move closer.

"I don't need to explain anything to you."

"We saw what you did, Reece," said one of the others. "The way you knocked down poor Mr Brownlow here."

Destry smirked. "For all we know," he said, "you did the same with the sheriff."

"Now hold on …" said Reece but was almost immediately cut off.

"Take his gun, boys and throw him in jail until the sheriff is recovered enough to deal with him."

"Destry," exploded Bessy, jumping to her feet, as the men surrounded Reece, relieving him of his revolver, "Mr Reece hasn't done anything save for listening to me. Is this why you're doing this? Because of your jealousy?"

"Damn you, woman," returned Destry. "Jealous? I couldn't give a fig what you get up to. But Reece, you're a different matter. You're here to get your greedy hands on what's inside the mine. That's why you attacked me because I know of your schemes!"

Reece raised his hands as the men grabbed him. "This is a mistake, Destry. I put you down because you are a conniving, twisted little—"

"Shut up," snapped Destry and watched with a good deal of amusement as the men forced Reece down the porch steps. "And you, my darling," continued Destry, taking Bessy by the arm, "you can come back to the guesthouse and make me something good for my supper. I need it."

"You idiot," she snapped, wrenching her arm free. "You have no idea what you're talking about. Reece, why would he want what's in the mine? There's nothing there, damn it. Reece is innocent for God's sake." She stepped past her husband and shouted, "Reece, you hang on in there. I'll get this sorted."

Shuffling across the street, the two men covering him with their guns, Reece turned to give her a downcast look. All he could do was say, "It'll be fine."

As Reece was being frog-marched to the jail, across town in the doctor's surgery, a group of men stood around the table inside the town doctor's surgery. Stretched out before them Sheriff Fieyn, his pallor a deathly shade of grey, struggled to breathe. The doctor, a short, rotund man, breathed heavily before placing the stethoscope he wore against Fieyn's chest. He listened for a moment, concentrating hard, eyes closed frown etched deep.

After a few seconds, the doctor stood upright and shook his head. "Shortness of breath coupled with an irregular heartbeat. Palpitations is what we call it." He looked at each of the assembled men in turn. Doc Turner spread his duties far and wide, a peripatetic practitioner who visited the town of Whitewater whenever he was passing by. When not in town, any medical problems were dealt with by his assistant, Brad Swail. At this time, Brad was nowhere to be seen.

"Is he gonna die?" asked Dimitri Gusanov, who owned a small dry goods store in town. His accent was thick with the sound of his Russian homeland.

Turner unclipped his stethoscope and ran it through his fingers. "I'll need to run some more tests and keep him under observation for a couple of days, but I believe he has had a heart seizure. From the color of his complexion, the weak, fluctuating heartbeat and this," here he touched Fieyn's blue lips, "it's not looking good."

"I'll sit with him," said one of the others and went to pick up a nearby chair.

"No need, Ira," said Turner. "Brad will be along soon enough."

Ira pulled a face. "I want to help."

"Ira," put in Gusanov, "you think you're up to this. It's a big responsibility looking after someone so sick."

"I'm fifteen now, Dimitri. I'm old enough."

"As long as you're sure."

"I don't mind staying," insisted Ira and sat down. "The sheriff here is a good man. He helped my family out even before the fire burned down our stable, killing them poor horses. He was a great comfort to Jilly and my grieving ma. I'll sit with him."

The others mumbled, exchanging troubled looks.

"All right," said Turner forcibly and motioned the others to leave. "You just holler if he wakes up or if you notice any change."

"I will."

"Make sure he stays warm."

"I'll stack up some wood in the potbelly."

"Thank you, Ira."

Raising his hand in a small gesture of farewell, Ira waited until everyone left before turning his gaze towards the ailing sheriff. Smiling, he said in a low voice, "Don't you worry none. I'm gonna make sure you suffer, Fieyn, and I'm gonna enjoy every moment of it."

Two summers before, the unrelenting heat of the sun making grass and woodland tinder-dry, Sheriff Fieyn came calling, as he always did. From his bedroom window in the converted hayloft, Ira had a good vantage point. Often, he'd witnessed Fieyn taking his mother to the stable where they'd remain for quite some time. He'd never felt brave enough to go and take a peek but his young mind filled in the gaps. They were lovers, Fieyn taking advantage of his mother's grief after the news of his father's death fighting in the War arrived. Ira didn't know the details of their relationship, nor did he want to. His one concern was for the welfare of his younger sister, Jilly, who seemed to cry constantly over the loss of her pa. No amount of comforting words made any difference and Ira often thought she was going to cry herself to death. Until the day she went running into the barn. This day.

Dipping back into his room, Ira did not see it. Did not see his sister running across the yard. He didn't know until he heard his sister's scream.

He took the loft ladder at a rush, gripping the arms and sliding down to the ground. Pausing only to pick up a pitchfork, he raced to the barn. There was Jilly, pummeling Fieyn with her tiny fists, and Ma trying to intercede, her blouse open to the waist. Ira stood in the doorway and watched Fieyn sweeping up Jilly in his hands. "Please stop," the sheriff said. Ira wanted to do something, if not physical then at least a shout, a yell of outrage. But he couldn't. Nothing worked, every tendon, every sinew frozen solid with fear, a fear so intense it turned his guts to mush, shriveling his testicles, forcing him to finally lurch out of the doorway and throw up into the dirt. Overwhelmed with terror and shame, he staggered back to the hay barn and collapsed amongst the straw, weeping for himself, his weakness.

He tried to rid his mind of the pictures playing out there, but he couldn't. Fieyn had stepped so easily into the space provided by his pa's passing. His mother ... what did she see in him? Was she willing? He didn't know, he didn't dare think about it. He cried himself to sleep.

He awoke to the unmistakable smell of a cigar wafting in from outside. And something else. Shouts and screams, the crackle and splutter of flames. Fieyn must have tossed away the match without thinking. What other explanation could there be,

Ira wondered, as he lay propped up on one elbow, listening, trying to make out what was going on in the yard. Clambering to his feet, he staggered outside, still shaking with the memory of what he'd seen. He didn't know how long he'd been asleep but already the sky was darkening. His eyes locked on the figure of a man striding across the yard to the house and his waiting horse.

Without a look, the man slowly rode away, continuing to chomp on his cigar. Jilly ran after him, arms waving, screaming like a banshee. The man merely kicked his horse into a gallop and Jilly fell to her knees and it was only then that the first tendrils of smoke made their appearance.

Rousing himself, Ira stepped out and gasped. The barn was alight, flames already lapping from the bottom planks to stream over the walls. Rooted, Ira gaped, indecision now grappling with his fear. Unable to conjure up any strength or courage, he stumbled backwards, aware only of Jilly's screams. "Mama, mama!"

Her voice never left his thoughts.

Much later, Doc Turner introduced the children to Maisie May, a woman the Doc said who would look after them from now on. When Ira gripped Turner by the lapels and shook him, screaming, "It was Fieyn, it was Fieyn who lit up the barn, doc. It was Fieyn who killed her," Doc Turner held him close and held him until his sobbing subsided.

Breathing into his ear, Turner said, "We'll find out the truth, Ira and we'll make amends, I promise you."

And now, here was the person responsible, stricken down by some sort of heart attack. Amends come home. Ira always dreamed of killing the sheriff but knew he lacked the grit to do so. Now, here he was, so close, the opportunity too good to miss. And all it would need would be a pillow, pressed down on the bastard's face. A few moments. That's all.

Grinding his teeth as he contemplated such an act, Ira's eyes fixed on the pillow propping the sheriff's head up, and, with a surge of determination, made up his mind.

CHAPTER TWENTY-EIGHT

Rooted to the ground, fear overcoming every sensation, Ezra swayed backwards and stared at the man standing before him. If indeed it was a man. It was difficult to tell with so much dried blood masking his features. It seemed as if someone had modelled his head from clay, someone not overly adept. Misshapen, features crooked, nose bent, a large bulge on the right side, a massive indentation on the left. And blood, blood everywhere, covering his entire face, his eyes shining brilliant white from within the blackness. Breathing laboriously, he brought up his gun hand and eased back the hammer. "How you know?" he croaked.

Perplexed, eyes focused on the gun, Ezra tried his best to remain calm. But it proved difficult. The man was like a vision out of hell. "Know?" was all he could manage.

"You have another map?"

All Ezra could do was offer a shrug, knowing for certain that this man wanted answers and wanted them quickly. So, he stepped aside slightly and gestured towards the door. "Indian told me," he lied.

"Indian?" Alarmed, the man spun around, sweeping the area around them both with his gun. "What Indian?"

Ezra needed to think fast. He was backing himself into a corner and such a strategy could prove beyond the capabilities of his limited imagination. Nevertheless, he had little choice. The man before him, beyond agitated, appeared close to losing control. His entire body was shaking as if gripped by an immensely powerful fever. The sweat ran through the encrusted grime of his face, revealing the deathly looking flesh underneath.

"Big fella. Wore a buffalo headdress. Pointed me in this direction."

As he spoke, Ezra recalled something similar had indeed happened. When was it? Earlier today, the day before, some years ago? Perhaps his lie wasn't so very far from the truth after all. "Yeah, that was it. Indian, had to be."

"Buffalo, you said? A buffalo headdress?"

"Hell yes," said Ezra with more enthusiasm than he felt only moments earlier. This wasn't so bad after all. The man with the gun could be a newfound friend, a confidant, someone to spend time with. "Listen, why don't we break through this here door and find out what's inside." The man faltered and Ezra plunged on. "Listen, there's a stream yonder. You should wash up, get all that shit off your face. I'll show you."

Cautious now, Ezra moved towards the tiny, gurgling brook that seemed to bubble from underneath the ground. The water ran milky white, and it glowed mysteriously in the semi-darkness.

Grunting with his exertions, the man dropped to his knees and splashed the water over his face, running more of it through his hair until, at last, he managed to wash away the majority of the caked blood and grime from his skin.

The man stood but almost immediately teetered to his side, the strength leaving him. Ezra took his chance, stepped in close, grabbed the man's gun and cracked it across his neck and followed it up with a solid punch in the solar plexus. A sudden rush of stale smelling breath erupted from the man's mouth. For good measure, Ezra swung his foot into the man's groin.

Screaming, the man doubled up, hands clamped around his crotch. He vomited violently, rolled himself up into a tight ball, and set about wailing, high-pitched, amongst the dirt.

Checking the revolver, Ezra grunted with satisfaction and decided to check through the man's pockets. He came across some dollar bills, which he pocketed, and an often-folded piece of paper. Standing up, he studied the badly drawn sketch map, looked towards the woods, then the door. He smiled. "Seems like that Indian was right," he said.

The man groaned loudly and rolled over onto his back. "You better kill me," he said through gritted teeth. Still partially bent double, his eyes were fixed on Ezra and they were full of murderous intent.

"Now why would I do that, friend?"

"Because if you don't, I'll sure as hell kill you."

Grinning, Ezra put the map into his pocket. "Is that so?" he asked, drew in a large breath, and smashed his fist into the man's face, throwing him backwards into the stream. Floundering around in the milk-white water, the man rolled over and remained still for a moment, before propping himself up on hands and knees. Giggling, Ezra turned to study the door. "Let's think about that, shall we? Thing is, I'm gonna need you to help me get this door open." To emphasize his words, he put his shoulder against the timbers and pushed. Nothing happened. "It's fairly solid. I think if we both have a go, we might break it open. What do you say?"

Raising himself from the water, the man stepped onto the tiny bank and spat a stream of blood onto the ground. "I'd say you are somewhat touched in the head. Give me back the map."

Ezra scanned the door and took several large breaths. "You smell that? Sweet. Like the very best homemade cooking. Not unlike that water you've been gulping down."

"It is sweet," said the man, peeling off his coat and shaking it. He shivered in the cold air. "You think there could be someone inside?" said Ezra, his ear still pressed against the door.

"I think you are a prime idiot." Clutching his head with both hands, a low whimper seeped from the man's throat. He was clearly in considerable pain.

"Boy, you have taken a mean whipping, that's for sure. What were you hit with, an iron bar?"

The man gave a sharp laugh. "Very nearly so, yes." He pointed in a vague, northerly direction. "I'm not feeling so good."

"Hell boy, you is close to death, I think. Go and get yourself a good drink and then we'll try and get this door open." He waved the gun. "No point in us falling out over this." He put the gun in his waistband.

"And the Indian? What if he comes back?"

"What Indian?"

"The Indian you told me about – the one with the buffalo headdress?"

"Oh him? Hell, he's well gone. I don't think we'll be seeing him again, not now we have the map."

"My name's Bourne," said the man. "I'm sorry to come up on you the way I did but my brain, it's all rattled, and I can't think straight." He massaged his forehead with one trembling hand. "I need water."

"All right," said Ezra, "go get some."

Sometime later, sitting on the bank of the stream, Bourne wrung his shirt out. He'd plunged into the rushing water on his own volition this time, sliding through the mud to land face-first and fully clothed into the shallows. He took great gulps to quench his thirst before he took to scrubbing exposed body parts with his nails. Soaked through, the blood washed from the exposed parts of his body, he stepped clear and grinned like a small child on Christmas morning. "Damn, I feel good now."

Ezra grunted. He stood staring at the water. "If I ain't mistaken, this water looks like milk."

"Huh? Milk? Who knows, maybe it is." He peered into the depths. "It gives off a sort of glow, you see that?"

"I can read by it," said Ezra, pulled out the map and studied the spidery drawing. "According to this, the stream seems to come from the mine." He jabbed at the paper with his finger. "Says here, 'Mine' and 'White stream'. There's a drawing of the wood I walked through too and just here," another tap, "there's a mark with 'Shack' written next to it. Might that be the shack I came across with that fella tied up inside?"

"What fella?" said Bourne, shrugging on his shirt. He struggled a little as it was still damp.

"There was a man tied up in there. Terrified he was. But, not only terrified. Almost as if he was crazy. Wild eyes, jabbering, like some men I saw in the War. Too much cannon fire everyone said. Made some go crazy. He was just like that."

"I wouldn't know," said Bourne. "What happened to him?"

"A bunch of men came from the town, set him free. They seemed mighty keen on finding out what had happened. I managed to slip away as they were talking."

"They didn't follow you?"

"Not as far as I know." Ezra put the map away. "Kinda weird, ain't it, this water being like milk? You said it tasted sweet?"

"Like the smell from within the mine."

"Wonder what it is."

"Who cares? There's gold in that mine. I mean to get it."

"How do you know there's gold?"

"Don't see no point in lying," said Bourne, reaching for his dripping jacket. "I work for Richard Quince, the biggest landowner around these parts. He has employed me to find out if there is gold in that mine. A seam was found in there but that was a while back. That man you found in the shack, his name is Destry, and he is the last man alive who went inside the mine."

"You mean *you* left him in the shack? Why?"

"To make him sweat. I wanted him to tell me what he knows

but since our conversation together, I came across that map there ain't no need for Destry's help anymore."

"Where did you find it?"

"I didn't. One of Quince's men did. He's dead now."

Ezra swallowed and considered the man before him. He knew without any doubt that he would have to kill him once they had reconnoitered the mine's interior. "So, once you discover the gold, you'll take it to Quince?"

"That was the idea." A grin slowly developed across his swollen face. "I'm thinking I might just take it for myself. Or," he brought up his hand in a gesture of peace, "the both of us could take it. Seems crazy to put in so much effort without any reward."

"Well, hell, let's both get it. You got any tools?"

Bourne spread out his arms. "Does it look like it?"

"I saw some tools back at the shack. There were picks and shovels, buckets. All that we need."

Bourne turned his face skyward. "It's gonna be night soon. I say we sleep at the shack and start early tomorrow. We'll be hungry, but if we work fast enough, we could be away from here by mid-morning."

Nodding, Ezra could find no reason to argue. There'd be time enough during the following day to bring this man's life to an end.

CHAPTER TWENTY-NINE

Hanson came through the door, face awash with sweat, his eyes burning bright. "What the hell is going on here?"

They had Reece against the bars of the cell. There was blood dripping from his nose.

"Easy Hanson," said one of the men who had escorted Reece into the jail, "everything's taken care of."

"What the hell does that mean?"

"It means," said Destry emerging from the shadows, feeding cartridges into an 1860 Henry carbine as he spoke, "he tried to get away, so we had to make him see sense." He chuckled. "He is gonna wait in here until the circuit judge passes through and he can be tried."

"Tried?" Hanson scanned the others in the tiny room but received nothing but blank stares in return. "Tried for what?"

"Insurrection, attempted murder, intention to commit theft. Plus," he grinned and touched his cheek with the back of one hand, "felonious assault."

"Are you out of your mind? He joined us in searching for you, Destry! He helped us *save* you from the spot you were in. Insurrection be damned – he persuaded Fieyn to—"

"Enough already," snapped Destry, engaged the Henry with a

forceful working of the lever. He turned the carbine directly towards the big blacksmith. "Now get the hell out, Hanson, before you join him."

Hanson puffed up his chest, deliberated for a moment, then shrugged and sighed. "The circuit judge may not be here for months – if at all. How long will you keep him here?"

"As long as it takes." Destry gestured with the carbine. "Now scoot."

Shooting Reece a meaningful look, the blacksmith left.

A noticeable relaxing of the atmosphere within the jailhouse followed and the two men turned to Destry. "What shall we do?"

"Watch him," said Destry. "Take it in turns, four hours each. I'll come back early. You," he looked at Reece, "behave yourself."

Reece glared but didn't respond. Instead, he swung himself fully across the bunk, tipped his hat over his eyes and breathed a long, slow sigh.

"Destry," said one of the others quickly, "there were two of Quince's boys locked up in here. Looks like they've been let out."

At the door, Destry stopped. His head dropped for a moment before he took a long inhalation. "Well, not much we can do about that, is there. Maybe it was the sheriff but I can't ask Fieyn, not until he wakes. No doubt it'll all work itself out."

There were few townsfolk in the street outside the sheriff's office. The cold kept most people inside once the sun had gone down. Destry checked both ends nevertheless, pulled his collar closer around his throat and, carbine in the crook of his arm, strode down towards the livery stables. He checked his wife's guesthouse on the way. It was in darkness. He wondered where Bessy might be, guessed she would be with the town gossip Miriam Clapham, the old hag who ran the coffee shop. God alone knew what they talked about, thought Destry, hawked and spat. Before moving on, he decided to take a look inside the guesthouse, wondering if there were guests. He'd need to give them some sort of explanation for the absence of their host.

As he stepped inside, he noted how chill the air was, much colder than in the street. His breath steamed, his teeth clattered. A depressing gloom seeped from every inch, every corner of the entrance hall. Ahead of him, the small reception desk, empty, forlorn almost. There is a sadness in this place, one he does not recognise. It is as if he has entered an unknown building, not the guesthouse, the one which Bessy has worked so hard to maintain, to make a success. Perhaps it is her absence which created this uneasy air.

He edged around the small desk and groped around underneath it, his hand at last enclosing around the bottle he kept hidden there. He shook it and, relieved, blew out a long breath. He took a long drink. It tasted as it always did. Pure and sweet.

The all-pervading silence, however, continued to cause him intense concern. Perplexed, he returned the now empty bottle to its hiding place and, a little uncertainly, walked forward, unconsciously bringing the carbine to aim ahead of him.

The kitchen was black. Impenetrable. He thought he sensed something. A shape, or perhaps it was nothing more than a shadow, or the drink dulling his senses like it always did. He made a conscious note to refill his stock as soon as all this nonsense was over.

Almost at once, as he stepped inside the kitchen, the smell hit him, a sharp tang which struck the back of his throat and caused him to cough. Shaking himself, he did his best to squint into the darkness but found that nothing came into focus. The smell dominated everything.

He waited, hoping his eyes would grow accustomed to the gloom. To accelerate the process, he squeezed his eyes shut and made a countdown in his head. Slow and deliberate. He wanted his sight fully restored to register what was going on because something was. He was certain of it. When he reached ten, he opened his eyes and screamed.

CHAPTER THIRTY

"There," said Mrs Clapham, setting a cup of coffee down on the table. "You drink that. I've put a splash of whisky in it, to warm you."

Smiling, Bessy lifted the cup to her lips and took a sip. A wave of cosy security wrapped itself around her as the steaming hot liquid percolated through her body. "That's delicious," she said and smiled her thanks.

Miriam Clapham sat down opposite. They were in the back room of the little coffee shop, closed up for business before the usual time. "I think you should stay here tonight," she said, her tone serious, her eyes like a hawk, penetrating.

Bessy tried to look away, but those eyes would not let her go. She wilted under their power. "I couldn't impose upon you that way, Miriam."

"Nonsense! It's not an imposition, Bessy. You shouldn't be alone, not after what you've been through."

Bessy knew she could not face returning to her guesthouse. The idea held more fear for her than anything else, even what happened in the bank with that horrid Weasel. She knew that from now on, every time she set her eyes on her kitchen, she would see Bourne stretched out on the floor, his skull cracked open, the blood ... A shudder ran through her and to disguise her discomfort, she took another, longer drink.

Miriam stretched out her hands and enclosed Bessy's. "You don't have to tell me what has happened, but I want you to know that, when you're ready, I'm here for you."

"Thank you, Miriam, I appreciate that."

"I saw they arrested Mr Reece."

Bessy brought her face up, a slight frown creasing her forehead.

"Do you know what it was for?"

Taking in a breath, Bessy held her friend's gaze. She knew she could trust her but even so, confessing anything at present, was going to be difficult. "Destry. He concocted some outrageous story about Reece pitting everyone against each other in order to get his hands on the gold."

"Gold? You mean from the mine? But we all know—"

"There's no proof to any of it, only Destry's insane jealousy. Why he feels that way when he hardly ever speaks, let alone touches me, is beyond my understanding."

"Perhaps Mr Reece heard the rumors, somehow? These sorts of things tend to travel far and wide. And now, with the War over, all sorts of people will come and go, looking for a means to start again. Maybe he is one such person?"

Bessy stared, recalling how Reece looked at her. He struck her as kind, as well as strong. Well aware of the effect she had on men, Reece was so different to others. He had an air of civility about him, a gentleman through and through. Unlike Bourne, whose groping hands she recalled with a shudder. He'd warmed her bed but there was no tenderness there, no affection. If anything, he proved the opposite – forceful, rough, and selfish. She felt dirty afterwards, empty, dissatisfied. She knew that with Reece it would be so different. If he ever saw the light of day again, if ever someone could sort out this ghastly mess.

"I sense you have some feelings for Mr Reece..."

Blinking, Bessy came out of her reverie and, a little embarrassed finished off her drink, which was cold now. "I hardly know him."

"But you believe him to be a good man?"

"I do. There's something about him. A gentleness. Honesty."

A smile played at the corners of Miriam's mouth and she went to stand but stopped when a series of gunshots rang out, causing her to yelp.

Without hesitation, Bessy sprang to her feet, whirling around to face the door. "That came from the guesthouse."

Miriam came around the table at a run and gripped her arm. "Wait, Bessy. It could be anything."

Bessy glared, knowing full well what it could be. "I have to go," she said, her voice breaking.

"Then I'll come with you," said Miriam, went to a cabinet full of cups and saucers, reached behind and produced a Winchester, which she engaged with a determined snap. "We've had enough killings without yours being added to the pile."

Together they went out into the night.

CHAPTER THIRTY-ONE

Hanson stepped from behind the corner of the sheriff's office and watched Destry disappear into the night. He guessed he was heading for either the livery or the guesthouse. There were no streetlights in the small town of Whitewater. A patch of yellow oozed from underneath the saloon doors on the opposite side of the street, and a trickle from between the shutters of the lumber office window. They were all he needed. He contemplated placing his neckerchief over his mouth as a form of disguise but dismissed the notion almost immediately. They'd recognize him easily enough as there was no one else of his size in the town. Besides, once this was done, who would ever listen to Destry and his wild ideas ever again?

He went through the door in a rush. The office was as before, save for the two inside helping themselves to copious amounts of whisky. The one nearest the small wood burner turned as the other, pouring yet another glass, gaped in surprise.

"Hanson? What the hell ...?"

Hanson punched him hard across the jaw, sending him crashing across the desk where he writhed and moaned. The other made a wild grab for his handgun but Hanson got there too soon, slammed a right blow into the man's guts and broke his jaw with a swinging left. As the man crumpled, Hanson swung around in time to see the first struggling to sit up and sent him into unconsciousness with a solid left fist into his temple.

Someone whistled.

Hanson turned. Despite the dimness of the single oil lamp burning in the corner, Hanson saw Reece standing up, close to the jail bars, and gave him a smile. He swept up the keys and opened up the jail. Reece stepped out and nodded to the giant blacksmith. "I wouldn't want to be on the receiving end of your fists, my friend. But thank you all the same."

"I know you ain't guilty of anything, Reece, except being a stranger. Sometimes that's enough. But you helped find Destry and whatever it was that happened up at the shack, we need to get to the bottom of it."

"I agree." Reece went to the man closest to the wood burner and relieved him of his gun.

"We'll put them both inside," said Hanson. He picked up the one sprawled across the desk first as if he were nothing more than a child and threw him into the jail. The other followed quickly, Hanson slamming the door shut with a crash before locking it. He went to the wall rack behind the desk and took down a scattergun. He checked the load. "I pray we don't need to start any shooting, Reece," he said as he put a handful of cartridges into his pocket. Snapping the gun closed he blew out a sigh. "Why did Destry get so wild up there?"

"I have no idea."

"The sheriff too. It was almost as if ... They were possessed."

"Possessed? What does that mean?"

"In my country, we have many stories which tell of horrifying events – attacks, hauntings, all that sort of thing, but one of them is something I know well. One of the most frightening is the Nattmara, a hideous creature that enters your mind as you sleep. It brings nightmares, nightmares so real that when you finally wake the images and experiences stay with you. Change you."

"Nightmares. Well, I doubt either Destry or the sheriff were asleep before they came over all strange."

"No, but the way they acted is similar to what happens when the Nattmara gets inside your head. Changed personalities, inexplicable actions, words ... Destry was inside that shack for a long time and Ezra, something strange also happened to him when he was in there."

"So, whatever caused them to change was inside the shack?" Reece remembered how the sheriff, in particular, changed, acting as if he were another person, blaming Reece with such harshness. "But what? I ain't one who gives credence to ghosts and demons, Hanson. Hell, I fought through the War and saw and heard a helluva lot. Most of it bad. I heard Indians talking about such stuff. Bad spirits and the like. Bad medicine. But I ain't never seen anything. I reckon the mind if it believes it, can make up all sorts of things."

"I just about think the same, Reece. There are only two persons in town, other than Destry, who were around when White came back from the mine. That's Brad Swail, Doc Turner's assistant, and the Doc himself."

"I reckon we go and talk to Turner. He's an educated man so won't be easily convinced by stories of the unnatural kind. We can also check up on the sheriff at the same time."

Hanson grunted. "Let's hope we get some answers because once those two wake up," he pointed towards the jail and the two inert men slumped together inside, "we're gonna have a lot of explaining to do if we're wrong."

The shots, when they came, caused both men to jump, Reece instinctively crouching low and drawing his gun with lightning speed. Dropping to his knees, Hanson breathed hard. "Damn, you are fast with that, by golly."

"What the hell..." Reece put up his palm and crept towards the door. "Put out the lamp."

Hanson did so and Reece slowly creaked open the door and peered out into the night. Distant laughter filtered out from the saloon but other than that there were no further sounds. Until that is, he saw the dark shadowy shapes of two men cutting across the street. "Damn," he whispered and stepped outside. *"Bessy? Bessy, is that you?"*

A short silence before her voice came through the darkness. A voice he didn't think he'd hear again for a long time. "Reece? Oh my God, Reece?"

Aware of both Hanson and Mrs Clapham growing restless beside them, Reece slowly released Bessy from his embrace, pausing only for a moment before brushing a lock of hair from her face. "All that Destry said, it was all lies. I didn't do anything, you must believe that."

"I do," she said. In the dark, the whites of her eyes sparkled.

Abruptly, her mood changed. She stepped away, face down, wringing her hands.

"What is it?" asked Reece, placing his hands on her shoulders. "Is it Destry?"

"No," she said, giving a sharp laugh. "Never. No, it's ... Reece, there's something you must know."

"Bessy, there ain't no need. You've told me all I need to know, and it makes no difference to me."

"Listen, what happened in the guesthouse with Mr Bourne, he—"

"The guesthouse?" interjected Hanson sharply. "I saw Destry heading that way."

"Oh, dear God," said Bessy in despair. "Then it's already too late. I may as well tell you all now ... Mr Bourne, he made advances."

"Bessy, whatever happened is in the past." Reece's hold on her shoulders tightened. "You have to let it go. It don't mean anything."

"No, Reece. I didn't tell you what really happened. He ... *forced* himself on me."

Instantly, Reece released her and crammed a fist into his mouth. "You mean he—"

"Yes. I didn't want you to …. He tried it again," she said quickly, "and if I hadn't hit him, God knows what might have happened."

"You hit him?" interjected Hanson. "What do you mean, like a slap?"

"A lot worse," said Mrs Clapham.

"I think I might have killed him," Bessy said.

Reacting swiftly, Reece motioned for Hanson to keep the two women from entering the hallway. "Wait here," he said and, drawing his gun, he went up the guesthouse steps and slipped inside.

There was an oil lamp spluttering on the small reception desk, its fuel almost spent. Crossing to it, Reece held it aloft. The entrance to the kitchen yawned black before him. He waited, listening. There was no sound.

He could barely pick out the details and the lamp was almost out when he spotted another over by the range. Swiftly, he put his gun in his waistband and, fumbling with the glass bowl, he tilted the larger lamp towards the still burning wick of the second and managed to light it. He turned up the flame, repositioned the bowl and swept its much stronger light around the room.

The sight of the two dead men did not cause him to start. Something inside him had already prepared him for such an eventuality. What did surprise him were the identities of the dead. Neither one was Bourne. The one crammed into the corner was Frank, the cowboy tough who had confronted him on that first evening. The other he did not know. Both were shot, the unknown one at close range.

Returning to the reception area, he caught sight of Bessy, her distraught, face awash with tears. She looked at him with such heart-rending pain that he simply had to go to her, comfort her. He put down the lamp and opened his arms.

"Destry is he...?"

Reece held her face in both his hands. "It's not him." Her eyes grew wide with disbelief. "It's not Destry nor Bourne. There are two men in there. One is Frank, the other—"

She didn't allow him to finish. Tearing herself free of his arms, she sprinted into the kitchen and almost immediately returned. "I need the lamp."

Reece picked it up and went with her.

Despite the light being dismal, a great moan escaped her lips when she settled her eyes on the second corpse. "It's Nathan."

Hanson was with them now, Mrs Clapham close behind. She gasped. "Nathan Hoffstedder? Why would anyone kill him?"

"That man," said Bessy, unable to answer as she pointed towards Frank. "He wasn't ... Reece," she whirled around. "I hit Bourne. Twice. With that pan." She picked up the utensil, the great dints clearly visible on the rim. "He went down, and he was dead. I swear to God he was dead."

"But Frank," put in Hanson, "how did he get out of the jail?"

"I let him out. He and Weasel. I needed them to help me, to hide the body. I suppose that is what they did but who shot Frank ... Oh Reece, what have I done? I wasn't thinking. I panicked and didn't know what to do." She sank onto a nearby chair, her body shaking, lips trembling.

"Bessy," said Mrs Clapham sternly, "I've told you already – you have nothing to reproach yourself for. He was forcing himself on you and you reacted instinctively."

"Whatever the truth of it," said Hanson, "someone has murdered these two men. Shot them and I'm assuming that wasn't you, Miss Bessy?"

"Dear God, no! They demanded more money for what I asked them to do. I went to the bank with Weasel to get them two hundred dollars. Mr Morrison can give witness to what happened next."

"All right," said Reece, giving her a reassuring smile, "what we need to do now is take a look at Bourne's body."

"They put him in the outhouse, I think," she said.

Mrs Clapham cried with horror and, trembling uncontrollably, groped for another chair. Bessy leaned across to her and said, "I think we need to get out of this hellish place."

"You're right," said Reece. "Bessy, you go back to Mrs Clapham's. Hanson and me will find out what the hell has happened here."

"Are you sure?"

"More than anything," said Reece and helped first Bessy and then Mrs Clapham to their feet. Eyes averted, Bessy headed for the door, looping her arm around Mrs Clapham's shoulders, and together they moved outside, both women shaken by the scene in the kitchen.

"It must have been Destry," said Hanson when the two women were out of earshot. "He came back looking for Bessy, found Frank and killed him. Then poor old Nathan comes in and gets much the same."

"Could be. Let's go and see what they did to Bourne."

But Bourne was not there, the outhouse empty. Getting down on his haunches, Reece shone the oil lamp to reveal the large patch of dried blood across the floor. "He was here, I'd say, but Bessy didn't kill him, although she probably meant to." Shaking his head, Reece stood up. "I reckon we put those other bodies in here and then try to get some sleep. We'll set out early in the morning and find 'em. I'm thinking that we'll catch up with 'em up at the mine."

"You believe it was Bourne who shot them and not Destry? He recovered, went back into the guesthouse and confronted Frank. But why kill him?"

"Hanson, your guess is as good as mine. All I know is that people around here act mighty strange and there is no predicting what they might do."

CHAPTER THIRTY-TWO

It was cold now. Not only in the evenings, but in the early morning also. Winter would soon make itself felt even in the daytime. Quince, a blanket wrapped around his shoulders, sat at the great dining table, slurping steaming broth as Manchester hovered and served hot coffee.

"It's awful early, Mr Quince, sir."

"I know that, Manchester. I can't sleep. Thanks for the soup."

"Can I get you anything else, sir?"

"Rouse everyone, but not the ladies. I need to talk to Weasel again, get the story straight in my head."

Manchester bowed slightly and shuffled out. Quince, finishing his broth, pushed the bowl away and leaned back in his chair, both hands wrapped around his coffee cup.

From somewhere deep within the house, raised voices complained about being woken so early. Quince waited, drumming his cup with his fingers. At last, Weasel came in, hair ruffled, bleary-eyed, disheveled looking. "Trouble boss?" he muttered, his voice still thick with sleep.

Quince did not look up. "Sit down Weasel. I want you to tell me again exactly what it was you saw back in town. And what happened to Frank."

Weasel dragged a hand through his wild hair and slumped into a chair. "I told you, Mr Quince."

"Tell me again."

"Well, all righty. But my story ain't changed none. We was in the jail, thanks to that Reece, and Miss Bessy comes in. She's upset. Shaking, crying. She asks us to help her move a body and we agree, but at a price. You understand?"

"Just get on with it."

"Yes, sir. From there, she unlocks the jail and we goes to the guesthouse where Bourne is lying in a pool of blood. We take him outside—"

"He was dead? Are you sure of it?"

"To be honest, we didn't check or anything."

"He was a good man was Bourne. Came highly recommended. You say Miss Bessy told you she hit him?"

"With a cast-iron pot. Smack!" He slapped the side of his head and giggled a little. "Anyways, we picked him up and carried him out back, put a pile of straw bales over him and then, when we were in the guesthouse again, Frank he demands more money. So she says ..."

"Weasel, get to the part where you go back to the guesthouse."

"Oh, yes. Well, I am about to go back to see Frank because they've locked the doors to the bank and ..." He noted Quince's furious look. "I hears this shot see. Two shots I think. Yes, yes two it was, so I run and there is Frank. He's dead and there ain't no one else there, so I'm wondering who might have done it when I see Destry. He's ... Jeez, Mr Quince, I ain't never seen a look like the one I saw on his face. Like the Devil himself, with spit drooling from his mouth, his eyes ... Damn ..." He rubs his face vigorously with both hands. "Can I get a cup of coffee?"

"When you're done. What happened next?"

"I gotta tell you, Mr Quince, I was spooked. Now, I ain't

easily spooked as you well know, and I turn to go when this young fella comes in. Tall and gangly, he's mighty afraid, waving his hands like he's warning us of a fire. And Destry, he shoots him. Just like that. *Pop!*" Weasel turned in his chair and shouted across to Manchester who was hovering against the far wall, "Can I get a coffee?"

"Who was this guy he shot," said Quince. "You recognized him?"

"No, sir. He could have been anyone, but I wasn't stopping to ask. I ran."

"You ran?"

Manchester came over with the coffee pot, refilling Quince's cup first before going to Weasel.

Weasel took a sip of coffee and nodded his thanks to Manchester. "Yes, sir. I did, I don't mind me saying so. Destry had that murderous look in his eye that I know so well. But there was something else. A *madness*. He'd been drinking, I reckon, and was not about to discuss anything with me or anyone else. I got on my horse and high-tailed it out of that damn town as fast as I could."

Quince looked at the scrawny cowhand without speaking. The heavy silence pressed down on them all, a silence broken only when Henry came in, breathing hard, tucking his shirt into his trousers. "What's going on, boss?"

"Weasel's just been telling me about what happened over in town," said Quince. "Seems like Destry shot young Frank and another fella."

"Why would he do that?" asked Henry, sitting down next to Weasel at the long table.

"Weasel here thinks it's because Destry has gone mad."

"I didn't actually say that," put in Weasel quickly, shooting a nervous grin towards Henry, "but he was acting strange. Wild," he waved a hand across his face, "with a murderous look in his eyes."

"Are we talking about the same Destry who spends most of

his time either drunk or trying to catch something nasty over at Saint Francine's?"

"The very same," said Quince.

"So, what do we do?"

"You take some men, and you ride over there, find him, and bring him back. I want explanations. I want to know where Bourne is and where the map to the mine is. I need that gold, Henry. I aim to expand my holdings here and to do that I need more money. I reckon Destry is the key to whatever is going on, so bring him back. We'll have all the answers before the day is out."

CHAPTER THIRTY-THREE

The sun was barely above the horizon when Reece entered the surgery to find Doc Turner, shoulders sagging, eyes downcast, slumped in a chair, staring into space. He turned and blew out a sigh. "Sheriff has gone, Reece. Dead. I have been sitting here trying to work it out but nothing I can think of gives me an answer."

Stepping over to the table on which Fieyn lay dead, Reece drew in a long breath. "You're sure he didn't ... you know, just *die?*"

There was no reply.

Reece moved closer, pulled up another chair, hard-backed and somewhat past its prime. It creaked as he sat. "Doc? How did he die?"

"Not from heart failure, that's for sure." His head came up, his eyes piercing. "And don't question my credentials or my ability to—"

Instantly, Reece swung up his hands, "Hey, Doc, I'm not questioning anything about you, just the nature of the sheriff's death."

The doc's face remained an impassive mask as he said, "He was murdered."

Turning away, Turner pulled out a drawer from his desk and produced a bottle. He unscrewed it and took a long pull. Gasping, he handed the bottle to Reece, who took a much shorter drink. Pulling a face, he gave it back.

Hanson, standing in the doorway as he had done since walking into the surgery to find the dead sheriff, said, "So now we have another mystery to add to the growing pile."

Reece sighed. "Give me another drink."

The doc passed across the bottle and Reece drank.

"Biggest mystery for me is why Destry had you arrested," said Hanson.

"It wasn't so much an arrest," said Reece, "as something more like a kidnap. He wanted to keep me out of the way whilst he did whatever he needed to do."

"Whatever it was," continued Hanson, "I'm saying this in front of the Doc here. I didn't witness anything you did up at the shack that might have justified your arrest, unless, of course, there's something you ain't telling us."

Reece shook his head. "I was talking to Fieyn when we noticed that Ezra, the fella we'd found at the shack, had disappeared. Fieyn and Destry went into the shack and I went to have a look in the woods."

"Yeah, I saw that."

"Then, when I came back, they were acting strange. Eyes were wide, they were shaking..."

"That might have been when Fieyn's heart started to give out," said the Doc.

"Maybe. All I know is that from that moment everything changed."

"So, you're thinking there's something in the shack?" Leaning back, the Doc folded his arms, eyes staring with a burning intensity. "Something inside they may have drunk or eaten?"

"Or smoked," said Hanson. "Over in San Francisco, I saw lots of Chinese – and plenty of others come to that – who visited opium dens and smoked themselves into oblivion."

The Doc gave him a look. "Yes, I've heard of that myself. So maybe there is something inside there? What do you think, Reece?"

"Could be. Destry was tied up inside," said Reece. "Ezra, he goes inside, looking for something, spends time inside. Later on, he tells us he saw his old ma." He looked from the Doc to Hanson, "Only thing is, his old ma has been dead these past five years or so."

Hanson sighed. "According to Ezra."

"I got no cause to doubt him," said Reece looking directly at the big blacksmith. "Why would he make that up?"

"Make us believe him. Perhaps *he's* hiding something? Maybe there is something in that shack and it's something Ezra didn't want us to know about. But the sheriff and Destry, they *did* find it."

"I know there's a map," said Reece. "A map old man White scribbled down after he'd first discovered the gold. Maybe it's that."

"How do you know there's a map?" asked Turner. He shot a glance towards Hanson who shrugged.

"On my way here," said Reece, "I stopped off in Lancaster. In the saloon, I met up with a couple of fellas and got into a card game with 'em. We got to drinking and talk turned to the old abandoned mine over at Whitewater. As I left, my pockets a lot lighter I have to tell you, one of 'em steps up to me. He's drunk and doesn't make much sense, rambling on about secret treasures. He passes me a note." Reaching into his shirt pocket, Reece produced a well-creased piece of paper. He showed first to Turner and then to Hanson. "He said I should look for this."

"So that's why you're here," breathed Hanson. "To find that?"

"I don't even know what it is. Treasure can mean a lot of things to different people." He looked again at the paper before returning it to his pocket. "None of it means anything without the map."

"And Destry is the only one left who might know the whereabouts of that map," said Hanson, "now that the sheriff's dead."

"I left young Ira watching over him," said the Doc. "Maybe he could shed some light on this. If it was Destry who came back and murdered the sheriff, then it all makes sense."

Reece grunted. "I agree. We need to find Destry, get some answers to what the hell is going on. All of it is linked to the mine, I'm sure of it." He gestured towards Fieyn. "Perhaps even this."

"From what you've told us, it can't be about gold, can it?" said Hanson.

"Something more valuable."

"There is one person I know who could give us some answers," said the Doc. "An old Indian lives just outside of town. Goes by the name of Winter Hair on account of his hair being white as snow. As is the rest of him."

"How do you mean?" asked Reece.

"He's an albino. Even his eyes are pink."

"Jeez," breathed Hanson.

"All right," said Reece. "The sheriff won't be going anywhere so let's go and talk to this Winter Hair. Hanson, could you stay, just in case someone comes back."

The big blacksmith shrugged. "I'll do what I can."

"And if you happen to see Ira," said Doc Turner, "ask him why he left the sheriff alone."

"Yeah, and if Miss Bessy stops by," said Reece, "tell her—"

"I get the picture," said Hanson with a dismissive wave of his hand.

Nodding, Reece gave the blacksmith a knowing smile before he moved across to the door. "You know how to get there, Doc? To where this Winter Hair lives?"

"I take it that means you'd like me to accompany you?"

"If that's not too much trouble for you, I'd be obliged."

The Doc gave a resigned smirk. "Doesn't look as if I got any choice." Shaking his head, he pushed past Reece, saying in a heavy voice, "I'll get some things and then we'll go."

CHAPTER THIRTY-FOUR

I t was a desolate place, the landscape scared as if blasted by numerous explosions or artillery shells. It reminded Reece of certain areas he'd fought in during the War, whole sections of earth blown wide open, the shell-holes deep and treacherous. The only difference here was the lack of mangled, ruined bodies.

Doc Turner picked up on Reece's mood. "You been here before?"

"Eh?" Reece shuddered, pushing the memories aside. "No, no, it's not that. I ain't ever been here but this place reminds me of somewhere, that's all."

"Yes, I get that. I was at Fredericksburg." He reacted to Reece's wide-eyed surprise, adding hastily, "On the side of the Union. My military rank was Major, but I was, then as now, a doctor." He turned and regarded the nearest hillside, pock-marked with caves. "Even now I have nightmares."

Taking a breath, Reece said, "So do we all, Doc."

Doc Turner nodded and blew out a long sigh. "We'll find Winter Hair in one of those caves. Not sure which one – I haven't been here for a long time."

Reece kicked his horse and urged it forward, the Doc falling in beside him. Before they had taken a dozen paces, a man emerged from one of the larger gashes in the hillside. Short in stature and stooping forward, he wore ragged clothes made from animal skins and sported a buffalo headdress, the large horns protruding from the sides glistening in the sunlight. Tufts of bone-white hair sprouted from the edges of the impressive bonnet. He was open-handed but Reece noted the large Bowie knife at the man's hip.

"Is that him?" asked Reece, reining in his horse.

"Indeed, it is. Winter Hair, so-called for obvious reasons although I do believe he was born that way." He chuckled. "As he's an albino, he was shunned by his tribe who drove him from their village at an early age. They believed him to be a bad spirit but recently they have seen him as more of a shaman – a medicine man. He's lived up here as a virtual hermit for well over forty years, so they say. He knows everything there is to know about these parts, including the mine. I think if we're going to get any answers, we won't find a better source. But be careful, he's known to become as wild as a mustang if he thinks you're a threat." He nodded towards Reece's gun belt. "So, if I were you, I'd unbuckle that and leave it here, with your horse."

Reece didn't argue. He dismounted, looped his gun belt around the pommel and waited for Doc Turner to follow him.

"I'll introduce us," said the doc, slipping down to the ground. "He knows me, or at least he should. I took a piece of jagged tree root from his calf muscle about fifteen years ago. He's walked with a limp ever since." He sniggered as he detached a large canvas bag from his addle. "I gathered together some things, which I hope he finds to his satisfaction."

"You've thought of everything."

"Let's hope so," said Turner as he looped the bag over his shoulder.

Outside the entrance to his cave, on a wind-blasted ledge, Winter Hair got down on his haunches to study the two men intensely as they approached.

The hill was gentle but even so, Doc Turner was breathing

heavily when he reached the ledge and stepped onto it. Reece hovered a little behind, holding Winter Hair's questioning gaze.

Winter Hair's skin shone with the lustre of alabaster and Reece could not take his eyes off it. Gnarled, sunken belly, nobbled legs and stick-thin arms, vivid blue-green veins running along their length, like symbols on a map. Reece believed he only needed to curl his fingers around the limb for it to shatter beneath his grip.

Waving them inside his cramped, barren cave of a home, the old Indian squatted in front of them both. The wind howled through the cave's entrance, but he didn't seem to mind. He was colder than any ruffled air, be it winter or fall. This was a man who had suffered much and conquered every exterior assault on his wizened frame.

At last, as if rousing himself from a trance, Reece cleared his throat and looked to the Doc for some sort of guidance.

"Greetings to you, Winter Hair. We have come to talk about ..." the Doc began but stopped as the old Indian turned his pink eyes towards him.

"I know why you are here. You wish to go inside the old mine." He looked at Reece, "Is it not so?"

Reeling back from the old Indian's piercing eyes, Reece sputtered, "How do you know...?"

The old Indian's hand came up slowly and, amazingly, he smiled. "Ask me how I do not."

The Doc chuckled at this but Reece, still entranced by those eyes, could not find any words.

"Can you tell us anything about the mine?" said the Doc, leaning forward. "We know men have died in there but others ... Others have entered the mine and have returned *changed*."

"This was so before you were born, old man. I watched the old one who took gold from there and used those riches to buy land. To build your town. I watched him close up the mine knowing what was inside. I know other stories, of men who came with murder in their hearts, of how they fled to the mine and died there, screaming in their agony. And in these past days, I have seen others come, greed clouding their minds, the way they have fought each other. The man who forced the murderers into the mine, how he himself was tied and left in the broken work shack. The shack Old Man White built. How another came and went and how a man cried for his mother, who spoke to him there."

Reece, gripped by the man's words, the way his voice seemed to be the only thing that ever mattered. He leaned forward, his voice a mere whisper when he spoke. "How do you know all this?"

The Indian regarded Reece keenly. "I told you. I watch. I listen. Nothing happens here that I do not know."

"You spoke of White," put in Doc Turner quickly. "Why is it that he did not die or change the way others have?"

"He did not return to the mine, nor the shack. He stayed away and built his ranch, his town."

"The town that bears his name," said Reece.

A frown developed on Winter Hair's otherwise smooth, unmarked face. "It is called White Water. Not because of old Man White, but because of the water that runs from the nearby spring. It begins beneath the mine, deep down, and the water mixes with the rocks and turns white. *That* is why it is so-called."

The two others exchanged wild looks. "I've heard that. It makes sense," said the doc, his voice trembling.

"No one who has come after has ever questioned the name, believing it to be from Old Man White. But the water, it is not good. The man in the shack, he drinks that water." He grinned again. "All the time."

"Your wisdom is as deep as the world around us," said Turner. He produced the items he'd collected from the canvas bag. Blankets to guard against the cold, fur boots, a leather pouch stuffed with tobacco and intricately designed wampum belts. Winter Hair picked up each gift, studying them closely, grunting his appreciation.

"This water," said Reece, keen to return the conversation back to the mine, "it is poisonous?"

"If taken too many times," said Winter Hair, placing the gifts in a neat pile behind him, "the mind, it can be altered. I have known some bucks who could not go a day without drinking it. They liked the changes it brought. But even the water is not as strong as the invisible gas in the mine itself, or in the work shack where it lingers in the smallness of the building. In the mine, it can disperse, becoming less potent the further you move from the source."

"The source?"

"Deep below the ground is where it begins. And when the ground rumbles and splits, the gases come out, sweet-smelling, not unpleasant. And there is its danger. Your mind is captured by the feelings that follow. Such feelings..." Shaking his head, he looked down and for the first time seemed disturbed. "The man in the shack who called out to his mother, its power ensnared him. He will wish to breathe it in again." His face came up. "Or drink it. Many drink it, filling their water bottles from the stream. They mix it with their whisky, and they become its servant."

"Destry drinks all the damn time," muttered Turner.

Reece grunted, knowing Destry wasn't the only one. "You think the man who called for his mother will return to the shack?"

Winter Hair nodded and held Reece's stare, "He will, as does anyone who breathes its air."

"Except for White," put in Turner.

"White was tormented with demons for many weeks after he first went to the mine. He killed. The shame of it broke him, made him become like a ghost, a man hiding in the shadows."

"Yes," said Turner, "people say he became a recluse. Towns-folk thought he'd been made mad by the lust for gold, that when he exhausted the veins in the mine, he raved endlessly about trying to find another source."

Reece felt a jolt run through him. "He did not exhaust the gold?"

"Gold is not the lure." The two men looked as if they were one and waited, holding their breath. Winter Hair held their gaze and nodded. "Treasure is still there. In abundance."

CHAPTER THIRTY-FIVE

A powerful and intense smell filled the fetid air within the shack. Heat rising, Ezra threw off his blanket and struggled to his feet. His head pounded and his guts churned. It was as if he'd been drinking and he swayed drunkenly, throwing out his arms to find something to anchor onto. There was nothing and he slid to his knees, nausea rising from the depths of his stomach. "Oh God," he groaned.

"What the hell is the matter with you?" It was Bourne, coming through the door, arms filled with wood collected from the nearby forest.

"I'm sick. Oh, Jesus." Ezra staggered forward, pushed Bourne aside and fell outside onto the ground. He writhed there for a moment, struggled to push himself to his hands and knees and then, retching horribly, he emptied his guts onto the dirt.

Other than shaking his head in disgust, Bourne ignored him and went over to the squat pot-stove. He filled it with smaller pieces of wood and bark. He'd already found a small leather pouch containing a flint and steel on a shelf and now used this to set the stove alight. Prodding the spluttering flames, he blew on them until the thinner pieces caught, flaring up and creating a few moments of glorious warmth. Rubbing his hands before the flames, Bourne added more, thicker pieces of timber then closed the small lid at the top of the stove. A satisfying roar developed within the belly of the stove and Bourne set about rifling through the various sagging shelves and warped cupboards in search of something to drink.

"I feel so ill," said Ezra, returning to the interior. Bathed in sweat, he shivered uncontrollably. Pulling his blanket tight around him he collapsed in front of the still-developing heat of the stove and rocked himself forwards and backwards. "I must have eaten something bad," he said, screwing up his face and squeezing his eyes shut.

"Like what? We haven't eaten for hours. Neither of us. And there's nothing here." Bourne slammed one of the cupboards shut in exasperation and it immediately crumpled into pieces at his feet. "This whole stinking place is rotten. We need to get to the mine, find the gold and get the hell out of here. We can stop off at the town to eat on the way back."

"Eat?" Ezra shook his head, "I never want to eat again."

"Well, I do." He had a canteen looped over his shoulder. He pulled it free and opened the stopper. "At least we have some water. The stream is not so far. Do you want me to boil it up? I could gather some berries and the like from the woods, brew up a sort of tea if you wish."

"Tea? What the hell, Bourne, are you planning on poisoning me?"

"You ungrateful cur. I could have killed you while you was snoring your pretty little head off. But I didn't, did I! No, I was out getting us wood to keep us warm."

"I ain't ungrateful, Bourne, I just don't think I could stomach anything right now. Maybe some water – *cool* water, that is."

Bourne handed over the canteen and Ezra drank fitfully from it. He pulled a face when he'd taken a good swallow. "That don't taste right. Not like water, anyways. Where did you say you got it?"

"Stream. Here," he yanked the canteen from Ezra's grip, "I'll boil it up anyway and make that tea." He went outside and headed towards where he'd tied up the horses, so long ago now he was confused about where he had left them. Uncertainly, he searched the immediate surroundings, the woods looking forbidding. He entered them, nevertheless. He didn't recall tying the horses there but surely...

He stopped, hands-on-hips, and scanned the immediate surroundings, turning in a wide arc, eyes not missing a single detail.

No matter how hard he looked it was clear the horses were no longer anywhere to be found. Deeply worried, he scrambled around and found bunches of nettles. He'd heard somewhere that they made a good tea, so he gathered them up in his gloved hands and strode out of the woods.

Back inside the shack, he found Ezra waiting, head between his knees, lank hair masking his face. A trail of spit drooled from his mouth. He breathed shallowly and did not stir until Bourne was almost upon him. He raised his head and Bourne gasped, taking an involuntary step backwards.

"Dear God," Bourne said, "you look like death."

"I feel like death," came the response in a frail, tiny voice. "I need a drink, but I ain't drinking that white piss."

"Listen," said Bourne, holding up the bunch of nettles, "I got some ... I ain't got nothing to put the water in. No pots or canteen I mean."

Ezra frowned. "What? You fool, Bourne, I got some metal ware on my saddle. All you need do is—"

"That's just it. The horses ... they've gone."

Ezra's mouth fell open. He spluttered, "I don't get yeh. How can they be *gone?*"

"I don't know. Someone took 'em, I guess. When we was sleeping."

"That can't be." Ezra slapped his palms on either side of his body and pushed himself to his feet. He stood swaying, as if on a sailing ship's deck. "There ain't no one else here, Bourne. Damn your eyes, what are you trying to do, kill me?"

"I told you, you idiot, the horses have gone, and I don't know—"

"You *liar!*"

Without any warning, Ezra launched himself forward. Frothing at the mouth, his eyes ablaze with hatred or anger, he stretched out his hands to seize Bourne around the throat. In a tangle of thrashing arms and legs, the two men fell heavily to the ground. Bourne, desperate to free himself from those hands which squeezed with such alarming strength, did his best to break away, but he could not.

"I'll kill you, you miserable bastard!" screeched Ezra, shaking his opponent's neck. "You'll not murder me, you'll not!"

Gripped by some diabolical power, Ezra was in a frenzy, uncontrollable, fingers like claws biting deep into Bourne's flesh, intent on ending his life.

But Bourne, despite the rising panic coursing unchecked through his body, the red veil falling across his vision, at last found some reserves of energy and used his superior strength to good effect. He jabbed his fists into Ezra's ribs over and over until there was the slightest loosening of the grip. Instantly, he brought up his knee, slamming it into Ezra's groin, three, four times. Each blow accompanied by a squeal of pain. As Ezra drew back, Bourne swung his right first across the man's jaw with all the power and leverage he could muster and sent him sprawling across the ground.

Breathing hard, but with no time to waste, Bourne got to his feet and put a boot into Ezra's ribs. Resolute but breathing raggedly, Bourne whipped up the gun lying on the table. He checked the load and, grunting with satisfaction, turned.

And there was Ezra, arms swinging low, eyes blurry, the spittle frothing all around his mouth. "Bastard," he growled and ran forward.

This time, Bourne was ready. He nimbly sidestepped and

smashed the revolver hard across the back of Ezra's head. A loud yelp erupted from Ezra's throat. He crashed into the table, his jaw hitting the edge, and jack-knifed to the floor. He lay there, the blood bubbling from his shattered mouth.

Taking a deep breath, Bourne brought up the revolver and aimed it unerringly towards Ezra's head. He eased back the hammer just as the footfall made the timbers creak at the shack entrance and caused him to stop and turn.

Three men stood there, the central one filling the doorway with his wide-shouldered frame.

"I'd put that down if I were you, Bourne," said Henry, coat pulled back, hands mere inches away from the revolvers at his waist, "and then you can tell me what the Be-Jesus is going on here."

CHAPTER THIRTY-SIX

Less than an hour earlier, riding hard with their faces set into the rising wind, the bunch of riders, some seven men in all, soon found themselves skirting the town of Whitewater. Weasel, coming alongside Henry, shouted across to his boss, "We is going into town? I thought we was going straight to the mine?"

"No point if we ain't got that map. We'll ride into town, find Destry and start to get to the bottom of this."

"Not sure I wanna go into the town again, Mr Henry. Seems that every time I do, I end up in some sort of trouble."

Henry could barely suppress his laughter. "You is all bluff, ain't you boy. With them fancy guns stuffed in your belt you like to think of yourself as a gunfighter, but when the chips are down you ain't nothing but a momma's boy."

Chewing up his mouth, Weasel went to speak when another rider, scouting ahead, came thundering into view. Henry raised his hand and the bunch reined in and waited.

"You find anything?" asked Henry as Mulehead O'Reilly, the best tracker the Quince Ranch had, pulled up and paused a moment to catch his breath.

"I sure did, Mr Henry. I saw Destry riding away from the town like he had the hounds of hell at his heels."

"We can catch him?"

"I reckon."

Without another word, Henry tore off his hat and, beating his horse's rump with it, careened away towards the distant woods. The others soon fell behind him.

They found Destry near a small creek, up to his waist in the water, scrubbing at his hair and face. He froze when he saw the approaching riders, calculated the chances of getting to his gun before they were upon him, and thought better of it. Instead, he stood and waited, his off-yellow colored long johns soaked through with the milky white water.

Henry motioned for a couple of his men to dismount. It didn't take them long to haul Destry out of the water and now, here they all were, at the shack with Bourne in the open, hands clasped in front of him as if in prayer, whilst Otis tended to the stricken Ezra inside.

"I'll ask you again," said Henry, still mounted, leaning forward with hands resting on the pommel, "what's been going on?"

Bourne shrugged and locked his eyes on Destry. "His pretty wife almost near killed me. Laid me out with a frying pan or some such thing, then got this idiot," he nodded towards Weasel, "to throw me into an outhouse and leave me for dead."

"That ain't exactly true," began Weasel but stopped when he noted Henry's glare.

"Go on," said Henry.

"Well, here I am, with this," Bourne dipped inside his jacket and produced the well-folded map. "I'm guessing this is why you're here."

"No," said Destry, "*I'm* here to kill you."

"Is that right?" sneered Bourne.

"You're damned right."

"Not before me," said Weasel quickly, his fingers already creeping towards the butt of his revolver.

"All right," barked Henry. "You cut all of that out, you hear me! Mr Quince wants this situation tidied up without any more bloodshed. If any of you butt-wipes have an issue with that, you'd best spit it out and I'll finish it for you." His eyes ran across the three men. "Each and every one of you."

"Ah shoot, Mr Henry," said Weasel in despair, "one of these shot poor old Frank. I know it because that there map Frank found at the guesthouse. We find out which one it was, and we can hang the sonofawhore right here and right now."

"I have to say," said Henry with a smile, "this must be one of the few times I find myself in agreement with you, Weasel. So, which of you two did it?"

"Listen here, Mr Henry," said Bourne, getting his explanations in first, "it was Mr Quince who employed me to find that map and learn anything I could about the mine. I'd like to think I've done that but that don't mean I killed Frank. Why in hell would I do that if we is all on the same side? It just don't make sense."

"I understand your reasoning, Bourne," said Henry. "The way Weasel told it back at the ranch, he says you were not yourself lately. Taking Destry up to this here shack, to beat the hell out of him no doubt, seems to have changed you."

"No, sir, it did not."

"So how you got the map?" snapped Weasel, his eyes mere slits in his grime-encrusted face. "Tell us that you silver-tongued piece of rat-filth!"

Bourne moved faster than almost anyone had seen before and landed a solid right haymaker square into Weasel's jaw which dumped the grimy little cowpuncher onto the ground. He lay there, flat out on his back, unconscious. Bourne slowly turned.

Henry already had his gun drawn but there was obvious amusement written across every line of his face. "I reckon he deserved that," he said, "but I'd still like you to tell me how you came across the map."

"Frank had it. I took it from him after I found him dead but … I don't know, I just felt I no longer needed it."

"You mean you already knew the route it laid out?"

"Yeah, that's just about it." He put his finger and thumb into his eyes and squeezed. "I get headaches, flashes, lights, all sorts of things but inside them, *amongst* them, I could see a trail leading through the woods to the mine's rear entrance. I still see it and it's much easier to get through than the front door if you get my meaning." He dropped his hand, "I can take you straight there, with or without the map."

"What about Frank?"

All eyes settled on Bourne, expectancy crackling in the air.

"As I said, he was already dead," said Bourne evenly. "All I did was lift that map from his dead fingers and studied it."

"So, who killed him?"

Bourne shrugged and gestured towards Destry who sat astride his horse, sullen, downcast, he did not flinch. "I reckon he knows more about it than just about anyone."

"Is that right, Destry?" snapped Henry, turning around to glare at the livery owner. "You know who killed Frank?"

"I found him," said Destry, at last lifting his head. "But he was already dead. He was lying there in Bessy's guesthouse, but I don't know who killed him. I'm thinking your friend Weasel knows more than he'd be willing to say. Interesting how he tried to blame Bourne here, ain't it."

"Mr Henry?" It was Otis. Emerging from the shack, he wiped his hands down the front of his shirt and shook his head, a dark look on his face. "Ezra, he's flat out cold but he'll live. Perhaps, when he wakes, he'll be able to tell us a lot more about what's been going on here."

"I reckon that's about right," said Henry.

"And there's more," continued Otis. "I been listening to what these two have been saying and Weasel, yeah sure he's rough, talks tough, likes to think of himself as a stone-cold killer but, to be honest, I just don't think he's got the guts or the brains to kill Frank."

Nodding, Henry took a long cold look at Weasel, lying unconscious in the dirt. "What do you reckon, Bourne?"

"I reckon he shot and killed Frank, thinking to take the map and go find the gold for himself."

Henry nodded. "We should send him for trial."

"That's right, Mr Henry," put in Otis quickly. "We should do the right thing."

Grunting, Henry smiled. Before anybody knew what was happening, he turned around, aimed his revolver, and shot Weasel through the head.

The enormous blast caused the assembled horses to scream and kick out with fright and every rider struggled to bring their mount under control. Otis, ashen faced, stared in abject horror, Bourne appeared mildly satisfied at the outcome and Destry returned to his former silence. Turning his horse, Henry said, "We ain't got no time for trials or hearings or any such thing. We're going to the mine. Otis, you stay here with O'Reilly. When that Ezra is awake, you bring him to the mine. Bourne, you lead the way."

The riders fell into a ragged line and Otis, still shaken from the sudden killing of Weasel, stood and watched them go. O'Reilly, sighing heavily, stepped up next to him.

"You think that Ezra will be able to tell us anything?"

"I'm not sure," said Otis, staring down at Weasel's corpse. "I'm not sure if any of this makes sense anymore."

"It's gold-fever, boy. Makes men do the most heinous of things."

"Yeah, but it's not that which is bothering me, Mulehead." Otis turned to face his companion. "It's something Bourne said."

"What was that? He said a lot, from where I was standing."

"He said that Weasel must have shot and killed Frank to take the map."

"Yeah. So?"

"But Bourne has the map. And he didn't get it from Weasel."

"By golly, that's right – he *did* say that! So then why didn't Mr

Henry say something? He shot Weasel stone dead without just cause, just like that!" He snapped his fingers to underline his last word.

Nodding, Otis drew in a deep breath. "I'm thinking Mr Henry knew exactly what he was doing, and justice has got nothing to do with it. As you said, Mulehead, the lure of gold, it makes men do the most terrible things."

"Dear God Almighty," said O'Reilly, staring after the swiftly disappearing line of riders. "I'm thinking we're the lucky ones being left behind like this."

Otis nodded. "Indeed we are, Mulehead. Things are going to get a whole lot nastier before long. And a whole lot more deadly."

CHAPTER THIRTY-SEVEN

"Dear God," gasped the doc. Reece quickly grabbed his arm to prevent him from saying anything more and gave him a withering look. In reply, Doc Turner put his head down and released a long sigh.

They'd arrived at almost the same time as the men from the ranch and were now hidden amongst a nearby thicket with a clear view of the shack.

"They murdered that man in cold blood," said the doc when the riders finally moved away. "I never thought I'd live to see such a thing."

Remaining silent, Reece stood up and stretched out his back. "We'll check the shack then go after 'em."

"What, are you mad? We're two against how many ... eight?"

"I counted ten, with Destry and Bourne."

"Oh well, that's so much better, isn't it!" He shook his head vigorously. "We have to think of a better plan than simply charging straight at them and—"

"Doc, I never said anything about charging at anyone. Trust me. Something will turn up." He shrugged. "Maybe breathing in all that stale air down the mine will send 'em half-mad."

"As if they aren't already."

After a meaningful pause, Reece took a step out into the open. "Doc, you fetch the horses, I'll check the shack."

"Be careful, for pity's sake. Otis is there, with that idiot of a tracker, O'Reilly."

Smiling, Reece drew his revolver and slowly made his way towards the small, sagging building some one hundred or so paces away. He moved stealthily, as a cat, and knelt next to the partially open door. He heard Otis and O'Reilly talking.

"It's best if we leave him," Otis said. "He'll make his way back to town, I shouldn't wonder. Once he's recovered."

"He looks awful, Otis. I don't give much for his chances."

"O'Reilly, I'm not sure he's gonna be any use to anyone. I say we go back to the ranch. I don't want any more to do with what's happening at the mine."

"Mr Henry ain't gonna be too pleased with any of that, Otis. He told us to stay here."

"All right, then let's say we go back into town, find the doc, bring him here to tend to Ezra. That's the Christian thing to do."

"I don't exactly class myself as a Christina, Otis."

"You go to church, don't you?"

"Not for a long time. Not since I was a young'un."

"Well, this is the way we make amends. The doc will know what to do, better than use."

O'Reilly grunted.

Reece swiftly dropped back around the corner of the shack as the two men emerged. Soon they were mounting up and galloping off. Reece watched them go and slipped inside the shack.

He found Ezra little more than a weeping wreck and it took some effort for Reece to bundle him outside. Sitting on the porch, Ezra, body racked with sobbing, slowly began to recover. Reece looked towards the woods. He felt resolute. His mind wandered back through the years, picking out some of the more desperate episodes in his army life, searching for something similar with which to gauge his current situation. He'd always been so resourceful, grim determination and a natural courage meant that few obstacles stood in his way for long. But now, with ten opponents to face down, to find what lay within the mine ... nothing had prepared him for anything like this.

"Those two seemed as if death itself had spoken to them, young Otis especially. Were they heading for town?"

Reece nodded as Turner stepped up close to him. "We need that Indian," he said. "Winter Hair? What possible good could he be? He's already told us everything."

"Not quite." Reece regarded his companion carefully. "He held me back as we left, gave me something."

Doc Turner frowned. "What was it, some sort of magical pendant to ward off those evil spirits?"

"Perhaps something a damn sight more useful. When I go into that cave, Doc, you stay outside. Our friend here," he nodded towards the blubbering Ezra, "he's just about done in. I believe his mind is addled and if he doesn't get some sort of medical help, coupled with prolonged rest, he's gonna be no use for anything."

"So, what do you suggest?"

"Take him back to town. See what you can do for him."

The doc didn't look convinced. "I'm in partial agreement with you, Reece. He's broken. But I doubt there's anything I can do for him. He's too far gone. Besides, you can't go up against Henry and the others on your own. It's suicide."

"Not if things go my way, Doc. Trust me, it'll be fine. I'll see you back in town."

Reece went across to the horses and mounted his. "There was a canteen in that shack, and it was filled with milky water. I reckon Ezra's been drinking it all day and all night."

"He'll be desperate for more. Once we're at Whitewater, I'll have to put him in the jail. He'll be as wild as a mountain lion if he doesn't get any more of that stuff, so it'll be best to keep him away from everyone."

"Yeah, I think that's just about so. You take care now, Doc.

Once you get back, tell Hanson what has happened and maybe he can get some men together and come over and help me."

"Hanson's a good man, capable too but I doubt if even he would want to go up against Quince's men."

"As these things always seem to pan out – I'm on my own."

Doc Turner led the way with Ezra close behind, head lolling, drooling over his shirt. He did not speak, and his breathing sounded labored as if every inhalation required a huge effort. Every now and then, Turner would turn and check that his charge was still alive. He was not absolutely certain if the stricken man would make it.

Arriving at Whitewater, Turner led Ezra to the surgery but as he reined in his horse and dismounted, the doctor noticed Hanson emerging from Miss Bessy's guesthouse. The big blacksmith was deep in thought and did not notice the doctor until Turner lifted his voice and beckoned him to come closer.

"Where is Reece?" asked the big man, his voice tinged with a note of concern.

"He's gone to the mine."

"On his own? Dear God, is he mad?"

"There wasn't much I could say to dissuade him. The old Indian gave him something, something Reece felt sure would give him an edge."

"And the others? What about Destry?"

"We think he'd gone to the mine also, together with Bourne. There were quite a few men from Quince's ranch there – including Henry."

"Then Reece really is a fool. To go up against Henry is foolish enough, but with all the others?" The big man shook his head, chewing at his bottom lip as he fell into deep thought.

"Did anyone come to the surgery?"

Hanson's snapped his head up. "Surgery? Why would anyone

...." A sudden light seemed to come into his eyes. "Ah! The surgery. No, no, nobody came."

"Then I wonder where Ira got to?" Dismissing any growing concern before it took hold, Turner turned to Ezra. "I need to check him over. He's delirious."

"What happened to him?"

"I don't know. I *think* it's got something to do with all the water he's been drinking but I won't be sure until I've given him a thorough examination. Could you help me get him inside?"

Almost as soon as Ezra settled into one of the beds in the surgery, he fell into a deep sleep, all of the pain, confusion and anguish leaving his face.

"I think we better take the sheriff over to the Undertakers," said Hanson, sniffing loudly. "He's beginning to smell ripe."

The Doc ran a hand through his thinning hair. "I guess so. I can't begin to imagine ... I mean, he was bad enough, not unlike Ezra here, but I never suspected he would die. If he wasn't murdered, I can only assume that his heart was worse than I at first thought. But if it has anything to do with what be in that old shack then I'm afraid our friend here," he pointed at Ezra, "may well be heading the same way."

"I don't understand," said Hanson, sounding more confused than ever.

"It seems there is something in the mine – something in the air. Winter Hair explained there's a gas, released from the rocks below. It has a kind of hypnotic effect and, if exposed for too long, can lead to changes in anyone's behavior, making them violent and unpredictable. It somehow leaks into the shack too."

At that point, Miss Bessy came through the door, that beaming smile of hers causing Doc Turner's heart to jump as it always did.

"Why, Doctor Turner, how happy I am to see you returned safely," she said, coming up close. She struck out her hand and

Turner took it without hesitation and kissed it. "Where is Mr Reece?"

"He's fine," said Turner, gazing at her hand. She smelled of honey and almonds and had clearly just emerged from a bath. He smiled, feeling himself drifting into a dreamlike state.

"I'm so glad to hear it," she said, flashing her smile to Hanson and back to the doctor. "But where is he?"

"He is searching for your husband, Miss Bessy."

Her smile instantly disappeared. She stiffened, her eyes losing their lustre and her voice, when she spoke, was without emotion. "I see."

Not wishing to pursue the conversation further, Turner returned the subject to the sheriff. "We should move him."

Hanson grunted and, with Miss Bessy watching, they carried the body unceremoniously across the street to the undertakers.

Brad Swail stood outside the entrance, smoking a thin cheroot. He stiffened when he saw them, tipped his hat, and gaped at Fieyn. "What in tarnation has happened to him?"

"I thought everyone knew," said Turner, breathing hard. "Help me get him inside would you, Brad."

Swail tossed away the cheroot and relieved Turner of his part of the burden.

After they'd put the body on a worm-ridden table, the undertaker, Conrad Phipps, emerged from a back room. "What's this," he demanded.

"Sheriff Fieyn," said Turner breathlessly, stepping up next to the others. "I'll do the paperwork, Conrad, make it all legal."

"Legal?" Brad Swail frowned. "In what way legal?"

"Doc seems to think the sheriff may have been the victim of murder," said Hanson.

Phipps's hand flew to his mouth. "Dear God! Murder? We'll need to bring across a US Marshal in that case, Doc."

"Can you keep him, er, on ice, so to speak, until we can get such a thing arranged?"

"Now, Doc," said Swail, studying the corpse with keen interest, "we don't need no Marshal to get involved, do we?"

Turner frowned. "It's the proper thing to do, Brad. He's the town sheriff, who else is going to investigate it?"

"If there is anything to investigate. Perhaps he really did die from his heart. All that shock and everything, it was all bound to take its toll."

Before Turner could answer, it was Hanson who interjected. "Shock? What in the hell do you know about any of this, Swail?"

"Nothin', nothin' at all. The whole town is buzzing with it. I just think we should all just step back a little, let things simmer down before we involve anyone from the Federal government. You know how they like to snoop."

"You could be right," said Turner. "Whatever else, please Conrad, do your best to preserve him until I can do a proper examination."

"I will, Doc," said Phipps. "I'll keep him as fresh as a daisy."

"That's not quite what I had in mind, but thanks anyway." Turner tipped his hat and returned to the street. Hanson was close behind but Swail remained inside with Phipps.

"What was Swail going on about in there, Doc?"

"Brad? Oh, he's just … He's never been one for outsiders, Hanson. Doesn't trust 'em and, well, he was a Confederate sympathizer. He doesn't take too kindly at the thought of having anyone from the government coming here to ask questions."

"He fought for the Confederacy?"

"Not sure. He may have done." Frowning, he shook his head. "He's assisted me for just over a year now, showed some promising medical skills, but other than that I don't know too much about him. He's a good friend of Destry's, by all accounts."

"Well, that ain't much of a recommendation, is it?"

"No," said Turner slowly, as if a distant thought was developing in his mind, "indeed it isn't."

. . .

Later, with the surgery smelling of carbolic, Turner, sleeves rolled up, face covered with sweat, did his best to make Ezra comfortable. Hanson had wandered off to his shop and Brad must have remained at the undertakers. Turner made himself a pot of coffee and wondered, once again, about Brad Swail, his words, his agitation at the mention of a US Marshal.

Finishing his coffee, Turner settled down in his armchair, wandered off to sleep and dreamed. By the time he woke, it was late afternoon and Ezra, far from succumbing to whatever he had inhaled, was gone.

CHAPTER THIRTY-EIGHT

Halfway to the town, Otis pulled up his horse and remained still, staring into the distance. O'Reilly, who didn't notice at first, reined in and turned, deep furrows on his face. "What is it?"

"I don't know. Something."

He swiveled in his saddle, looking across the wilderness that separated the woods from the town. There was nothing, save for the sweeping plains, the distant mountains. Somewhere overhead, an eagle screeched.

"Something?" O'Reilly, a man who had scouted for the Union, who knew his way through forests, across mountains, could tell which tribe used what bird feathers for their fletchings, could sense nothing. Otis's agitated state, however, caused him concern. "You can see something? What?"

"I don't know."

He doesn't know. O'Reilly blew out his cheeks. "All right, let's hold up here for a few moments, see what occurs."

With his attention not fully on his companion, Otis shook his head. "I can *feel* someone is watching us. Can't you?"

"No. not a thing." To be sure, O'Reilly slowly ran his eyes across the surrounding plain. He took his time, deliberately so.

Otis did not strike him as someone prone to fancy. "Nope. I don't see or hear anything." He considered the young ranch hand. He'd seen so many like him during the war. Innocent, inexperienced, yet full of vim, ready to step up and do their duty. A lot of them died, their youthful exuberance giving them a false sense of invincibility. The curse of the young. "What do you propose we do, Otis?"

"I'm thinking ..." His expression grew grave. "I'm thinking I'm going back. Meet up with Henry and the others."

"What? But I thought you said we should—"

"I know what I said, and I thank you for coming along with me but, damn it all, there is *someone out there.*"

"You think they've been following us?" Unconsciously he scanned the ground. "I could ride ahead, pick up any signs."

"I think you should carry on into town, speak to Doc Turner or anyone prepared to listen. Maybe they could gather together a group and ..." his voice trailed away.

"No one is going to come out here, Otis. If we are being followed, better for me to pick up their trail, circle around 'em and find out what's going on. Don't you think?"

"Yes." Otis sucked in his lips, deep in thought. "All right," he said finally, "do that if there is someone and, if not, go to town and talk to Doc Turner anyway. I reckon he's the only person we could trust in that damned town."

Nodding, O'Reilly readjusted himself in his addle and flashed a smile at Otis. "You take care out there, young fella."

"I will. And you too. God speed."

Grunting, O'Reilly turned away and kicked his horse into a canter.

They stood in front of the rear entrance. Set within the rock face, the door appeared flimsy as if the merest pressure would cave it in. Henry checked his Winchester and motioned that the others should do the same. "I'll stay out here. The rest of you make your way in. Destry, you lead, with Bourne close behind.

"Don't think I like the sound of that," said Sam Pettigrew, one of the oldest of the ranch hands assembled outside.

"Tell you what," said Henry, "why don't you wait outside too."

Pettigrew liked the sound of that and visibly relaxed.

"Go and tie up the horses and stay with 'em. The rest of you, let's get this done."

Muttering and shuffling, the group edged their way towards the doorway. Destry sucked in a large breath, put his shoulder against the warped and partially rotten timbers, and broke through. The others pressed forward, Bourne urging them onwards.

Henry stood for a few moments before making his way to a cluster of boulders and settling himself down. Pettigrew waddled up to him, rubbing his grizzled chin. "Not wishing to question your authority or anything, Mr Henry, but ..."

"Spit it out, old man."

"You think it's wise sending them inside like that? We all know the stories, especially what happened with them bush-whackers."

"You were here when that happened?"

"I was over in Lancaster so never saw anything. Stories soon got round though. Like they always do."

"You hear anything about gold?"

"Not a whole lot. Some believed White had mined it all out, others weren't so sure. Indians though, they said it was cursed. That there was bad medicine inside. They never did say what exactly, but it was enough to keep them well away."

Stretching out his legs, Henry rested his carbine across his knees. "No doubt we'll learn the truth soon enough."

They both heard the unmistakable sound of an approaching horse. Instantly, Henry dropped behind the boulders, bringing up the carbine, whilst Pettigrew, bleating like a goat, moved well to the rear.

A few minutes passed before horse and rider appeared.

Henry released a long sigh of relief and stood up. "Otis? I thought I told you—"

"Sorry Mr Henry," said Otis, breathing hard. He dismounted, beating the dust from his clothes. "We decided to head back to the town, get help for Ezra, but ... There's someone shadowing us, Mr Henry."

"Who?"

"We couldn't tell. O'Reilly has gone to Whitewater to get some help." He pointed towards the mine's rear entrance. "You've sent some of the boys inside? What for?"

"Mr Quince wants that gold. I'm here to see he gets it, or..." He glanced at Otis. "Explain to him why we've returned empty-handed."

"You think that's a possibility?"

"Son, anything is possible right now."

"And for now, we wait?"

Grunting, Henry produced a small leather pouch of tobacco and, with great precision, rolled himself a cigarette. "You want one?" Otis pulled a face and shook his head. "We might be waiting out here for some time."

"I'll rustle up some coffee," said Pettigrew, pushing past them.

"A good idea," said Henry.

"I'll make myself comfortable then," said Otis and made his way to a clump of fallen tree trunks, sat down on the ground in front of them and settled his hat over his eyes. Within seconds he was snoring.

Chuckling to himself, Henry lit the cigarette and, eyes fixed on the entrance, smoked and waited.

He heard a dry tree branch snap loudly in the stillness and he swung around, fully expecting to see Pettigrew returning with a steaming pot of coffee. He gasped.

It was Pettigrew, but not as he expected.

An arrow protruded from his neck, the blood running thickly

from the wound to splash over his open shirt. Groping forward, he appeared like a blind man feeling his way. As Henry ran forward, the old man fell headfirst onto the ground.

"What's happening," spluttered Otis, rousing himself and drawing his gun.

Henry, down on his knees next to the prostrate Pettigrew, peered towards the woods. "Indians," he whispered, gun in hand. "Find cover and don't—"

An arrow streaked inches above his head and, without a pause, he rolled over to a nearby outcrop of rock and pressed himself behind it. He shouted across to Otis, "Keep low, son. I don't know how many there are but we is in a fix, that's for sure."

Head down, Otis sprang into action, weaving across the open ground towards another cluster of rocks. An arrow, swiftly followed by a second, scorched a trail through the air. Otis fired from the hip but never slackened his pace until he reached those rocks and dived into cover. He put his gun arm over the top and fired twice more in the general direction of the woods. "They must have been the ones following us," he shouted.

"Yep, and they're here to kill us. Don't waste your bullets, son," cried Henry. "Reload now before they move in. Which they will, the heathen bastards."

Following his orders, Otis worked feverishly at his Colt Navy, pouring in powder from his flask, pressing home the ball and fitting the cap. It all took time, and his fingers were shaking uncontrollably. He'd never been in any form of gunfight before, the closest being the run-in with Reece, but this, this was on an altogether different level.

He chanced a peek around the boulder and cried out in despair.

Across the narrow stretch of rough ground separating him from the woods, the first Indian came charging, tomahawk raised. Otis shot him through the chest, but his momentum kept him careening forward and Otis put another bullet into him before he fell dead into his arms. Rolling over, Otis quickly got to his feet as another warrior came from nowhere. Catching the downward blow of the hatchet high up on the man's arm, Otis swung up his knee and finished this second assailant with a vicious club of his gun.

"Otis!"

He looked up to see Henry struggling with a third Indian, who had the range boss at his mercy, his arms pinned by strong, muscular legs.

Advancing, Otis shot the Indian high up on the left arm and blew him off his boss. Even as he began to rise, the Indian must have sensed the futility of his actions. He let out an ear-splitting scream before Otis shot him again through the head.

The scream, however, was some sort of signal. At least half a dozen savages erupted from the woods, brandishing knives, axes, and war clubs. One had a lance.

"Oh, sweet Jesus," wheezed Henry, clambering to his feet.

Otis sidestepped the one with the lance, swiveled and cracked his pistol into the man's nose. He wrenched the lance free, turned, reversed it, and plunged the tip into the Indian's stomach. But this time, there was little chance of preparing himself for another assault. The attackers were too close, too fast, and too numerous. One leapt at Henry's body as a second tackled him around the legs. Three more closed swiftly on Otis and although he blocked and thrust with the lance, each action took so much out of him that he knew he couldn't last for much longer. And then, unbelievably, he saw another group charging forward.

There was nothing left to do except try and delay the inevitable.

Until the figure came riding on the back of his horse, his revolvers blazing. Two, three, four of the Indians went down as bullets struck home. Energy and resolve renewed, Otis dispatched one of his attackers before turning to those swarming over Henry. At the same time, the rider was dismounting and working the lever of his Winchester carbine. He fired quickly and methodically, making every bullet count until, at long last, the attackers broke and fled, whooping with frustration and the ignominy of defeat.

There came a prolonged yet expectant pause. Silence fell. Otis, ignoring the man with the Winchester, feverishly reloaded his revolver again. He caught sight of the stranger doing the same with his carbine. Their eyes met and Otis recognized him for the first time. "Reece?" he spluttered.

Reece nodded. "You fought well, I gotta say. Where you learn to fight like that?"

Otis shrugged as he worked with the last load in the cylinder. "My pa was a wrestler in a travelling circus. He taught me some things." He snapped the cap cut-out closed and turned his gaze towards Henry who was sitting up, coughing raucously. "Mr Henry?"

Henry's hand came up. "I'm all right." He rubbed his throat, coughed some more, and got to his feet. He swayed a little. "Reece, I'm indebted to you." His voice sounded strained. "A couple of minutes more and that heathen would have killed me for sure."

Surveying the surroundings, littered with the bodies of the dead Indians, Reece sighed loudly. "This was a scouting party. They'll be back and there'll be plenty more of 'em." He pointed to the mine entrance some way off. "The rest of your men gone in there?"

"Yes," said Henry. "But right now, I'm not so sure that was a good decision. We should get out of here."

Reece grunted. "I'll get them out. There's more in that mine than gold, Henry, and none of it is good. My advice is for you and Otis to ride back to town and gather together as many townsfolk as you can. Those Indians, they won't hesitate in attacking the town if they believe it is to their advantage."

Otis came forward. "You'll follow us on?"

"As soon as I get your men out of there." He produced a

piece of padded leather. "This was given to me by an old Indian who said it'll protect me."

"What the hell is it?"

"A mask of some sort. It's got some herbs and the like stuffed inside. I'm hoping it'll work."

"Why?" asked Henry, now troubled. "What the hell is in that mine, Reece?"

"I don't know for certain but from what the Indian tells me, it'll change you. Make you go mad."

"Sweet Jesus." Henry ran a hand over his face.

Otis cleared his throat and, not allowing his eyes to fix on Reece, said, "You wouldn't be planning on taking all the gold for yourself, would you?"

"Son," said Reece easily, "if there was any gold in there, I just might. But there ain't. I do believe, however, there's something a darn sight more valuable." He pointed towards one of the corpses, "At least to them it is."

"You mean they attacked us because we thought we were trying to take something that is rightfully theirs?" asked Henry.

"Seems that way. I was hoping to stop you, but I got here too late. But if the natives is thinking their mine has been pillaged, they'll kill every man woman and child they come across."

"Then we'd better get going," said Henry.

"Good luck," said Otis as he fell in behind Henry.

Reece tipped his hat and watched the two men stride away. He blew out another long sigh and made his way slowly towards the mine's rear entrance.

CHAPTER THIRTY-NINE

It was an easy ride across to the next town of Lancaster. It was a journey Doc Turner made every other day or so as he was the peripatetic surgeon for both towns and had been for almost ten years. During the war it sometimes proved treacherous. Wandering bands of renegades occasionally drifted this far west but not often. Turner always offered up a prayer of thanks for that. Not that he was overly religious, simply that he was never one to hedge his bets. Even the slightest chance that God could be looking down at him was enough. He prayed, he rode, he did his best not to concern himself with the various problems confronting him back in Whitewater.

He calculated that Ezra, suffering from delusions, hallucinations, or both, must have decided to return to the mine. Turner had no intentions of doing the same. If Ezra did go that way, then Reece would confront him. Thoughts of Reece loomed large in Turner's mind. The meeting with Winter Hair had gone well - up to a point. The doc did worry over what it was the old Indian said to Reece when he pulled him aside, out of earshot. What was so important, so *secretive* that it couldn't be shared? Reece himself had not been forthcoming and Turner decided not to press the point, preferring to wait. Everything would work out fine in the end, he convinced himself. Nothing was going to go wrong. Nothing.

Arriving in town, he went directly to his tiny surgery at the end of a narrow side street. Although Lancaster was bigger than Whitewater, it was much quieter. Whereas Whitewater's inhabitants busied themselves with the various work associated with the lumber business which dominated everything, Lancaster was little more than what has come to be known as a dormitory town. Turner felt it would soon cease to be even that as the lure of a better life out west in California took hold.

Mounting the stairs – his surgery was situated above the Carson and Jones Cattle Association office – he paused a moment to view the street. He felt confident nobody had followed him, but he needed to be sure. He was a cautious soul and these past few days had reaffirmed his belief that life was essentially made up of two types of people - those who cruised through everything and those who were shat on almost every day. He placed himself in the latter group.

His surgery was cold, the sun barely able to penetrate the gloom of the narrow street. Ignoring the chill, he crossed to his desk and rifled through the bottom drawer to find the eight-year-old Bourbon he kept there, together with a glass. He peered at it and felt sure it hadn't been that low the last time he'd checked. He poured himself a healthy measure into the tumbler and downed it in one. A tiny shudder ran through him, which he ignored, and he poured himself a second glass.

The first indication he had of somebody approaching was when the surgery door creaked open. He hadn't heard any steps on the staircase, which was unusual given how old and warped the woodwork was.

"Hi, Doc."

A little surprised, Turner grunted and indicated his visitor should take a seat. He poured the man a Bourbon. "You saw to Fieyn?"

Brad Swail nodded, took the drink, and swallowed half of it.

Smacking his lips, he winked and said, "Things must be serious, you giving me your best whiskey."

"They are," said Turner and went behind his desk. "We found Ezra in the old mine-workers shack. He'd been seeing ghosts."

"Ghosts?"

"At least I *think* they were ghosts. He was in a deplorable state. Someone had bashed him up pretty bad too. I was planning on taking him to Whitewater, but I drifted off to sleep and when I woke up, he was gone. It's my guess he's gone to the mine."

"That's understandable. Gold-fever is everywhere in Whitewater. The saloon is full of talk, as usual. It's no surprise that Ezra would fall for it too."

"No, perhaps not. Reece has gone there also. You remember Reece, don't you?"

"Lean guy, good with a gun, and his fists, so I hear."

"He's curious, a do-gooder. He thinks he can go and find gold and help Miss Bessy get back on her feet. He ain't easily dissuaded, even when he's confronted with the facts." Turner shook his head and sat down. "I made a mistake."

"You? You never make mistakes."

"Well, I did this time. I took him to Winter Hair. I was hoping the old Indian would scare him off, fill him with some wild stories of evil spirits and the like. Instead, he seemed to encourage Reece to investigate. I think he gave him something. A potion."

"That won't work. We've seen plenty of folks come down with fever after wandering up there. We've tried everything." He grinned and finished his drink. He held it out for a refill. "Including lots of whisky."

"Yeah, but what if Winter Hair's concoction does work and he finds something. He has a drawing."

"A drawing? Of what?"

"Of what's in the mine. I think Winter Hair confirmed it."

Swail studied his whisky before draining it. "So, what do you suggest?"

Turner picked up the bourbon bottle and shook it. There was little more than a dribble of whiskey left in the bottle. "You ride up there and when he comes out, you kill him." He tipped the bottle to his lips and swallowed down the last of the alcohol. "You can then take whatever it is he finds and, all being well, we'll be rich."

His visitor did not argue. Standing up, Swail adjusted his gun belt and left.

CHAPTER FORTY

T hey had taken less than a dozen steps when first Bourne, then Destry came to a halt, hands pressed into eyes, breathing growing strained.

"What is it?" said one of the others, a cowboy called Rudy Malone. He groped forward. There was one torch amongst them. Malone had tried in vain to hold them all up before they went any deeper. The need for more light was now painfully apparent.

"I don't feel too good," said another cowboy, Johnny Ayres, stumbling towards a nearby rock. He fell down and immediately vomited.

"Destry," said Malone. "We need to go back, get more water. We ain't prepared for this."

"You shut your damned hole," snapped Destry, swinging on the much older man. "You go back if you want but we is going on." He pressed both hands against the sides of his skull and squeezed, "Oh God, my head."

"There is something wrong here," said Malone. "I don't like it. I don't like it one bit!

"Damn you, you wretched bastard, trying to stop us getting what is ours," shouted Bourne. He rushed forward. Too late

Malone saw the flash of steel and then the pain of burning erupting in his guts.

"What the—"

Ayres got to his feet. He was still not recovered, something Bourne noted by the way he staggered and retched, nausea overcoming him. Bourne pulled out the knife from Malone's stomach and swung, slashing with the blade. It hit Ayres across the side of the face and sent him screaming to the ground.

"Kill 'em all," screeched Destry, drawing his gun, "kill 'em all!"

"Destry ..." muttered Malone, falling to his knees, clutching at his stomach as the blood bubbled over his fingers.

Destry shot him through the head and laughed. He picked up the torch Malone had held and waved it from side to side. "Kill 'em, Bournie my boy, kill 'em!"

Bourne, dancing from one foot to the next, slashed again as Ayres tried to get up. This time the blow, delivered backhanded, sliced through the opposite side of the young man's face, opening up a gash so deep it exposed his teeth.

Destry was incensed, cackling insanely as he waved the torch ever more wildly.

The last remaining member of the group, another young ranch hand by the name of Adler, turned and tried to run. Destry emptied his revolver into the man's back then ran over to the body, held the gun by the barrel, and bashed in the back of the man's skull with the grip.

"We'll do Henry," spat Bourne, putting the heel of his boot against his stricken victim's chest and pushing him to the ground. "We'll do Henry and anyone else he has with him when we get out. This gold is ours, Destry. Ours! No one is gonna deny us." He fell upon Ayers like one possessed and stabbed him repeatedly in the throat and chest. By the time he was finished, he was awash with black gore.

"We is gonna be rich," said Destry, staring at his hands, the blood dripping from the fingers. He screeched high-pitched and threw the gun away, not caring where it landed.

"We'll go back to town. I'll take Bessy for yeh, satisfy her the way I know she wants. You'll be fine with that, won't yeh?"

"Lord Almighty, yes!" Destry put down the torch, propping it against a nearby outcrop of jagged rock sprouting from the tunnel wall. "I know you been visiting her, Bournie my boy. You and plenty of others."

"You don't mind it?"

"I have no feelings left for her." He rifled through Adler's pockets. "Truth be told, I ain't got no feelings for anything much more." He stood up and popped a piece of chewing tobacco into his mouth, "not since Lizzie made fun of me. Made me sort of reconsider things."

"Lizzie?"

"Lizzie Coombs, a whore I used to visit. Man, she was fine. Thighs as thick as tree trunks, a waist like a young boy's and those breasts..." Shaking his head, he slumped down next to the torch and leaned forward, head in hands. "Oh, Almighty Jesus, I slit her throat, Bournie my boy. I murdered her!"

"Why you do that?"

"I couldn't get it up and she laughed. Can you imagine? She laughed, waggling her finger at my pecker. Making fun of me. I don't know what was wrong with me, I truly don't. I'd always enjoyed her, the way her sweet mouth made me so damned desperate to get inside those glorious thighs. But that last visit, I just couldn't. I'd been down here again, searching for hours, and all I got for my efforts was such a case of loose guts the like of which I'd never had before."

"Maybe it was that?" Bourne came over and sat next to him. He slowly put his arms around Destry's shoulders. "You mustn't blame yourself. She was nothing more than a whore."

"You're right," said Destry, sniffing loudly. He raised his head and looked at Bourne. "You is a good friend to me, that is for sure."

"And to Bessy as well. We will be happy together, the three of us."

"I'll make you breakfast after you've satisfied her through the night."

"And I'll make sure she appreciates you for the man you are."

He held Destry closer and Destry smiled such a sweet smile that Bourne's eyes closed, basking in the love for his companion. Destry liked the feel of being in control. It was what urged him on and what had made him lose his mind when Lizzie said those terrible things to him. Well, that wasn't about to happen again, especially after he was rich. He deserved to be rich. By God, he'd waited long enough, and no one was going to deny him, not now. He turned into his newfound friend and plunged the knife he'd secreted from his belt deep into Bourne's stomach, twisting the blade and slicing upwards to the breastbone, opening him up like a fish.

CHAPTER FORTY-ONE

Reece felt a tingling developing along his back, a sensation he thought would never visit him again. A sensation buried, he believed, but not buried deep enough it seemed. Because the last time it had come to him, his world slipped into a dark abyss of horror and fear. Fear the likes of which he'd never experienced, before or since. A fear he had convinced himself was nothing more than a nightmare because it couldn't be true, it couldn't be real. A base, looming dread, something only to be found within the pages of the most terrifying of Poe's writing. Supernatural, inexplicable, not of this world.

Until this moment, he might have come to convince himself of all those things.

As it rose and threatened to engulf all of his senses, all of his reasoning, the memories returned and with it a trembling of every fiber.

With feet so heavy they seemed set in thick, clinging clay, he took a breath and forced himself to move forward.

The mine's interior pressed upon him, causing both the oppressive atmosphere and the humidity to soar. He lurched forward, pressing the mask tight against his nose and mouth whilst, in his other hand, he held aloft the torch. Wild, grotesque shadows danced across the craggy rock surfaces and now and again he'd stop, take his breath, still his heart. Faces peered out at him from within the orange glow cast onto the walls by the flickering flames, and noises, from deep beneath the ground, seemed to taunt him, rumbling, groaning disembodied voices urging him to turn and flee. He thought he recognized them but then his senses would take back control and he knew that none of it was real. At least, he hoped this was so.

Memories returned in that dim, lonely mine. Memories he thought he'd suppressed. He found a shelf of rock jutting out from a wall and he sat upon it. It wasn't long before flickering images from his past reared up in his mind.

It was in those early days when the War was full of uncertainty and it seemed the Union would never be healed. The north suffered setback after setback causing many men, Reece included, to doubt the rightfulness of his choice of side. Born in New York State, it was perhaps inevitable that he would muster with others from his hometown, take the blue, march down to fight the Rebs in their own backyard. He fought at First Manassas and fled with the best of them when the Union forces broke, never looking back, dreaming of home and the bosom of his family. He ran with privates Lord and Mayhew and made it to a river, throwing himself into its depths, emerging on the far side refreshed but terrified.

They rolled over the grass, clothes soaked, minds alive with fear. Reece forced himself to sit upright. He checked the others were safe. They were but none of them had a weapon. In the desperation of their rout, their only thought was to escape, to survive.

Downtrodden, they walked on throughout the rest of that day, convinced that at any moment the Rebs would burst all around them, take them and kill them. But the Rebs didn't come. Something else did.

That evening, with the sky streaked with grey, they came upon a scorched landscape, earth the color of ash, burnt tree stumps rising like stunted stone monoliths and bones, bleached white, littered everywhere.

Something dreadful had happened here.

"Indians?" asked Lord, his voice little more than a croak.

Reece shrugged and bent down to examine some of the remains. "This happened long ago. None of this is recent."

"Bad medicine," muttered Mayhew and hugged himself as he shivered.

They'd all heard the stories, of Indian burial grounds, sites of spirit magic. In the awfulness of war, most of the tales had been forgotten or pushed back in minds too consumed with the dread of battle. Yet now, confronted with this reality of death, misery, even barbarity, it was easy to envisage evil spirits lurking amongst the bones.

There were caves and in one of the largest, they sheltered. With nothing to make a fire with, they huddled together and shivered as the temperature plummeted. Alone, frightened, and uncertain what to do for the best, they longed for sleep. The sound of their teeth clattering in their skulls kept them awake. Perhaps they would never find rest. The more they strained to sleep, the more it remained unattainable. And then, sometime in the night, they heard something moving from within the depths of the cave.

It came at them, a huge, lumbering form, impossibly strong, its great hands seizing them. It took Lord first, ripping him apart as if he were made of badly stitched cloth. Reece and Mayhew managed to scramble out into the night. But they could not get far. A string of savages barred their way, eyes burning white in their dark faces. They overpowered both men with ease, stripped them naked, and bore them away, chanting as they went, some ancient heathen song, primeval, hellish, not of this world.

Pegged out upon the ground, they defiled Mayhew first. Young, innocent, his first journey away from home, he screamed and writhed, crying until he could cry no more, each savage taking from him whatever they wished. When they cast him aside, he was no longer the fresh-faced young man who had left Maine all those months before. Shame was now his best friend and a bullet in the brain was the only thing he yearned for.

They left Reece for the morning. They drank and laughed until sleep overcame them. For Reece, sleep no longer an option, he worked upon the bonds that lashed his wrists together, even managing to slither towards the campfire those monsters had made and tried time after time to use the dying embers to burn through the rope.

It was shortly before the sun crept above the horizon that he broke the bonds apart. Feverishly rubbing wrists, when one of them stood up and groped for a tree against which he could relieve himself, Reece took his chance, swept up the savage's knife, and plunged it deep into the man's exposed neck. Taking him by the throat, Reece lowered him to the ground without making a sound, then rushed to where they had put their rifles. Army issue. Single-shot carbines. And a brace of Navy Colts. It was these Reece chose, stepped away and eased back the hammers.

There were six bucks asleep around him. Each received two bullets as Reece killed them with slow, methodical precision. He did not flinch from this gruesome toil. No remorse, no sense of conscience. They were like wild beasts, rabid, and had to be put down.

When he was done, he dressed quickly. He helped Mayhew to his feet and, after finding water and some dried corn biscuits, they set off again.

Mayhew died on that journey. It may have been from blood loss or shock, but no matter what Reece did to save him, once his friend slipped into unconsciousness, there was no coming back.

Reece buried him high on a ridge and continued home, alone and never once allowed himself to think of what had happened and what the thing was that lurked in that cave.

Until now. In this mine. Dark. The damp, musty smell hitting the back of his throat despite the mask he wore. He wondered, not for the first time if it would protect him. Winter Hair had assured him it would but now, with the air so stifling, he doubted those words. Perhaps it was a trick. After all, what did the old Indian owe him? Hadn't the White men always caused him pain? Now, this was his chance to pay one of them back. Reece, the recipient of all his hate?

From somewhere deep within the network of twisting tunnels, several gunshots rang out. Reece waited, holding his breath, alert, ready to respond. There was no subsequent sound save for the steady drip of water echoing all around him. He waited, nevertheless, certain someone would arrive. Perhaps those men that Henry had sent into the cave had stumbled across others. More Indians, he wondered. The idea caused him distress, made his throat dry, his heart to hammer in his ears.

Rousing himself from his awful memories and other, equally frightening thoughts, he peered into the gloom and thought he saw something there. He rubbed his eyes. He'd fashioned a torch from pieces of broken branches, packing the end with bracken, lichen, and dried grass. The light it gave out was almost at an end now but, swinging it in a wide arc, he tried to make out what it was that loomed at the edge of his vision. A shape, large, looming.

It was here again, that abomination, that thing from the cave, come to tear him limb from limb. He leapt to his feet, drew his revolver, and fought down the urge to scream. But before he could do so, or utter a single sound, a voice came to him from the darkness, whispering, "Reece. Is that you?"

"Move and I'll plug you," said Reece, his voice cracking.

"Reece, it's me – Destry!"

And so it was. Bessy's husband stepped closer and the glow from the torch he held picked out his features. Reece didn't know whether to feel relief or horror. Destry appeared real enough but unrecognizable as the man he thought he knew.

Perhaps it was the unnatural pallor of the man's face, accentuated by the torchlight, or was it the awful grin, so ghastly in his twisted, distorted mouth. The features of a man close to the edge of insanity.

Perhaps, it was the fact that all of his clothing, including shirt and trousers, was soaked in a thick, black, greasy slime.

"What's the matter, Reecey?" said Destry, his voice shrill, unnatural.

Reece's eyes fell upon the knife Destry held, with the same colored slime dripping from its blade. The knowledge of what it was hit him like a fist.

Blood.

CHAPTER FORTY-TWO

H is chest wheezed and his shoulder, where Destry's bullet, still lodged deep in the muscle, had hit him all those years ago, hurt like sin. He reined in, unable to bring his horse to full gallop due to the motion causing the pain to increase. He took a long drink from his canteen and studied the surroundings, the mountains with their thinned out wooded slopes. White water's prosperity hinged upon its lumber industry, but the trees had all but gone now. He doubted whether there was little more than a year left before the place was abandoned. A far cry from how it was when he rode in at the head of his men, guns blazing, Rebel Yells erupting from their mouths. Good days, brought to an abrupt end by Destry and his interfering.

He squeezed his eyes shut. His mind returned to images of the mine and no matter how hard he tried, no matter how many years had swept by, the thought of that place filled him with cold dread. And the memories of what occurred there, all those years ago.

They made it to the mine in a mad dash, the townsfolk close behind them. Well-armed and organized, they had retribution on their mind. Not that Nathan Kelly, nor his men, had killed all that many. A few, that was all, but in a town as small as Whitewater was, even a couple would have impacted on several families. So, they rode, and they rode, not knowing where they were heading, until they came to the mine, smashed their way through the boarded-up entrance and decided to make a stand of it from inside.

Of course, they didn't know it was a mine back then. Kelly didn't notice the crudely scrawled warning sign hanging by a rusted nail from one of the boards. None of them was in any mood to stop and consider their options. They didn't have any.

Bowers took the horses to somewhere safe. Kelly paid him no mind. He was never to see him again. He gathered the remnants of his men and they rushed to fashion cover from boulders, fallen tree trunks, and anything else they could find that would slow their attackers down.

"Let's go deeper," said Taylor-Phelps, his trusted lieutenant.

"But we ain't got no light."

But Taylor-Phelps was grinning, and he pointed along the twisting passage in front of them. "There! Can't you see it?"

In the distance a tiny pinprick of light. A beacon in that darkness.

"Sweet Jesus," said Kelly under his breath. "Let's go."

Without thinking, they rushed forward. There were five of them left now. Not enough to muster any telling defense, so they plunged towards that light, uncaring, heady with the idea of escape.

After a dozen paces the light went out and the darkness engulfed them.

Sitting out in the open astride his horse, Kelly shuddered at the memory. He remembered the smell. Sweet, enticing, like the puddings his old ma baked in the oven back in Kansas. Irish immigrants, his ma made the best apple pie on the entire continent of the Americas. They were a throwback to the life they'd left behind, not that Kelly could remember much about that, but he did remember the aroma that filled the kitchen and that smell, in the mine, conjured up so many good feelings.

He took deep breaths and suddenly nothing much mattered anymore.

Placing the stopper in his canteen, he kicked his horse into a steady walk once more. That smell, there was something else to it, at its edges. Something sharp, unsettling. He was the first to be sick, so violently he could not continue. The others eventually succumbed and when Taylor-Phelps screamed and ran back towards the entrance, six-shooters blasting towards the cavern roof, Kelly knew something wasn't right.

The townsfolk, they killed Taylor-Phelps and then they came upon the rest of the gang. They fought and they died but by God, they gave a good account of themselves. Kelly managed to scramble out, shooting as he went, dropping at least two of them before he crashed out into the sunlight.

And there was Destry.

Of course, he didn't know then the man standing there, grinning like someone possessed, was Destry. He brought up his gun and fired. The dull click of the hammer falling on an empty chamber turned his guts to liquid. He whirled away and Destry shot him in the shoulder, throwing him to the ground.

Indians came from nowhere then, forcing Destry and the other surviving townsfolk to fight them. In the confusion, Kelly got away, found a horse, and rode in a red mist of pain, nausea, and confusion.

He didn't stop until he came upon another town and the doctor who tended him. The doctor who was so very interested in the mine and what Kelly had found there.

"The man who shot you sounds like Destry," explained Doc Turner as he probed away at the bullet. "This is deep, son. I'd have to operate, and I just haven't got the tools nor, sad to say, the expertise."

"Am I gonna die?"

"I doubt it," said Turner with a grin. "You'll always feel it, of course, and sometimes the agony of it will make you wish you were dead. But you won't die. You'll live. And any life is sweeter than no life at all."

The shooting and yelling brought him up short. Pulling up his horse, Kelly, or Brad Swail since changing his name several years ago, slowly dismounted and listened. He wore his twin holstered guns in a pair of cartridge belts crossed over his chest, the grips turned inwards so he could draw them with ease. He always preferred his left hand as his right shoulder ached too much to be of any real use and he now used this to draw one of the Colt Dragoons. More screams rang out from the distance. He led his horse to where the woods formed a solid wall and lashed the reins around a tree trunk. There was a path plunging into the woods or he could skirt around them. Doc Turner had informed him of two entrances but the rear one was more difficult to find. He had no map and no idea what might be waiting for him among the trees, so he decided on the longer route and, easing back the hammer of the enormous handgun in his hand, he slowly continued.

The soft plod of approaching horses forced him to dive in between the soaring trees. Crouching down, Swail peered out to where the land lay open, gnarled, and scorched. Two horsemen rode by, a big man in the lead with a much slighter, younger one behind. Swail thought he recognized them but he wasn't about to announce to break cover and announce himself to the pair and certainly not in the present circumstances. So, he waited until they were well out of earshot before continuing on his slow, methodical journey.

When he came upon the shack he considered going inside for a moment. Something, an odd feeling of trepidation, spurred him on and although that niggle of curiosity played around at the nape of his neck, he put his face forward and did not stop until he came to the clearing where the bodies were.

He stopped and stared. Indians. Half a dozen or so, blown

apart with bullets or sliced through with something sharp. Grotesque attitudes, one or two reaching to the sky, attested to their last, awful moments of life. They would lie like that, frozen forever until the coyotes and the buzzards came to pick their bones clean. Swail trembled and looked away. Death, his old friend, was here again.

The entrance to the old mine gaped open before him. He stood and waited. The memories rose again, the horrors of what went on inside invading his mind. And the smell. Would it still be here, or had it disappeared, lost in the vastness of the air?

Should he venture inside? Should he wait, but for what? What lurked for him in those dark depths, ghosts, demons, murderers? Unable to bring himself to take those steps towards the entrance, he slumped down on a nearby fallen tree and fought to overcome the shaking which threatened to defeat his senses. From somewhere far away, thunder rumbled. Ignoring it, Swail took in a deep, resigned breath. He never guessed, not for a single moment, how difficult this would be, not until he had arrived here. Not until the past loomed like a living thing and wrapped its vice-like grip around him to crush, to smother. He believed he could win them over, these debilitating fears that often came to him in the dead of night, but he was wrong. Here, so close, he understood the folly of agreeing to return here. Turner had no comprehension of the terror that dwelled in those tunnels. No one had, only those who had ventured within. Those men of his, those companions, they'd died in there, their minds scrambled, their senses mangled. It happened so many years before but the resonance of it all remained so clear, so vital. Swail, or Kelly as he was then, knew he could do no more. He had come far enough. This, for him, was the end of the line and Turner would have to accept it.

CHAPTER FORTY-THREE

The two men rode hard, Henry in the lead, head down, leaning over his horse's neck. A man possessed, Reece's words ringing in his ears. They had to get to Whitewater before the Indians attacked.

Behind him, whipping his reins across his own mount, Otis kept up as best he could, but his horse was smaller, nowhere near as fast. His boss was steadily out-distancing him. Determined not to lose too much ground, he gritted his teeth and urged his horse on as fast as it could go.

Despite their best efforts, the time diminished more quickly than their race. Every minute they spent galloping was another minute given to the Indians. For all those two men knew, the attack could already be underway.

As they burst out across the ragged plain, they could see the town, its one main street a dusty, yellow snake moving in between the squatted rows of businesses and homes. People were milling about.

The Indians had not yet arrived!

Spurred on by this realization, Henry turned in his saddle and barked, "I'm going straight to the sheriff!" And, taking off his hat, he beat his horse's rump with it and ate up those last few, precious yards of ground.

Hanson worked on an old iron gate, its hinges rusted away, when he heard the shouting. Dragging his forearm across his sweating brow, he looked up and instantly threw down his tools. Without removing his thick, leather apron, he burst out of his shop and ran towards where Henry battled with his horse, shouting out, "Indians! Indians are coming!"

Several townsfolk screamed; others demanded to know more details. It was as if someone had put a light to their tails as they ran around, confused, frightened, everybody talking at once.

Hanson pushed through them, seized Henry's reins, and helped the ranch boss down from his horse. He was a big man, almost as big as Hanson but he appeared diminished with terror. Breathing hard, he blurted, "You have to get out of here – there's an Indian war party coming this way. You all have to leave – *now!*"

Coming upon them at a gallop, Otis dismounted at the run, flapping his arms as if he were trying to take off. "It's true. They're coming and we don't know how many."

Henry quickly recounted what had happened outside the mine, how the Indians had attacked, how Reece had appeared and helped them overcome the savages.

"It was Reece who told us to come here and tell you to get ready," said Otis. "I believe he is right in warning us. We should either set up some sort of street barricade or quit the town."

"Quit the town?" squawked an aged storekeeper, sporting a striped apron. There was blood on his arms and his hands. "My livelihood is in this town. I ain't quitting for some half-baked notion of an Indian war party!"

"And what Indians, exactly," demanded a feisty, red-headed young woman, an infant clinging at her skirt tails. "We ain't had trouble with Indians for at least ten years, maybe more."

"That's right," put in another, much older woman, standing pale and drawn, wringing her hands constantly. "My Neville is too old to move anyhows. I say if we have to do anything, we stand here and fight!"

Henry and Otis exchanged a look. Exasperated, Henry blew out a loud sigh and flung out his hands. "All right then, we'd better get to it – they could be here at any moment!"

Once again, as Hanson stepped into the kitchen it was to find Bessy on her hands and knees, brushing furiously at the stone-flagged floor. He watched her for a moment before dropping to his haunches beside her. "Big ol' Henry has ridden into town, warning us of an Indian war party headed this way."

She stopped, brushed away a lock of hair from her glistening face, and looked at him. "How does he know that?"

"Reece told him."

"I thought Reece was up at the mine."

"So he is – it was there that he came upon Henry and some young 'un. Saved them, from what Henry tells us."

"And Destry?"

"No mention of him, only those Injuns heading this way."

"Damn," she snapped and stood up, groaning with the effort. "It doesn't matter how many times I scrub this damn floor, his blood is never cleaned."

"Bessy," said Hansom placing his big, gnarled hands on her tiny shoulders and turning her to him, "for all we know they're dead already, all of 'em. The mine will do for them all like it did before."

"Maybe Reece was hallucinating when he spoke of Indians coming."

"Maybe. Or maybe Henry is."

"Could be. Anyone who gets near that place goes crazy, we both know that."

"What do you suggest we do?"

"Find Doc Turner. If anyone knows what's going on it'll be him. This is all coming to a head."

"I reckon so. But what if the Indians do come?"

"Then we fight them, I guess."

Hanson grunted. "I'll find the doc, then help organize a barricade. There are maybe six or seven able-bodied men left in this poor excuse for a town. I doubt it'll be enough to hold back a war party."

She nodded, dried her hands on a threadbare cloth and crossed to the far side of the kitchen and a large wall cupboard, next to the range. She opened it and brought out the Henry carbine she kept in there. It was Destry's but since the drinking took hold, he could barely lift it never mind shoot it. Plunging her hand into a box of cartridges, she began to feed them into the weapon. "Six or seven has now become eight." She winked at him. "There are some guns at the sheriffs. Load 'em and distribute 'em. Bring the women and the children here. They can hide in the upstairs rooms. Then, put some carts and wagons across the street. There's only one way into town unless they come down from the hills, which I doubt."

"Damn it, Bessy, you are something else."

"I'm alive Hanson," she said, engaging the lever with a hard snap, "and I intend to stay that way."

CHAPTER FORTY-FOUR

"There's Indians," said Reece, his hand creeping towards his gun. "They were attacking Henry and that young kid when I got here. We managed to drive 'em off but they'll be back, in numbers."

Destry barked a scoffing laugh, "Jeez, Reecey, you just don't get it do you? There's *always* been Indians, even when we all thought they were safe in their reservation. Arapaho mostly. Blood-thirsty, determined. This was their land." Suddenly, as if all of the strength drained from him in an instant, he slumped down on the ground, the knife dropping from numbed fingers. He began to weep. Gut-wrenching, uncontrollable sobs consumed him. Reece took his chance and stepped closer. He kicked the knife out of reach and moved back, drawing his gun smoothly and easily.

"What the hell has happened to you, Destry?"

"Oh, sweet Jesus," the man wailed, pressing both hands over his face. "I get these visions, Reecey, visions of hell. We're running through fire, Bessy and me, naked as the day we were born, and the rain is coming down so hard. Blood red rain. It's a shower of fire, you see." He dropped his hands. "You get me?

Fire, from the pits of hell. And it hurts, oh my Lord how it hurts!"

"Destry," Reece looked down both ends of the narrow passage in which he stood. "We have to get out of here. Have found any gold, Destry? Tell me the truth because I've been told there ain't no gold in here."

"Oh yes," said Destry, sniffing loudly, "there's gold. But not the type you mean." He pointed towards Reece. "That mask. What is that?"

Reece unconsciously brought his free hand up to the padded scarf Winter Hair had given him. "Old Indian gave it to me. Told me some things, but not enough I reckon. He said there was a kind of gold in here, that old White had worked out the whole seam but left something else behind."

"I believed all of that once. When White got back, we stood in his shop and he spread out those bits of jagged, yellow metal and we both knew we was rich. He said then that was all there was. A tiny lode, all gone now. I didn't believe him, so I came back here, and I found it."

"Found what? The gold, another seam?"

Cackling, Destry shook his head. "No. There is no more gold, Reece. He was right, told me the truth. He was sick for a long time after he got back into town. Bessy, she was so good, so kind. She was young then. Fifteen but her mother helped. They nursed him, tied him to his bed as he screamed and fought to get free. I never understood what that was. Bessy's mother said it was demons. Demons from hell. And that's why I get these damned visions!" He pounded his head with both fists. "Those same demons have come for me."

"Destry," Reece holstered his gun and got down on his knees. He reached out and took Destry by the wrists. "Tell me then. What is it, what is the gold that Winter Hair told me about?"

"Winter Hair, is that the Indian that spoke to you?"

Reece nodded. "I'm here to try and find it, Destry. For Bessy, for her business, the town."

"Winter Hair, he's the albino Indian, lives up in the mountains? The Arapaho, they fear him, Reece. They say he is bad medicine. You shouldn't have listened to him, Reece."

"He gave me this mask," said Reece, releasing Destry and sitting down on his backside. "Without it, the gases in here will overpower me, make me like you, like the others."

"He gave you that mask? Oh, dear god, Reecey. He's poisoned you." Now it was Destry who reached forward and held onto Reece's forearms. "He's put something in there, stuffed it with some potion. He doesn't want anybody coming down here, Reece! Nobody. He'll do anything to keep you out, even it means killing you! You don't get it, do you? You just don't get it." He stood up, pulling Reece to his feet. "Come on, I'll show you and then we'll get out of here before I start feeling murderous again."

"Murderous? What do you mean by—"

"Never mind about that. For the time being, I'm feeling all right but we ain't got long, and you need to get that mask off before whatever it is he's put in there kills you."

"Look," said Reece, reaching inside his jacket and pulling out the crinkled piece of paper he kept there. He opened it, showed it to Destry. "Is this what's in here, Destry? Is this what lures so many to their deaths?"

As if touching something precious, he delicately took the paper and with deep reverence took in the drawings. Helmet, shield, sword. "This ..." he swallowed hard. "The Spanish. They left these things here, Reece, so long ago. They are pure gold, valuable beyond words and the Indians, they revere them as sacred objects. They won't let anyone take 'em." He lifted the paper. "This is the treasure everyone has sought. Not gold, Reece. This."

And then, as if he were taking control of a child, Destry strode off down the passageway, holding on to Reece's wrist in a vice-like grip.

CHAPTER FORTY-FIVE

Manchester stood on the balcony staring towards the horizon, the blood-red sun ribboned through with dark, purple clouds. He did not flinch as Eva came up and stood beside him. "It's beautiful," she said."

"There's a storm brewing. Hopefully, it won't come this way, but it may already have hit the town. But there's something else too..." He gestured towards the nearest paddock, the way the horses appeared jittery, almost as if they were expecting something. But not the storm.

"Shouldn't we put them in a barn, keep them dry?"

Manchester shook his head. "Nah. Besides, we ain't got the hands to do that. Half the men have gone to the mine with Mr Henry, the others are way over at the far end, repairing fences and ..." He shivered and leaned across the balustrade, the tendons on his old neck straining against his reddened skin. "If I didn't know better..."

"Should I tell Mr Quince?"

"About what?"

"This *feeling* you have. Manchester, you're making me feel nervous."

Smiling, he turned to her and patted her hand. "Listen, do

me a favor. Go downstairs and make sure the bar is put across the main door. Then, go and ask Mr Quince to come and see me."

Without a word, Eva turned and ran off. After a moment, Manchester returned his gaze to the land sprawling out before him. If he could, he'd saddle a horse and ride across to where the men were. It would take him a good twenty minutes to summon them back to the house. Would twenty minutes be enough, he wondered.

In the near distance, a coyote howled. He flinched. Coyotes were not as dangerous as wolves, but they still posed a threat to the horses who, by now, were full of gathering fear, herding together as they often did when wolves were close. Or another danger.

The light was still good. True, shadows were lengthening and, if he allowed his imagination free reign, he could conjure up any number of shapes lurking out there. What little cover there was could conceal a man. Or two. Or a dozen.

He jumped as Quince came onto the balcony. Ruffled hair and dewy-eyed, it was clear he'd just emerged from sleep. He often had afternoon naps now, excusing himself that as this was the furthest south he'd ever lived, then he'd take up the tradition of having a siesta in the afternoons. He adjusted his housecoat as he came closer, stifling a yawn. "What is it? Eva's in a flap, shuttering the doors and windows downstairs."

"I'm not sure, boss. Take a look."

Quince went up to the balustrade. "What am I looking for?"

"I don't know, boss..."

"You don't know? If *you* don't, who does?"

"There's something..." That coyote howled again, closer now. Manchester stiffened. "You hear that?"

"Coyote? So what? Manchester, what is this? You're making me feel jittery."

"I think we should gather some weapons, boss because I think—"

An arrow scorched through the air and slammed into the woodwork of the wall behind where the men stood, missing Manchester by mere inches.

Below, Eva screamed.

It was as if the entire world had plunged into a maelstrom of fear.

"They're in the house!"

"They came in through the back," hissed Manchester, "while we've been standing here, discussing what to do, they've come in from behind!"

He was running through the double doors and slammed straight into a wild-eyed warrior, parallel stripes of white paint covering both cheeks. The knife in his hand went into Manchester's midriff with ease, right to the hilt.

Quince didn't wait. Gripping the balustrade, he vaulted over and plunged to the ground and hit it with bone-jarring force. Collapsing into a heap, he rolled over onto his side, screeching in pain.

He did his best, despite the fire raging through his ankles. He knew he'd broken them, but fear spurred him on and, dragging himself along by his hands, he slowly made his way towards the big barn and what he hoped was safety.

From inside the house came more screams. His wife and Eva, both defiled by the Indians rampaging within. Blocking out the horrors, Quince bit down on his lip and continued, determined to get away. If he could reach the barn, there were horses there, a couple of rifles too. If he could just fire off several rounds, those workers of his on the far side of the ranch, they would come. They would help. If he could just …

Unbeknownst to Quince, those workers were already dead. The first to die as the band of Arapaho came upon them like whispers from the mist. No sound, striking with tomahawks and clubs, dispatching every one of them with a final knife in the throat. It was quick and it was bloody and the men working on those fences didn't stand a chance.

The warriors took what weapons they could and now they were here, three of them easily overtaking Quince as he wormed his way forward. They laughed and jeered, kicking him in the ribs, putting a blade into the back of his thigh. They yelped with glee as Quince screamed and they left him there to bleed out, content with what they had done.

They took the women. It was rare to find such beauties. Tying them across the backs of their ponies, they then torched the house before galloping off.

These white people had paid the price for defiling what was sacred.

Others would follow soon enough.

CHAPTER FORTY-SIX

The rain came down like a wall, drenching Swail within
seconds. Cursing, he stumbled towards his horse, sliding
up into the saddle. He could barely make out the mine from
here, but he cared little for that now. This was a mistake, and he
should have told Turner so. Returning to this damnable place,
with those memories, those nightmares, he should have known it
would all end terribly. And here he was, giving truth to that
assertion. He'd confront Turner, tell him enough was enough.
There was no gold, no hope of riches. He wouldn't like it, but
what the hell ... he'd have to live with it. The way Swail had for
all these years.

He walked his horse through the rain. Bent over its neck,
wishing he'd brought a coat. The storm had broken so unexpect-
edly without any sign of its building. If he'd taken the time to
notice, of course, he would have read the signs, heard the
thunder rumbling. Too immersed in his self-pity, he's ignored it
all and now here he was, soaked through to the skin, miserable,
cold, defeated.

Coming upon the old shack he didn't hesitate. Reining in his
horse he jumped down and bounded across the wet earth and
burst through the door, slamming it closed behind him.

He stood there, breathing hard, the water dripping from his hat, his nose, his hair, and every fiber of his clothing. Soon a pool developed around his feet. At least now he could shelter from the downpour outside.

The shack was dry, the roof fairly sound, the walls still standing. But it stank of something. A dead rat perhaps. Something vile. Nose twitching, he pulled off his sodden neckerchief and wrapped it around his nose and mouth. Tugging off his coat, he laid it across the back of the one remaining chair. He then took to searching the disheveled interior, moving broken furniture, old rotten boxes, sacks full of things he'd rather not explore, and everything caked in dust. One cracked open crate offered him a glimpse of something promising and he cautiously probed around inside. Dynamite. Several sticks. Could they still be useable, he pondered?

Shivering, he realized how cold the shack was. The tiny wood burner in the corner was like an icebox. Packed with ash, it had not been lit for some time. He took to clearing it, heaping the debris into one of the empty jute sacks. Taking broken pieces of wood that littered the floor, he soon had them stacked and ready to be lit. But he had no matches, no flint and steel. Nothing. So, once more, he took to searching.

Soon he felt dizzy. He was over-exerting himself and needed to take a few moments. No longer young, he had had scares in the past, heart-murmurs. Doc Turner told him he needed to pay heed to the warning, that his heart was damaged. What was he now, almost sixty? He'd fought hard throughout the War, been in many a tight spot, but his body was strong back then. Not like now when some mornings he'd wake up and felt as weak as a kitten. Old age, something he'd never considered before. Would he end up like Fieyn, he wondered?

Dismissing such morbid thoughts, he returned to searching. There were some blankets and other assorted fabrics in the corner. Pulling them apart he fashioned a sort of bed but in so doing discovered a back door amongst the piled-up debris.

Putting his shoulder against it, he stumbled out into the rain again and instantly stepped back inside. There was a path leading to a privy some ten or so paces away. A creek ran beneath it, fed from a larger brook that roared close by and disappeared between the curtain of trees forming this part of the wood. He looked and saw the water ran white, like milk. What could that be, he mused, stepped back inside, and pushed the door closed. When the rain ceased, he may well need that privy but for now he needed rest. Stripping off his sodden trousers, shirt, and pants, he settled down between the blankets and tried to still his shivering. By now he was used to the smell and discarded the neckerchief. Soon the drowsiness became irresistible. Too weak to fight it, he allowed himself to slip into the warm embrace of sleep.

The groan of the floorboards as a heavy footfall pressed into the ageing woodwork caused Swail to snap open his eyes. For a moment he did not know where he was and he lay there, amongst his makeshift bedcovers, disorientated, confused. He waited, blinking repeatedly to clear the grey mist enveloping him. His head throbbed, his throat felt parched and deep within his guts a rumbling nausea developed. But he dared not move, not yet. It could be a rat mooching about, a raccoon sniffing out a tasty tidbit. Anything.

Something rustled and Swail froze. A breath, low but unmistakably human. Forcing himself to move as slowly as possible, Swail's fingers crept towards the revolver in his waistband. A Colt Dragoon is a big gun, and it took some time to draw it out completely. As he did so, the breathing from over by the door continued. It was as if the person was waiting but waiting for what, Swail did not dare mull over.

He drew a breath and sat up, the Dragoon aimed towards the door.

The light was dim, dribbles of morning sun leaking underneath the main door. It was enough.

There, ramrod stiff, stood Destry, the grin plastered on his face.

"So, here you are, back from the dead," he breathed, and his grin grew wider. "What you doing up here, Kelly?"

"It's Swail, you bastard. You know my name is Swail."

"Yeah, I knows it. Swail or Kelly, it makes no diff to me. I should have left you to rot in that mine all those years ago, but I thought you was a reformed character."

"As you are, I suppose?"

"Me? Hell, Kelly, I ain't *ever* gonna be reformed. But you, I gave you the chance to start a new life. And you have, damn your eyes. You have shown what true redemption brings. A life, free from hate. Free from avarice and greed. So," he sniggered, "what you doing here?"

"Come for the gold, Destry. Me and Doc Turner, we're gonna make it rich."

"I should have left you, that is the truth, but here you are. Back from the Hell to where I sent you."

Swail did not give him any more time to utter anything else. He squeezed the trigger and blew a hole the size of a melon through Destry's chest, blasting him through the door.

He waited until the cordite dissipated until the shack ceased shuddering. He got to his feet. Outside, sprawled across the ground lay Destry's remains, ruined body a mess of blood and gore. Swail, struggling to regulate his breathing, went to the doorway, leaned against the surround, pressed fingers into his eyes. A wave of repulsion came over him, knees buckled, muscles lost their strength, and he fell to his knees and vomited violently.

"Oh Kelly," came a voice.

He didn't want to, but he had little choice and no control any longer. It was as if invisible hands were lifting his head, forcing him to look.

A shape that might have been human once swayed before

him, the head at an impossible angle, the eyes clear, the mouth opening and closing, blood-drenched spit punctuating each word. "You can't defeat me, Kelly. Not anymore. I'm here to take you home. Home to the fires of Hell."

The voice was Destry's. The voice Kelly remembered. But how could it be? How was any of this possible?

It took a step.

Swail screamed, brought up the Dragoon and emptied it into the thing advancing upon him. Each heavy caliber slug slapped into the bloodied mess, spinning it around, tearing off chunks of corrupted flesh. The head erupted; internal organs spewed forth. It crumpled and remained still.

Sobbing uncontrollably, Swail slithered down the door jam, the Dragoon slipping from his fingers. And there he remained, a blubbering wreck, the pain behind his eyes lessening a little, but the nightmare vision of Destry's living corpse embedded into his brain.

An hour, perhaps several passed before he felt sufficiently strong enough to get to his feet again. With eyes averted, he reeled back into the confines of the shack. He knew what had to be done and, after pulling on his coat, he readied everything.

CHAPTER FORTY-SEVEN

A large depression, the bottom like a mirror, smooth and black, barred the way. Beyond it, Reece could make out a chink of light. The rear entrance. They'd slept fitfully, Destry waking every few hours to scream, as Reece, racked with fatigue, bundled himself into a tight ball and prayed for the morning. Their torches spluttered, giving off a feeble glow until, finally, they gave out, plunging everything into inky blackness. Now, the tunnel stretched out before him but Destry no longer remained. At some time in the night, he'd slipped away to leave Reece to find his way out.

To do so he would first need to cross the depression.

As his eyes grew accustomed to the gloom, using the distant light, he managed to pick out the features in and around the dip. Bones, dazzling white despite the muted darkness, littered the perimeter, many more arranged in curious patterns across the base. In the center, dominating everything stood a large obelisk of polished stone topped with the skull of a deer, the antlers so large, so black. Its gaping, black, empty eyes stared directly towards him, studying him. Held by its hypnotic gaze, Reece could not move, gripped as he was by this thing's invisible power.

What drew his attention more than anything, however, was

the helmet. He recognized it from the drawing. Made from bronze, perhaps even gold, it glowed with an inner life-force. In front, taking up the rest of the plinth, a bronze breastplate. Both objects bore intricately carved designs. An officer's armor from another age. Reece knew them to be of Spanish origin and, by the way their highly polished surfaces shimmered, these artefacts were of great value, preserved and tended by unseen hands over the years to maintain their elegance. Revered. Worshipped perhaps.

The ground gave a sudden shudder as if shaken by some gigantic hand. The very earth buckled and heaved, accompanied by a horrible and terrifying groaning sound. From the roof, pieces of ancient rock became detached and fell crashing to the ground. Stumbling to his right, Reece groped for cover as jagged stone shards rained down. The earth beneath his feet lurched and yawned ever more violently. Rocks split and from the depths came threads of smoke. But not from any fire. This was gas. Reeling in retreat, Reece pressed the mask hard against his mouth and nose. This was the poison Winter Hair had spoken about, that when the earth cracked, the gas would issue forth.

Taking a breath, he dashed forward, leaping over upturned rocks, ignoring the bones, the central monolith, the armor and crossed towards the far exit, head down, one hand clamped around his face, the other waving through the air to disperse the gas as he sprinted.

All around him, rocks fell and smashed across the ground, sending up blooms of dust and debris. Reece pressed forward, eyes clamped on the wooden door ahead, with its cracks and the promise of warm sunshine beyond.

He hit the door with all his might, blasting through those ancient timbers and shattering them as if they were not much thicker than paper. He fell flat on his face in the wet ground, the rain pounding down all around him. No sunshine but an abundance of welcome fresh air which he took into his lungs with great gulps. Rolling onto his back he lay there, allowing the downpour to wash over his face and restore some of his vitality.

Staring at the sky, clothes soaked through, he broke into laughter at the absurdity of it all, thankful he was free of the mine at last.

————

Sheltering close by, Destry studied his erstwhile partner with interest and a growing malignancy. Reece was an obstacle he needed to remove, to kill. He had not fulfilled what Destry had hoped he would, the hope being that Reece would find the treasures within but then the earth cracked, and dreams became nothing once again. He recalled what Winter Hair told him all those years ago on his return from the mine and the slaughter of those bushwhackers.

"There is gold within the mine," the Indian, old even then, had said, "but not the gold you think you know. The spirits of our forefathers reside in there, alongside the tomb of those who came to plunder and kill so many years before. Men clad in burnished copper, bronze, and gold. My people lay their chiefs alongside those men, believing them to be guardians against the evil spirits which lurk in those dark passages. The poison that seeps from below, tainting the water of the nearby river system, is a natural barrier to the curious. But I tell you this, the poison infected even those ancient invaders and they turned upon each other and murder once again put an end to their adventures."

Destry's head was clearing now. The air smelled fresh and clean out here amongst the trees. An hour or so, perhaps a little less, he would have the mindfulness to know what to do. The effects of that mine, the gas, would no longer cloud his judgement, distort his thoughts. He barely remembered killing Bourne or the others but knew, with stunning certainty, that he had.

Reece, his usefulness no longer of any value, would have to

die. Destry fingered the handle of his knife. It would have been best to have slit his throat as he slept but there was always the hope he would uproot the tomb, reveal those ancient treasures which lay amongst the bones of the Spanish. Plans needed to be changed. With Reece lying there, laughing like someone possessed, now would be the perfect opportunity. Grinning, he slowly drew the knife from its scabbard and took a step.

As if it were a signal, his first movement from the trees resulted in a distant explosion. Not like before, this sound was different from that of the earthquake that had ruptured the mine's floor. This sound was manmade and that, Destry said to himself, made it even more dangerous.

CHAPTER FORTY-EIGHT

The dead man had a horse. Head down against the rain, Swail approached the animal, calming it with soft, gently cooing sounds. Eyes wide and white with terror, it struggled to free itself from where the dead man had tied it to a tree, the repeated blasts of Swail's Dragoon spooking it. Swail, however, well experienced with horses, their moods, their personalities, brought all of his considerable knowledge into play as he smoothed its mane, stroked its neck, and smiled as it slowly relaxed, nickering quietly.

Beneath the overhanging branches, the horse remained fairly dry. Swail rifled through the saddlebags, finding hard tack, a change of clothes, some powder and shot, and, at the very bottom, a piece of flint with its accompanying steel. Also were a couple of pieces of char rope, which caused Kelly to stop for a moment and think. Destry was many things, but a man adept at outdoor living he was not. At least, Swail did not think so. During the War, living on his wits and the land, Swail developed skills that enabled him to survive, even in the most extreme of circumstances. But Destry?

Swail looked across the sodden ground separating him from the tree line and the shack. The obliterated body lay there as it would for eternity. The more he looked, the more Swail realized that unless Destry had lost a mass of weight in the intervening years, the corpse was nowhere near corpulent enough to be that of his old nemesis. However, knowing there was little he could do about any of that now, Swail gathered together his fire starter kit, ran across to the shack and went inside.

Using pieces of a broken crate, he soon gathered sufficient kindling to place inside the wood burner, preparing it for lighting. He worked at the flint, striking it hard with the steel, the sparks flying. With a small piece of the char rope set across the flint, soon a tiny ember glowed, and he quickly placed this inside the wood burner, blowing on the smoldering beginnings of the fire.

It wasn't long before the flames took hold. Swail added more pieces of wood until the warmth embraced him. He sat back, clothes steaming, and luxuriated in the glow, closing his eyes as life gradually returned to his cold, aching limbs. He dozed.

Waking with a start, he noticed, that the rain no longer pounded upon the shack roof. The fire had burned low. Not knowing how long he'd slept, he stood and took a cautious look outside. The rain had ceased, and he sighed with relief, despite yet another headache building up behind his eyes. He longed for some whiskey, anything to dull the pain.

With grim acceptance, he knew he could no longer put off his plan.

Taking the crate of dynamite, he carried it outside, skirted around the corpse and moved to where the horses stood at what he hoped was a safe distance. He checked the reins of both his horse and the dead man's, tugging at the leather to tighten them as best he could. Then, with four sticks in his hand, he returned to the shack.

He would need to move fast. He placed three of the sticks in strategic positions in the interior. With the one remaining stick in his hand, he took a dying ember from within the wood burner and retreated to the doorway. He felt faint and nauseous. The longing for whiskey grew stronger. What he wouldn't give for a good, long bath, a couple of glasses of the best Bourbon, and a warm night in a soft bed.

Something with the weight and scorching pain of a red-hot poker slammed into his back. He gasped, more in surprise than agony, and dropped to his knees. Before him, the shack wavered in and out of focus. Hadn't Doc Turner warned him about spending too long in the shack and the mine? What was it he'd said? That the smell, sweet, pleasant, was the foulest of all things he could find there? Well, it was sweet. Comforting too. It brought a kind of peace to his soul, wrapping him up in a blanket of bliss. That was true ... wasn't it? He'd felt it before he'd drifted off to sleep only to be wakened by ...

He cried out. The taper had almost burned right down and had brushed the tips of the fingers holding it. Snapping himself back to reality, the pain between his shoulder blades unlike anything else. He made to stand but could not. Something flashed past the corner of his eye, inches from his head, and slapped into the shack's far wall.

"Oh, dear God," he managed to mutter, his eyes readjusting at last. An arrow, still vibrating along its length, protruded from the wooden wall. An arrow?

He turned and saw them. At least four of them stripped to the waist, faces daubed with white and black warpaint. They were screaming, one of them nocking yet another arrow.

"Damn this to hell," Swail spat, touched the tapper to the dynamite and watched with a growing sense of victory the way the fuse spluttered and fizzed before taking proper hold.

The arrow hit him in the throat, and he fell back, the dynamite falling from his fingers. He could just make out the shack ceiling, thought of his home back in Kansas, the childhood sweetheart he'd left behind and smiled. A liquid warmth flowed through him before something brilliant and white invaded everything and he heard and saw no more.

CHAPTER FORTY-NINE

Doc Turner came into town at a steady trot and noted the barricade across the main street. He chuckled and raised his hand in greeting. Someone waved him forward and when he reached the wagons, he negotiated a path along the side. There were several men crouched behind the two upturned wagons, all armed. The largest of them stepped forward and held out his hand. "Welcome, Doc."

Turner took Hanson's proffered hand and shook it. "I have a rifle," he said and, patting the holster at his hip, he added, "and my old Colt Navy. Never thought I'd need to use it again."

"Doc," said Hanson, "we need you here to help us man our defenses."

"There's a war party heading this way," said another big man from the steps of Miss Bessy's guesthouse. Turner vaguely recognized him. "Name's Henry," said the man, "the Quince ranch boss. This here is Otis." The young man next to him nodded. "You see any signs on your travels?"

"Not a thing," said Turner.

"Where you coming from?"

"Lancaster," said Turner, scanning the immediate area.

Around half a dozen frightened-looking townspeople were assembled behind the wagons. Turner doubted they would last for long if an attack ever came. "How do you know Indians are coming?"

"We got into a scrap with 'em," said Henry, moving down the guesthouse steps. "They would have scalped us for sure if it wasn't for Reece."

"Reece? I thought he was at the mine?"

"He was," put in Otis. "We all were."

Turner tried to keep the surprise from his voice. "I see. But what makes you think that a war party would make a detour to here?"

"We don't," said Henry, "but it's what Reece said, and, to my mind, it makes perfect sense."

"We think they were defending their mine," said Otis.

"*Their* mine?" Turner gawped and shot a quizzical glance towards Hanson. "Why they say it is their mine?" Hanson shrugged and pulled a face.

"Why else would they try and stop us from getting inside," said Henry. "Doctor are you?"

"I am."

"Well, *Doctor,* how come you are casting so much doubt on what we're saying? You know something we don't?"

"Me? What could I possible—"

"The Doc is just naturally skeptical," put in Hanson quickly, "ain't you, Doc?"

Turner laughed but he knew it sounded self-conscious and not at all convincing.

"I'll go talk with Miss Bessy," said Turner quickly, before Henry could attempt any further probing questions. He walked off without looking back.

Miss Bessy was in the small breakfast-cum-dining room preparing tables when Turner came in. She stopped and, putting her hands on her hips, gave him a withering look. "You look like I feel. Have you returned with Destry?"

"I don't know where he is," said Turner. He felt weary and sat down heavily on the nearest chair. "Have you got any coffee?"

"What do you mean you don't know? I thought you were the one to sort everything out?"

"And how was I supposed to do that?"

"You've always sorted things out before. You've helped save lives, talked sense, made people feel safe. Now that Fieyn's dead, who else have we got?"

"Reece?"

Bessy frowned as her face drained of color. "Please don't tell me—"

Turner held up his hand, "Don't fret none, Miss Bessy. I haven't a clue what Reece is up to. All I do know is he received some help from Winter Hair. I'm sure he'll be just fine."

"But you can't be sure." She sank into a chair. "Dear God, I wish none of this had happened. That damned mine... It turns everyone against each other. It's evil, I tell you."

"Maybe so. Swail has gone up there to find out what's happening."

"Brad Swail? Why would you send him?"

Turner shrugged. "Better than anyone else. At least he knows the way."

Bessy's frown grew deeper. None of this was making any sense to her. "First Destry, then Reece, now Brad. That mine sucks everyone in."

"Bessy," said Turner slowly, "there's a lot you don't know and some of it is going to come as a big shock to you. You're right, the mine has a hold over us all." He smiled. "Even me."

"I don't understand."

"No reason why you should. The thing is, there isn't gold in that mine. What little there was old man White dug out years ago. What's in there is treasure, Miss Bessy. It's priceless. I went to see Flying Eagle, the Arapaho chief. But our meeting didn't go well and when I mentioned unearthing the tomb, I thought my end had come."

"What meeting? I don't ... Doc, why are you telling me all this?"

"I guess it's because I like you, always have and therefore I think it's only right you know the truth, the truth your damned husband has kept from you all these years. Destry was never the man for you. He's a drunk and an adulterer." He took a hard-backed chair from the corner and placed it in front of her. Then he sat, his face grave. "You must listen to me. We have a chance to set things right, to start again. This town could still be a little goldmine if we do things the right way."

"I thought you said there was no gold?"

"I don't mean a goldmine in the literal sense, Bessy. The West is opening up more than ever. There are fortunes to be made as the trails are developed, stagecoach services expand, and the railroad, of course. With a little luck and the money we can make from selling that treasure, we could make a go of this place, Bessy. A *real* go." Turner leaned forward and held her hand between his. "The one problem was the sheriff, but young Ira put paid to that after he'd convinced himself that Fieyn had killed his mother."

"He did *what*?" Appalled, Bessy threw herself back against the chair and clamped a hand to her mouth. "Sheriff Fieyn killed Ira's mother? What evil is this?"

Spreading out his hands, Turner chuckled. "It wasn't Fieyn. I just made sure Ira thought it was."

"You? Why on earth would you...?"

"As I said, he was a threat. As is Quince and that damned ranch. Flying Eagle took a lot of persuading, but he eventually agreed to attack the place, get rid of them all." Pressing his lips together, Turner pointed to a nearby coffee cup. "Any chance? I'm feeling all done in, Bessy, I have to say."

"You're done in? After all this so am I! I never would have believed that you, of all people, could conjure up anything so wicked. So sinful."

"I'm old, Bessy. Old and tired. If I'm going to make anything of my last few years, now is as good a time as any."

As if in a dream, Bessy stood up, fetched the coffee pot, and poured Turner a cup. She watched him drink.

Turner smacked his lips. "Thank you."

"These plans of yours, how do you think you will get away with it?"

"Who is going to stop me? I'll give it an hour then when everyone is certain there's no war party on the way, I'll take Henry and Otis across to the ranch. Flying Eagle will be waiting for me there."

"Then you find Reece and Destry?" She stepped closer and re-filled Turner's coffee. "And what, you murder them?"

"If they haven't already killed one another thanks to that damned gas. I want nothing or no one to stand in the way of our plans anymore." He turned the cup around in its saucer. "Winter Hair gave Reece something. A mask. To protect him from the gas."

Her voice almost broke, "So there's a chance he might live?"

"I might have made a mistake introducing him to that old Indian, but I think in the end, if he can extract the treasure, things will work out for us all." He winked. "Except for Reece, of course. I'm afraid he's going to have to die, Bessy."

"He'll stop you, Doc. You won't get away with any of this."

"I believe I will and as head of this guesthouse, you will be the most attractive thing in this town, Bessy. That's why you're still alive. You're valuable."

"You bastard!" She swept up the coffee pot and was about to raise it when Hanson stepped into the room. He stood in the doorway, mouth falling open.

"Oh Hanson!" cried Bessy, threw the pot down and ran into the big blacksmith's arms. "Thank God you're here." She turned in his embrace and glared at Turner who remained sitting, grinning like someone possessed. "He's a monster, Hanson. He's responsible for so many deaths, and he's now planning to kill everyone who stands in his way. Destry, Quince, even Reece. He's already seen to it that Sheriff Fieyn was taken care of." She turned to him again. "He's confessed everything to me. We have to—"

"Bessy," said Hanson gently and pressed one thick finger over her lips. "Shush now, little one. You have to be brave."

"Brave? What the hell are you talking about?" Her eyes locked on his and then she saw it, all of it. "Oh my God," she said incredulously. "You? You're in all this, with him?"

She struggled to release herself from his grip but failed miserably. As she writhed against his impossible strength, she took a breath and prepared to scream. Acting quickly, Hanson placed one huge hand over her mouth to suppress the sound and looked across to Turner as she kicked and fought. "What do we do with her?"

"Keep her here and keep her quiet. I'll check what Henry is planning on doing. He's a thorn I can do without." He stood up. "Later, we can tie her up, go to the mine and find Reece. Knowing him, he'd have survived. We'll kill him and then we can have free reign."

Leaving Bessy struggling in the arms of the blacksmith, Turner stepped out into the early evening air and glanced over to the assembled defenders. They looked scared, and so they should, he mused. Shaking his head, he went to step down into the street when a figure materialized next to him.

"I heard what you said in there." It was Ira Rush, emerging from the shadows. His haunted eyes roamed over the doctor and the gun in his hand seemed impossibly big.

"Ira? What are you doing here?"

"You fed me lies about the sheriff, didn't you?"

"I did no such thing, Ira. He was responsible for your family's death, just as I told you."

"No, it wasn't like that, was it. I listened to you from out back. I heard it all. I also been talking to other folk. After I smothered him, I couldn't sleep, couldn't eat. I'm not a murderer, Doc, what I was looking for was revenge, you understand?"

"Of course I do, Ira, but everything I told you was in good faith. If I got some of the details wrong, then I—"

"You did more than got them wrong, Doc. Millie Burrows came across me in a side street. I was all crouched up, crying like a baby. She took me in. We have always been close, me and Millie. After I'd calmed down, I told her what I'd done, and it was then she told me the truth."

"Ira, for God's sake, Millie Burrows is not of sound mind – you know that! Ever since those bushwhackers rode into town and gunned down her pa, she ain't ever been right in the head! She was little still as she watched him die, right there." He pointed towards the merchandise store some way down the street.

"I know what she saw, and I know the effect it had on her," said Ira, his voice a growl now. "What I didn't know was how sensible she is, how she's handled everything so well. You and a lot of other people dismissed her as some sort of dullard because she has always kept herself to herself. But you know why that is? Because of her mother. She had to tend to her night and day. Night and day, you understand? It ain't any wonder she's never had time to socialize or reopen her pa's store. Yeah, she was grieving and grieving for a long, long time, but she's fine up here," he tapped his head, "and she told me everything. About the sheriff and what he did."

"Well, there you are then..."

"No. She told me *precisely* what he did. Sheriff Fieyn had nothing to do with what happened – it was Destry and *you*."

The young man slowly brought up the enormous gun and levelled it towards the doctor's guts. Turner eyed it with horror. It was a Walker Colt and would blow him apart if Ira fired. "Ira, listen to me," he said quickly, desperation in his voice, "none of this is right. What I told you about Fieyn, it was all true."

"No, it wasn't. You wanted him out of the way, that's all. He was sick, probably would have died anyway. I should have thought about it before. Why me? Why of all the people in this town would you ask me to look after him? Me, the one person who had every reason to see him dead?"

With deliberate slowness, Ira eased back the hammer of the handgun.

At that moment, a shadow passed over them and Henry, the Quince ranch boss, appeared. He took in the situation in a glance. "What in the hell is going on here?"

"Henry," spluttered Doc Turner, "oh thank God. This fool here, he—"

"I ain't no fool," said Ira through clenched teeth. "I have a grievance is all. And it ain't anything to do with you," he shot a look towards Henry. "No offence."

"A grievance? Well, boy, seems to me that if you fire that piece, you is gonna be put up for murder. At this time, we need every man we got. So let it rest, son. We can work it all out after we've overcome the Indian attack."

"There ain't going to be an Indian attack," said Ira, a tiny smile flickering at the corners of his mouth. "It's just another lie from this scoundrel."

Henry frowned and swayed backwards. "Doctor, is what this boy says correct?"

"Oh hell, Mr Henry," said Turner, "you gonna believe the word of a mad idiot like this? He murdered Sheriff Fieyn for pity's sake!"

"He did what?"

"Our good sheriff, murdered as he slept! And Ira here, he did it."

"That's right, I did," said Ira. "I ain't gonna deny it, but there's a good reason why. One I'll gladly tell any court of law."

A shot rang out and a bullet scorched through the air and missed Ira's head by a hair's breadth. Everyone ducked and turned. Henry drew his gun in a blur.

On the steps of the guesthouse, Hanson busy worked the

lever of a Sharps rifle and brought it up in preparation for another shot.

Ira bolted. He wasn't about to stand around and present himself as a simple target. Swerving left and right, keeping low and moving as fast as a buck-rabbit, he disappeared down the narrow street running along the side of the guesthouse just as another bullet flew next to his head. It slapped into the opposite wall, but Ira wasn't paying much attention. He simply ran.

CHAPTER FIFTY

The shaking grew louder and stronger. Close to the town and stretching back through the woods to the mine, the ground seemed to buckle and groan. Around the remains of the shack, burning embers surrounding the dead bodies strewn amongst the dirt, Reece negotiated a path. His horse had bolted with the initial eruption so his was an arduous and slow journey. Aware of Arapaho eyes on him, he only stopped when he reached the exploded shack. Studying the debris, he took note of the two white corpses, one a blackened, burnt mess, the other, some distance from where the shack once stood, perforated with gunshot wounds. Identification of either was impossible.

"That's Nathan Kelly," came a voice.

Reece whirled in a half-crouch, gun whipping up from his holster.

Destry threw up his hands, "Easy boy, it's only me." He tilted his head and smiled. "Kelly was the surviving bushwhacker. But he didn't die all those years ago. Changed his name, started a new life. That second one, the one I think Kelly must have killed, went by the name of Ezra. They knew one another back during the War. Seems like they had not learned to get on."

"How you know all this?"

Shrugging, Destry kept his arms raised. "I also knew 'em, of course. I believed Kelly was dead. I believe he's been holed up in Lancaster all this time, but I didn't know until dear Ezra informed me of his encounter with old Doc Turner. Seems that the doc has been sheltering Kelly all these years. Made him his assistant. Called him Brad Swail."

"Why would the doc get involved?"

"For the gold. In the mine."

"But there ain't no gold. Only poison gas and a few trinkets."

"You know that's not quite true, don't you Reece? Winter Hair told you, didn't he? Told you the truth. And now you've seen it for yourself. Don't deny it."

Reece eased back the hammer of his Colt. "Loosen your gun belt before I plug you."

Destry laughed. "That would be a tad foolish. Together we might make it back to town, with me dead those Indians will almost surely split you asunder."

"And why would that be, Destry? You got some sort of pact with 'em?"

"Pact? What's that, a deal? Now, what makes you think I'd make a deal with a pack of savages, Reece?"

"Because they ain't savages. Sure, Winter Hair told me about what's in that mine, but he told me some other stuff too. That the Arapaho, they have deep beliefs and a lot of 'em are centered on that mine. The burial of old Spanish Conquistadors. The white men with beards. Originally those Indians down south, they thought of the Spanish as gods, until they started killing 'em and enslaving them. Those original beliefs, they have a way of clinging on."

"I never took you for a scholar."

"You don't know anything about me, Destry, that's your problem. You've underestimated me every step of the way."

"You could be right."

Reece smiled. "Since the treaty of Medicine Lodge, the Arapaho have been a lot more peaceful, which makes me think someone must have got them all stirred up, causing them to attack Henry outside the mine the way they did."

"Clever, ain't you, Reece."

"What did you trade with 'em? They let you take that Spanish treasure, you give 'em free-range across the Quince ranch once you've gotten rid of everyone there?"

"Something like that."

"But now the mine has been made virtually impassable thanks to this latest earthquake, your plans might have to be redrawn, so to speak."

"Maybe, or maybe I can just go on in and help myself to whatever's down there. The tomb is cracked open, I guess?"

And saying that, he beckoned with his left hand, his grin widening as he did so.

Taking his time, Reece turned and looked over his shoulder. Sure enough, his worst nightmare became reality as he saw a group of Arapaho approaching, weapons at the ready.

"I guess you might call this a deciding moment," said Destry. "You either decide to put that gun of yours away or my friends here will kill you."

"Kill?" Reece looked again at Destry. "Seems like you don't leave me much choice."

Destry feigned surprise. "They kill you slow, Reece. It won't be easy. They'll split you wide open and leave you to bake in the sun, watching the buzzards peck out your gizzard."

Reece thought about that and dropped his gun back into its holster. "All right. Maybe we can come to some arrangement."

"Time for arrangements is over, Reecie," said Destry with a cackle and drew his own gun. "Time for you, my friend, has run out."

CHAPTER FIFTY-ONE

With his mouth gaping open, Henry swung around and shouted out to no one in particular. "What the hell is going on here? Who was that young fella and why you tryin' to kill him?"

"Shut up, Henry," spat Turner.

"*What?*"

Young Otis came forward, eyes shifting in all directions, "Mr Henry, I think it's time for us to get out of here."

But Henry was no longer listening. Purple with rage, he pierced Turner with a glowering glare. "Don't you *ever* speak to me that way! Have you any idea who I am?"

"We know," said Hanson, working the lever. He brought up the Sharps, peered down the barrel, and blew a hole the size of an orange through Henry's throat.

A great fountain of blood sprayed outwards, splashing across Otis who, screaming, backed away, fumbling for his gun. He watched in horror as his former boss buckled at the knees and fell in a bloody heap to the ground.

A hand of immense strength gripped him by the shoulder and turned him.

Otis looked up into Hanson's face.

He saw the fist too late. It cracked into his jaw and sent him sprawling. Senses reeling, he battled hard to clear his head, but the world pitched and yawned in front of his eyes, he had no feeling in his arms and legs, and the only sound he could discern was the pounding of his own heart.

Stepping down the steps to her guesthouse, Turner met the incredulous eyes of the bedraggled townsfolk who had witnessed what had happened.

"It was always my belief," he said, voice assured, with no hint that the killing of Henry had affected him in any way, "that Quince, the ranch owner, had designs on this town. That he would use any gold he may have discovered from the mine to buy everyone out, extend his land holdings and take over the lumber business which remains the lifeblood to us all."

"How you know this?"

Turner turned to the owner of the voice, a small, aged man by the name of Peter Winston. "Reece told me."

"Reece?" asked another.

"Yes. He told me. He confided in me that he was working for Quince, that it was his job to enter the mine, discover its riches and help Quince in his plans. The other man, Bourne, was an accomplice. Henry here," he gestured towards the destroyed remains of the ranch boss, "was in on it too. Convince us that the Arapaho were heading this way to murder us all. This would leave the mine open for Reece and Bourne to explore at their leisure."

"So there ain't no Indians comin'?"

Turner shook his head. "I believe it was just such a ruse," he said. "I didn't want to believe it because I trusted Reece. But it's clear now that we have all been tricked."

· · ·

Later, as the townsfolk pulled apart the barricades they had so carefully erected half a day before, Hanson sat across the dining table from Turner and Bessy. The two men quietly sipped bourbon and the hand that Hanson used to lift the glass trembled.

"They'll hang you, Hanson," said Bessy. The blacksmith had loosened the ropes he'd used to tie her up, but the one around her waist remained, making it impossible for her to stand. "You know that, don't you?"

Turner sniggered. "Ain't nobody going to hang, Bessy. I sensed the people might start getting feisty, so I conjured up that story about Reece and Bourne and Henry, all of them conspiring to develop Quince's ranch. They believed it because it fitted their long-held suspicions."

"You lie like you are used to it," said Bessy.

"Don't be thinking I'm not," Turner retorted, mouth and stare hard as granite. "I will do whatever is needed to ensure this town remains under my control. I have too much invested in it."

"What of Reece?"

"Destry will deal with him," he said and took a long drink. He laughed. "He's come good these last few days. Something happened to him in that mine, something that changed him. He took to drinking and has gradually turned into a murderous, cantankerous old coot. But he has his uses."

"You believe Destry is capable of killing Reece? You're a fool if you think that."

"Brad Swail then," said Turner. "If Destry doesn't kill Reece, Swail will kill. All we'll need do then is remove Quince from the equation."

"You sound like a professor," said Hanson, smirking.

"It's true we need to ensure Reece is dead," said Turner. "He trusts me. We'll go to the old mine and if we discover him alive, I'll find out what he knows. If Swail has killed him then let us all hope he managed to get any information from him before he did so." He shook his head and stood up. "We need to bring this to an end. I am sick and tired of pretending I am somebody I am not. No more will I hide behind my smiles and my medicine bottles. Hanson, tie her up again and then we'll set off. Then, together with Swail, we'll ride across to the Quince ranch. This ends now." He strode out of the room, down the corridor and out into the street. He watched the townsfolk heaving together to return a wagon onto its wheels. He lifted his voice to them. "Well done everyone. We can go back home, put our lives back together. We're safe now."

It took a few moments for these words to sink in. Several townsfolk did not look too convinced nevertheless, after some hesitation, they started to drift away.

He glanced askance as Hanson joined him on the top step of the guesthouse.

"Did you tie her up well?"

Hanson gave him a look. "As well as I could."

"If we leave now, we'll make it before dark. Before you do, you take that miserable piece of offal to the jail and lock him up. I'll think about what's to be done with him later."

Hanson grunted but did not offer any comment. He went down the steps and crossed to where Otis remained flat on his back and lifted him as if weighed little more than a sack of oats. He threw the young rancher over his shoulder and crossed towards the tiny jailhouse. Clearing his throat, Turner shivered slightly before he too went down into the street and quickly followed Hanson, their horses, and their destiny.

In the dining room, Bessy, long since given up hope of loosening her bonds, stared at the floor, and pondered on what life could have been like if Destry had never gone to that damned mine. Bourbon infused with milky-white water had led to his ruin. And not only him. Turner, Hanson ... she hung her head and swallowed down her despair. If only Reece could manage, somehow, to turn everything around then possibly, just possibly, life could return to something like normality.

CHAPTER FIFTY-TWO

At least a dozen warriors, with possibly more lurking amongst the trees, moved forward like whispers in the fog, silent and alert. Reece pulled off his mask and looked askance at Destry whose grin was causing the anger to boil.

"You'd better unbuckle your gun, Reecie, these boys don't take kindly to their blessed sites being violated."

"No one's done more of that than you, Destry."

"Well, I'm not thinking these boys will look at it that way. They're my friends, you see, and, after all, it was you who was there when the earthquake struck. Maybe they think it was you who caused it and broke their little shrine." He cackled and turned to beckon the chief warrior to move forward.

The chief approached. A tall superbly muscled individual, his face a blank canvas, no expressions revealing what lay beneath his unruffled exterior.

"You are the one called Reece," he said, his voice flat, his English faltering but perfectly comprehensible.

Reece felt Destry flinch.

"Yes, he is," blurted out the old livery owner, "and he's been inside, opening up your tomb, pulling out those treasures. He's the man you've been looking for, Chief! The man you should hang out to dry."

Arching an eyebrow, Reece threw him a poisonous look. "You're full of it, Destry." He looked to the Chief. "An earthquake struck, not for the first time. But this one, it was big. Cracked the tomb."

The warrior tilted his head, "Earth...*quake*? What is that?"

"When the earth opens," said Reece. "That is when the poison comes out."

"We will go," said the Chief and before anyone could object, the warriors pressed in closer and herded Reece and Destry through the woods towards the mine.

They moved in silence, Reece always in control of his nerves whereas Destry was like someone gripped by a fever. Sweating profusely, he constantly looked from Flying Eagle to Reece, expression one of twisted rage in a face chalk white with terror.

They came to the main entrance and found it gaping open, the rock floor ruptured with jagged pieces arched upwards where the earthquake had torn everything apart.

"We need to be careful of the poison gas," said Reece. He lifted his mask. "This protected me before." He fitted it across his mouth and nose.

"Yes, Winter Hair made you a gift of it."

Destry stepped forward, his voice strained, "Don't listen to him, Chief. The man has committed sacrilege."

The Chief frowned.

"He means I have broken into the tomb. But I didn't."

"I know that," said the Chief. Destry gasped and the Chief abruptly halted any further interruptions with a raised hand, "You also know it is not a tomb."

Beyond him, the assembled warriors shuffled and stepped aside as through their ranks strode a wizened figure, his hair brilliant white, topped with a deer-antler headdress. Many of the warriors bowed in reverence and even the chief, giving way to the newcomer, lowered his head.

Reece met the newcomer's hard stare and smiled. "It's good to see you again."

"And you, my friend," said Winter Hair, and he thrust out his hand and seized Reece by the forearm. "You have done well."

"What the hell is going on here," squealed Destry, stepping away. "This man, he tried to take your gold, it was he who—"

"No," snapped Winter Hair. "Reece is here to do my bidding. To seal up this mine forevermore."

"That's what this is for," said Reece, pulling off the canvas shoulder bag. "Winter Hair asked me to set dynamite at both entrances and make this place inaccessible. Seems like the earthquake has done most of the job for me."

"You ..." Destry spluttered, shaking his head, feet moving in a little jig as he wrestled with this news, "This ain't how it was meant to be! That gold, it's mine you bastard – mine!"

"The gold has gone. A gold helmet and breastplate are all that remains, together with a bundle of old Spanish trinkets and weapons. There is a few silver goblets and plate, buried there long ago as a bunch of Conquistadors moved north. A gold sword, encrusted with precious gems is what old man White discovered all those years ago, together with the gas of course. He should have blown the place up back then, but he always hoped he could return and find some *real* gold. That's what he told you Destry – that there was more gold waiting to be mined out. The Indians thought the place sacred due to the siting of an old chief's tomb down there. It was a true story, and the lure of more gold was so good you and everyone else found it irresistible. But what nobody counted on was the gas. How it distorts your thoughts, changes your personality. Unless," he brought up the mask, "you have some form of protection."

"Bastard," hissed Destry and pulled his gun. Almost at once a dozen or more bows swung up and pointed in his direction.

"Do so and you die," said Winter Hair.

Furious but with little real choice, Destry returned his gun to its holster and, gnashing his teeth, said, "I'll fix you, Reece. You just don't see if I don't."

With that, he whirled around and broke into a run.

Winter Hair watched him go, said something to the chief in their language, then spoke to Reece, "We can track him and kill him if you wish."

"No," said Reece. He delved inside the canvas bag. "I'll finish off what I meant to do, then I'll settle my account with Destry later on."

"There are others who will side with him."

"I know." Reece blinked away his regrets. "I've been well and truly duped, Winter Hair. It's thanks to you I've seen a way through this."

The old man extended a hand and rested it on Reece's shoulder. "You will do us a great service by sealing up this old mine. For too long, people have come to this place to disturb the resting place of our great and wise chief-shaman, Gurcharan the Great. Close it up for us, Reece. Let peace return."

"There'll always be the earthquakes."

"The natural world holds no fear to us, Reece. Gurcharan's spirit flies no matter what."

Sometime later, crouching behind various rocky outcrops or deeper into the wood, they all waited for the gunpowder to spit and snarl its way towards where Reece had set the dynamite. There was a deathly pause. Reece pressed his hands over his ears, yelled, "*Get down!*" and threw himself behind a large boulder just as a massive, roaring explosion blew out gaping gashes across almost the entire mountainside, bringing down massive slabs of rock and scree to engulf the old mine's entrance. Seconds later another blast did the same for the rear entrance. The earth shook with the force of it all.

"You'll need to get your people away," said Reece, pulling on his mask as the dust settled. "That gas will pump out all around these parts, infecting everything hereabouts."

Nodding wildly, Winter Hair stood and called to his fellow companions, barking out a string of commands. Immediately, the warriors faded away into the surroundings, the Chief alone hanging back for a brief moment to offer Reece a single nod of gratitude.

Reece shook Winter Hair's hand. "We'll meet again," he said.

"In better times," said the old albino and loped after his people.

Checking his gun, Reece plunged into the woods to make his way back to the old shack and his horse.

He found his horse grazing some way from the remains of the shack. Pausing for a moment, Reece surveyed the destruction once again. The remains of the two men no longer concerned him. What took his attention now were small trails of gas worming their way through the splintered and shattered wreckage together with pools of milky white water punctuating the ground's surface. The explosion must have ruptured the banks of the nearby stream. As a precaution, he adjusted his mask before turning away, and as he did so, he heard the approach of more horses. He quickly tied his mount's reins to a nearby tree and retreated into the woods. He chose a place that afforded him a good view of the open ground between himself and the shack and dipped down out of sight. Within seconds, they came into sight. Hanson and Turner moving cautiously forward.

And with them, bringing up the rear, Destry.

CHAPTER FIFTY-THREE

Mrs Clapham was out back, scraping carrot and potato peelings into the bin she kept for the pigs when she stopped, ears pricked. Slowly, she turned and gasped as young Ira stepped into view.

"Please don't shout out," said the boy, his voice trembling with fear. He outstretched both palms.

"What are you doing here?"

She may have been an old, frail woman but her attitude conveyed a fiery courage. Ira looked away, ashamed. "Oh Mrs Clapham," he began, breaking down, "I've done a terrible thing."

"You'd better come inside and tell me all about it. I'm guessing that Indian attack is not coming, as we were warned it would be?"

Ira shook his head.

"I thought as much." Wiping her hands on an old, ragged towel, she stepped away and motioned for Ira to step inside the small coffee parlor.

With the evening coming on, the temperature in the small preparation room was dropping considerably. Ira, huddled up in a chair, shivered and Mrs Clapham draped a blanket around his shoulders. He looked up at her, his large, puppy-dog eyes awash with tears.

"Ira," she said, crossing to the stove and heating up a pot of coffee, "I don't know what happened exactly, except what we were all told by Doc Turner, but there must have been a reason why you did what you did." She poured him a cup of steaming coffee and placed it in front of him. "You tell me your side of it then we'll see what we can do."

And so, between the sobs, Ira recounted it all – how Fieyn visited his mother, how he'd set alight to the barn, his mother's horrible death, and Ira seizing the opportunity to avenge it, the sheriff laying there, so vulnerable.

"Did you ever talk to your sister about it, before she died?"

Ira's face came up. He sniffed loudly. "Jilly? No, I didn't think ... Why? She saw it, same as me. We watched Fieyn riding off and the barn blazing. There was no need to ... Why are you looking at me like that?"

"A few weeks before she died, with the cancer eating its way through her poor, wretched body, she came to me and told me."

Ira stopped, barely breathing. His voice, when it came, was small, frightened. "Told you what?"

"Who she thought she saw." She stretched out her hands across the small table and gripped his arms. "I thought you knew."

"I ... Maisie May, she knew, didn't she? Mrs Clapham, *please* tell me what you know."

"Sheriff Fieyn had left well before the blaze, Ira and had ridden back to town. Someone else came calling. Jilly never did see who it was, and she came to me and asked me if I might know. I didn't, of course, but ... It was sometime later that I got to talking to Bessy and she told me that ... there is no easy way to say this, Ira. Your mama, she took comfort from several men. The sheriff was one, true enough, but also ... Doc Turner himself."

"Doc ..." Ira ripped his arms free and stood up, face screwed up with rage, "Dear God, that devil! It was he who brought Maisie May into our home, who visited us and made sure all was well."

"I'm guessing it was Doc Turner who planted that seed in your mind, Ira. That it was Sheriff Fieyn who put a match to the barn?"

Gaping, Ira forced out his words. "I heard him talking to Miss Bessy. I couldn't make out everything but now, now it all fits. I confronted him, told him what Maisie had said. He denied it of course but before I could get to the truth someone tried to shoot me."

"Who would do that, Ira? If you were talking to Doc Turner, then who—"

"It was Hanson. Oh my God, Mrs Clapham, they're all in this together."

Mrs Clapham managed to force a swallow. "And Bessy?"

The young man shook his head and looked at her, his eyes welling up but before he could another word the strength left his legs and he collapsed to the floor.

CHAPTER FIFTY-FOUR

Somewhere from within the depths of the guesthouse a clock chimed out the hour, sounding Bessy like a death knell. She didn't count the hour, knowing only that time dragged and, with each ponderous minute that passed, her situation grew darker and ever more miserable. She sat straight-backed, the ropes cutting into her wrists. She's struggled against them but Hanson's handiwork was too good. With Ira's escape, the truth of it all might come out. She chided herself for not acting sooner. Hitting Bourne was only the start of it. Employing those two scoundrels, trying to deceive Reece, everything that could go wrong had gone wrong. Destry and Turner, those miserable curs, had been beavering away at the plans for months, possibly years, just waiting for the right moment. And Brad Swail. Dear God, was there no end to their deviousness, their greed? Madness, all of it. Until Reece came along. Reece, who seemed so much more *alive* than anyone she had ever met. Honest, true, a man to share a life with once Destry was out of the way. And Hanson, the way Bourne no doubt twisted him, seducing him with stories of riches, making him into something he was not. She blew out a long, despairing sigh. So many bad choices.

Mistakes. She no longer knew right from wrong. She no longer cared.

The creak upon the hall floorboards caused her to snap her head around to gaze towards the open entrance to the dining room.

"Oh, dear Lord, Bessy!" Mrs Clapham raced to her friend, feverishly pulling at the ropes.

"Get a knife, Miriam. Over there, in the dresser."

Without a word, Mrs Clapham rushed over, took up a carving knife and attacked the bonds with furious anger. "Who did this to you?"

Gasping, as the ropes parted, Bessy sat forward, rubbing the broken skin of her wrists. "Hanson."

"Oh no," Mrs Clapham collapsed into a chair. "This is so awful, Bessy. Hanson? Ira told me he took a shot at him."

"They're all mad with the lust for gold, Bessy. The promises of untold riches."

A dark look descended over the old lady's face. "How did we come to this, Bessy?"

"Destry, for the most part."

"That man has blighted everything he's touched. I've always supported you through the years, looked out for you as Destry grew more and more wayward. That dreadful incident with Lizzie Coombs..." She shook her head again, a slow, sad gesture this time.

"I've always appreciated your friendship, Miriam, you must know that."

"I do, of course I do. None of this is your fault."

"I'm not so sure, Miriam. If I'd been stronger, I could have stopped Destry years ago, when my feelings were still strong." She shook her head sadly. "On his return from the mine, he was already changed, even before the drink. Since then, he has become nothing more than a monster, his mind filled with schemes, all of them heinous, evil."

Tugging a small, silken handkerchief from her sleeve, Bessy

dabbed at her eyes as the first tears sprouted. "I've been a fool. A deluded, weak and manipulated fool." She sniffed loudly before standing up and crossing the room to the drinks' cabinet. She fetched out a cut-glass decanter filled with a dark red liquid and poured herself a generous glassful. "Doc Turner prescribed me this for medicinal purposes. To help me sleep." She lifted it to her lips.

"What is it?"

"Fortified wine." She took a sip, closed her eyes, and sighed.

"Bessy," said Miriam and stood up. She went over to her friend and gently took the glass from her. She sniffed and recoiled a little. "What is this *fortified* with?"

"Mineral water, spices, a splash of brandy."

Wrinkling her nose, Mrs Clapham carefully tipped the remaining contents back into the decanter. "Bessy, you need to listen to me. I've been talking to one or two people and you need to hear what I have to say."

"Whatever you have to say, it's too late. All of it is too late."

"Sit down." She squeezed Bessy's arm. "Please."

Returning to the table the two women sat across from one another.

"Ira came to me," Mrs Clapham began. Ignoring Bessy's sharp look, she plunged on. "I've known Ira since he was a small boy. His mother helped me out at the parlor for a number of years after her husband died fighting in the War."

"What has this got to do with anything, Miriam? For God's sake—"

"Hear me out, Bessy. I knew things were difficult for the family and I also knew Sheriff Fieyn visited Anita Rush on many occasions. They were lovers. He would often come into the parlor for coffee and sit, staring into the bottom of his cup, and one day he confided in me that they loved one another, that they planned to move away."

"Miriam, that's not what anyone believed."

"I know. The question you need to ask yourself is *why* you thought it wasn't so."

Frowning, Bessy struggled to recall from where she'd first heard the rumor that Fieyn was taking advantage of the widow Rush. "Destry, I think."

"Your husband. A drunk and a liar?" Chuckling humorlessly, Mrs Clapham leaned back in her chair, arms cross. "You believed him?"

Bessy shrugged. "I rarely believed anything he said but that seemed to make sense. We all witnessed Fieyn riding out in the evening, off on another of his jaunts. We chose not to say anything because ... Well, hard for you to believe, I know, but it wasn't anyone's business but theirs. I rarely thought about it."

"Ira too would see him arriving. He'd watch him leading his mother into the barn. He knew what was happening, of course, but he, like so many, never confronted his mother with his suspicions. Perhaps if he had things would have turned out differently."

"In what way? How can any of this be linked with all the horrors that have visited this town recently?"

"The night of the fire, you remember that?"

A shiver ran through Bessy and she held herself as if suddenly cold. "We all do. Awful, horrible thing ... poor Anita, those children ..."

"Not long after, Doc Turner sent them a woman to look after them. Maisie May."

"She was a squaw."

"Why do you say that with such bitterness?"

"Some people said she was a witch, that she fed those children poison. Jilly died young, did she not?"

Nodding, Mrs Clapham came forward. "I told Ira what Jilly had seen. That the barn was set alight deliberately and that she had seen who it was."

Bessy's felt as if an iron brace was tightening around her throat. "Who ... Who was it, Miriam? Destry? Sweet Jesus, don't tell me it was Destry. I know he is many things, but I never suspected he would be capable of—"

"It was Doc Turner. The same Doc Turner who put it into Ira's head that it was Sheriff Fieyn who was responsible. That is why Ira killed him."

"Fieyn? But ... no, he'd had a heart attack and he was—"

"Recuperating in Turner's surgery, with Ira left in charge. He smothered Fieyn to death with a pillow, Bessy. He's confessed everything to me."

This revelation did not leave Bessy as stunned as Mrs Clapham might have expected. "Turner told me as much," said Bessy unblinking, her face a perfect mask of indifference. "Nothing shocks me now, Miriam. Turner is as big a monster as Destry. They deserve each other. My only concern is why it took me so long to see through all the lies."

"They've hoodwinked us all, Bessy, so don't blame yourself unnecessarily. Turner and Destry are in cahoots with everything that's been going on and all of it linked with the mine. The wine everyone who is involved in this drinks is laced with water from the local stream. It's poison, Bessy."

"*Poison?*" Bessy frowned. "You believe Turner has poisoned the water? For what purpose?"

"Not Turner. It's poisoned from an underground spring that runs from the mine. Nobody knows the truth of it, Bessy. Not Turner, not Destry. But it's what's been making everyone's actions so difficult to understand. Destry has been drinking it for years. He's dependent on it. Turner too probably, although I think he had his suspicions."

"How do you know all this?"

"Reece."

That name, the one which ran constantly through her mind, struck her like a blow. Reeling back, eyes sprouting tears, this time unchecked, she tried to speak but could not.

"He called on me before he went to the mine. The shaman, Winter Hair, told him everything."

"And ... and he told you?"

"He said I was the only one he could trust. I didn't drink from the stream and the water was always boiled to make my coffee. My mind is clear, Bessy. Can you say the same for yours?"

Bessy couldn't. The headaches, the indecision, the changing moods, how one moment she felt a yearning for Reece, the next how she succumbed to the advances of others, most lately Bourne. "You're saying everything is down to us drinking the water? That's madness, Miriam. Utter madness."

"Is it? Think about it. Personality changes, the sudden eruption of violence, the fits, the delirium. Destry perhaps more than anyone else."

"And it comes from the mine?"

"There's a gas in there, deep underground, which seeps into the water system every time there's a tremor, no matter how small."

"And we've just had one."

"Yes. Stronger than usual."

"Miriam ... Turner and Hanson have gone to the mine with the hope of finding Reece and murdering him. Swail is to meet them there. Turner told me it all. He wants to come back here when he has the treasure that Reece is supposed to have discovered, sweep me off my feet, and turn this town into something special. He spoke of hotels, railroads, all sorts of things. The folly of so many is breath-taking."

"Greed does that."

"He talked about the Quince ranch. I never liked that man, nor the way his ranch hands would swagger around town, but Turner has something planned for him too."

"Henry is dead. Otis in jail. Quince has no more men in this town now. Perhaps it's the doc's wish to take over the ranch as well?"

As if sinking inside herself, Bessy's face crumpled, and she burst into tears. Rushing around the table, Mrs Clapham comforted her as best she could, throwing an arm around her shoulders, hugging her close. "We can fix this, Bessy. We damn up the stream, divert its course, get everyone well again. Once our minds are clear we can move forward. We can, I know we can."

"But how?" Her voice shuddering with the effort to remain calm, she gripped her friend's arm. "The only hope we have is with Reece but if they kill him ..."

"We have to pray they don't get that chance."

And together they remained like that, holding one another close, the horrors of what might happen playing out in their minds.

CHAPTER FIFTY-FIVE

The night encroached quickly, long shadows impenetrable, details difficult to discern. From his spot amongst the trees, Reece had to squint to gain a decent view of the three men who dismounted and kicked their way through the ruined shack. He recognized them all, his shock at seeing Turner only eclipsed by the sight of the big blacksmith Hanson. Why were they here? They did not seem particularly interested in the bodies and picked through the wreckage as if searching for something. As they did so, the still spewing gas slowly enveloped their ankles before coiling upwards, drawn inexorably to their open mouths. As they inhaled, their reactions grew spasmodic as if they were seized by spirit hands shaking them violently. Which, thought Reece as he watched and trembled, they probably were. Destry, perhaps the least affected and the one Reece had expected to encounter, stepped away, coughing and retching until he vomited. The other two, bent double in attitudes of great agony, seemed to rally before they turned upon one another, their voices booming across the stillness.

"Damn your hide, Hanson," spat Destry, "you should have killed him before now."

"Me?" The big blacksmith bunched his fists, "Your plans, doctor, your ideas. Don't put this on me."

"But I have seen it," said Turner, jigging from one foot to the next, "I saw the map in his hand, and it was here, I tell you. Here," he fell to his knees, clawing at the dirt. "He buried it, that no good, lying, son of a whore! It's here, it has to be."

From nowhere, Turner pulled his gun and waggled it in front of Hanson. The Doc's voice thundered, "I'll not be maligned or doubled-crossed by you, you dammed ape! You want the treasure for yourself, damn you, so where is it? The map – you *must have taken the* map!"

This would have been the perfect time to confront them but Reece, twisted up with indecision, didn't know what to do. The diminishing light made him reconsider his original idea – to jump out and surprise these three men, men he now detested, and force them to draw. Reece was confident in his skills with a gun. That was not the problem. The problem was simple – darkness could cause him to miss a movement, a sudden attack from behind, the side, anywhere. It would be to their advantage, not his. So, he hung back, gnawing on his bottom lip, calculating his chances of overcoming them.

Hanson, however, had no doubts. One massive hand snaked out, gripped Turner around the wrist and bent the much slighter man to the ground.

"You bastard," growled the big man and landed a stunning, sledgehammer right into Turner's jaw.

Reece winced at the power of the blow. Even from where he was, some distance from the altercation, he heard the sickening snap of broken bone. He doubted whether Turner would ever get up again.

Destry shouted out for them to stop. He rushed forward, hands aloft, and then, as if some invisible, god-like hand had reached across and pulled the sun up from below the horizon, the sky, the woodland, the ground flared with the glare of a myriad of lights.

Gaping, Hanson turned, and a single arrow struck him in the mouth. Blinking in disbelief, he crumpled to his knees as several more arrows slammed into his chest.

The clearing, alive with whooping, swarmed with semi-naked warriors. Those not brandishing torches held tomahawks and knives aloft, and they charged towards their victims. Destry, screaming, fired off several shots before turning and fleeing into the darkness, leaving Hanson and the still living Turner to their fate – overpowered with ease and scalped where they lay.

As if in a daze, Reece climbed to his feet, and stood swaying at the sight of the horror being enacted before him. Entranced, he did not hear the footfall behind him until the voice, low and gentle spoke.

"Lay down your weapon, Reece. No harm will come to you."

Holstering his gun, he turned to find Winter Hair, standing there in the darkness of the wood.

"You have done everything we have asked of you, my friend," the old shaman said, "and now we have repaid the debt by killing these vermin."

Reece nodded dumbly. He knew the reckoning with Destry would be next. He held his breath, not sure what to say or do.

"Leave now, my friend and never return."

The smile, frozen on the old man's face, slowly disappeared and Reece moved away with great care, went to his horse, and swung up into the saddle. He glanced across to where the Indians appeared in a frenzy, hacking the bodies of the two others to pieces. Closing his eyes and swallowing down the bile rising to his throat, Reece turned away and took the long route back into town.

As he rode it soon dawned on him that he could not continue for much longer. The inky blackness, accentuated by the closeness of the trees, meant any form of travel was impossible. Cursing his luck, Reece found a thicket, tied up his horse, and settled himself. Hunger gnawed away at his stomach and he did his best to relieve some of it by drinking fitfully from his water bottle. It helped a little but soon his guts took up its rumbling and gurgling once again. He rolled over and closed his eyes, doing his utmost to clear his mind and get some sleep. Any confrontation with Destry would have to wait until morning,

CHAPTER FIFTY-SIX

B essy accompanied Mrs Clapham to the entrance of the guesthouse and stopped in the doorway. They'd spoken at length all through the night and Bessy saw the sense in her friend's words. As her mind cleared of all its confusion, its hate, she saw it all set out so clearly before her. Now, with the first sprinkling of the grey dawn appearing on the horizon, she took Mrs Clapham's hand in hers. "You've helped me see it all so clearly, Miriam," said Bessy, her tired voice still sounding strong. "I've done some terrible things lately. Horrible things."

"None of it was your fault."

"That's good of you to say, but we both know my lack of determined action means I must take most of the responsibility."

"Bessy, the water ... How could anyone know?"

"I suppose you're right and I'll take a little comfort from that. I often refrained from drinking it due to its color."

"Your husband seemed addicted to it."

Bessy chuckled, "Either that or the oceans of whisky he added to it!"

Mrs Clapham smiled then grew serious. "We have to gather the town together, tell them what has happened." She took in a deep breath. "What will Destry do, once everyone knows about his plans?"

"I'm not sure. We'll have to get word to a US Marshal. Perhaps there is someone in Lancaster who could help..." Her voice dwindled into a whisper as the hopelessness of it all pressed down upon her. She sniffed. "Dear Lord, Miriam, this a nightmare."

"Not if Reece can help us. He is a man of indomitable spirit."

"If he survives Destry's attempt at murder. He'll be going up against four of them, Bessy. Even Reece couldn't ..." Shaking her head, Bessy lowered her gaze. "I think the wisest thing to do is to try and clear my head of the whole ghastly matter. Draw a line, start again." Her face came up. "It might be for the best if I leave this place. I could sell up, move back east, open up somewhere else."

Appalled, Mrs Clapham seized her friend's hands. "Oh no, surely there has to be another way?"

"Once news gets out that I did nothing, that I didn't warn anyone of Hanson and Turner's plan to commit such terrible deeds, I'll be hounded out of here anyway."

"You were tied up, Bessy! There was nothing you could have said or done."

"And Destry? I should have spoken up about him long ago."

"No, Bessy, people will understand. In time."

Bessy shook her head, the sadness overwhelming, the pressure unendurable. The strength leaked out of her limbs and she staggered and fell against the door jaw. As her shoulder struck the woodwork a bullet screamed through the air mere inches from where she had stood. Almost immediately, the crack of the rifle echoed through the town. Mrs Clapham screamed and dived into the doorway, taking her friend with her.

Scrambling around on the floor, both women fought to find their breath. Mrs Clapham managed to kick shut the door behind them as another bullet slapped into the timber framework.

Bessy, mind in a mad whirl of confusion and fear, shouted, "Who is it? Who's trying to kill us?"

Shaking her head, Mrs Clapham drew a breath and started to crawl down the hallway towards the tiny reception desk. "Come on," she said, "we have to try and get away somehow. Through the back. For the love of God, keep your head down."

Bessy couldn't help but smile, "You're certainly a good friend to have when things get nasty, Miriam."

"We'll soon see if that thought has any truth to it," Mrs Clapham rasped through clenched teeth.

"There's a gun in the dining room," said Bessy, shuffling next to her friend. "I think it's still loaded." Mrs Clapham gave Bessy a look. "It's one of Destry's. Ironic isn't it."

Nodding, Mrs Clapham continued worming her way forward. "Let's pray we don't have to use it."

Bessy swallowed down the reply formulating on her lips. She would like nothing better than to use it.

On Destry.

CHAPTER FIFTY-SEVEN

Having spent a cramped night in the tiny jailhouse, Ira stretched out his limbs and yawned loudly. He crossed the room and prepared coffee in the battered, blackened coffee pot before rousing Otis lying fully stretched out on the narrow camp-bed beyond the iron bars.

Nostrils full of the aroma of freshly brewed coffee, Otis had little trouble rousing himself. The previous evening Ira, who came to free him, told him everything. Sitting quietly, digesting every word, Otis had all of his fears confirmed. Everyone he knew was dead. Mr Henry, the Quinces, Eva, Manchester. Murdered for the love of gold. Gold that might not even exist.

"We've all been tricked," said Ira with feeling as the night pressed in. "Best if we do whatever it is it takes to set this miserable affair to rights."

"What about that gunfighter? The one they're all afraid of?"

"Reece?" Ira shrugged. "Who knows. Last I knew he was at the mine but what he was doing there is anyone's guess."

"Finding gold? For himself, or for Bessy? Everybody knows he has feelings for her."

"Maybe so. Come morning it'll all be a lot clearer."

And now the morning was here but nothing was any clearer.

Ira sat with his hands clamped around his coffee cup and stared into space. The idea of going up against Reece did not fill him with any kind of confidence. He let out a long sigh and raised the cup to his lips. He almost scalded himself when the crack of a distant rifle shot caused him to jump.

"What in the hell...?" Otis was already getting to his feet. He immediately went to the rifle rack and pulled down a Winchester.

"Maybe it's Reece," said Ira, checking the load of his Colt Dragoon.

Otis moved to the door and pushed it open, dropping to his knees. He peered out into the cold, still greyness of the morning. There was not a sound or movement from anyone. The street stretched narrow and empty on either side. A second rifle burst took him by surprise, and he automatically jumped back into the cover of the jailhouse.

"Who is it?" asked Ira, coming up behind him.

"I can't see. I think it's coming from the direction of the lumber yard, but I can't be sure." He engaged the Winchester's lever and took another look along the street. "The guesthouse is the only building which has a second storey, so whoever it is, they is shooting from ground level. On that side of the street, there's only—"

A third shot rang out. This time, Otis held his ground. In the lightening morning, there was still sufficient gloom for him to pinpoint the flash of the discharge. He grunted with satisfaction. "It's the lumber yard. He's squatting down behind the fencing and has a direct line to the guesthouse."

"The guesthouse? Why is he shooting at the guesthouse?"

"Maybe the gang have fallen out. It often happens, don't it, when gold is involved."

"Greed. Yeah ... Can you make out who it is doing the shootin'?"

"No. He's crouched down too low. I reckon if it was Reece, he'd have already found his mark."

296

"But if it's Destry ... Why he's shootin' at his own wife?"

"Ira, I reckon Destry wouldn't stop at killing his own mother where gold is involved."

"All right, then what do we do?"

"We flank him. Or, at least, you do. We'll skirt down the side of the street. You take the first passage and come at him from behind. Meanwhile, I'll concentrate on him from the front. As soon as I start firing, you step out and plug him. You get me?"

"Jesus, Otis, I don't think..."

"Ira, if it's Reece, he'll shoot you stone dead if you hesitate. If it's Destry you have every right to put him in the ground."

"Yeah, but I'd be shootin' him in the back!"

"Since when does chivalry come into any of this, Ira? They wanted us dead. Both of us. They ain't got no scruples and nor should we."

Ira considered the words for a brief moment. Swallowing hard, he gave a single nod. "All right. Let's do it."

"We move out real slow and real careful. Keep your head down and if he spots us and starts shooting, you head for whatever cover you can find."

"Jeez ... Otis, this is one helluva—"

Another retort from the rifle, swiftly followed by the sound of splintering glass, caused him to wince.

"Let's go," said Ira and they both crept out into the street.

Destry opened the breach and fed in another cartridge, closed the lever, and squinted through the rear sight towards the guesthouse. He'd had enough of being told what to do, of always being second best. First, it was Bourne, then that bastard Reece, and now Hanson. Well, he'd put paid to them all. Well, to be absolutely accurate, the Indians and that worm Winter Hair took care of them. He should never have trusted that old shaman. He'd said something to Reece, set him straight about much of it. Destry didn't know what had passed between them but he knew that Reece sealing the mine was something that should never happen. If there wasn't gold to be had, there was treasure. Enough to set him up for life. And nobody, not Reece, Turner *or* Bessy were going to get their greedy hands on any of it.

With his anger boiling, he squeezed off another round and blew out the window adjacent to the guesthouse door.

Grinning, he took a long drink from the leather bottle at his side. He was much the worse for alcohol, having drunk almost continuously since fleeing the destroyed shack the previous night. A night in the open had not tempered his mood and he felt cold, bad-tempered, and thoroughly determined to end it all that morning. He opened the breach and was about to slide in another round when he caught sight of a shape moving at the periphery of his vision. Smooth as oil, he turned, drawing the colt Navy from his waistband. He was nothing but fully prepared.

What he saw before him, however, froze the very marrow of his bones.

"Oh Brownlow, what has happened to you?"

The voice was that of his mother. The person mouthing the words appeared to *be* his mother. But that could not be – she'd been dead these past forty years.

The gun fell from his rigid fingers as he reeled away. There was no feeling there, no feeling anywhere. He gazed open-mouthed aghast. Disbelief coupled with abject terror conspired to overawe him.

"Why are you shooting at your lovely, Bessy? Oh my boy, what has brought you to this?"

She took a step forward and Destry pushed himself away across the dirt, the back of one hand pressing over his mouth, suppressing the whimpers escaping from his throat.

"Destry."

Another voice. Lower, much more severe. Destry snapped his head around and he felt his guts churn, his bowels loosening.

His father, always a big man, now appeared more enormous than ever before.

"Destry, you need to stop this. Stop, you hear me? Throw away your gun and make peace with Bessy. So help me, if you don't, I'll fetch my belt and whup your ass."

Other shapes materialized around him, forgotten faces, voices he thought he recognized but never believed he'd hear again. They rang out across the timber yard, crackling in the chill morning air, a morning full of blazing blues and purples. The very atmosphere danced with a myriad of colors, flashing lights, and smells. Old smells from his childhood – baked bread, apple strudel laced with cinnamon, eggnog at Christmas.

Unconsciously, he reached out for the leather bottle and took a long drink, the water laced heavily with whisky, hitting the back of his throat, and giving him some small relief from the nightmare playing out around him.

"You can't be real," he managed, recovering slightly. Enough, at least, to grab the Colt, bring it up and level it towards his father. "You always did beat me, didn't you, you bastard."

"Oh Brownlow. Please."

She came like a dream from beyond his parents, her blonde hair fluttering in whatever breeze there was, her full lips parting, her voice like honey sliding from her tongue. "I've missed you."

"Ashley?" The gun hand lowered as if of its own accord. "Ashley ... how...? Oh my God, Ashley."

It was her, his first love, come to him again from across the years, as lovely as she ever was. Her skin, alabaster white, fresh, smooth, perfect. Her bosom, full, the soft flesh blossoming above the top of her dress.

"No..." he whispered. Shaking his head, he did nothing to stem the tears rolling down his face. "No...you...You're dead, Ashely. All of you are *dead*."

It was true. He'd shot her the night he'd found her with Drew Stanton, kissing so openly. He'd shot him first, blew him across the narrow street that ran alongside the Starlight Empress

Variety hall. She'd screamed, saw Destry's face alive with jealousy, and shrieked, "Brownlow, *no!*"

He'd shot her then. She fell and he continued shooting until all of the bullets were used up. He ran. Joined the army. Disappeared. He thought forever.

"We're here, Brownlow," Ashley was saying, "here to save your life before you throw it away."

"Again," added his mother.

"Give it up son," said his father.

"Give it up, Destry."

Destry blinked. This new voice was one he wasn't at all sure of. Not one from his past. But one he knew even so.

He threw himself face first and rolled as the Winchester barked. Mother, father, and Ashley disappeared as abruptly as they'd appeared, leaving Otis standing in the open, working the lever of his carbine.

Destry fired three times and watched Otis buck and bolt, losing his footing and falling backwards, three fountains of blood bubbling up from his chest.

From his right came a terrific boom and a heavy slug smacked into the ground inches from him. Rolling over, Destry was coming up to a kneeling position.

"You shouldn't have done what you did, Destry."

There she was, larger than life, hands on her broad hips, her corset pulled tighter than he thought possible.

"Lizzie?"

The young whore cocked her head. "Surprised to see me? Your folks, they seemed to accept me, Destry. That young girl of yours too. They all knew what you are capable of and not one of 'em was in the least bit surprised when I told 'em how you'd murdered me."

This couldn't be happening, Destry thought, his scrambled wits unable to untangle anything and make sense of what was happening. He stood up on rubbery legs and groped for the fence beside him, gain some support however meagre. "I never meant to—" he began but got no further as a second heavy-caliber bullet slammed into his chest and blew him backwards.

Through the swiftly dispersing cloud of cordite, he caught sight of Ira, that young scallywag who delighted in causing trouble whenever he could.

"Ah shit..." muttered Destry. He fell onto his backside, back pressed against the fencing surrounding the lumber yard. The gun hung in his feeble grip, but he doubted he had the strength to fire it, not now.

A shadow loomed over him. Who was it now? Parents, Ashley, or that damned whore Lizzie Coombs. Why did she say his pecker was like a little worm? That made him so mad. So mad. He squinted towards the person stepping closer and felt a sudden rush of elation.

"Bessy..." he mumbled.

He half expected her to smile, relieved he still lived. Instead, without a flicker of emotion, she brought up the gun she'd taken from the guesthouse and blew his brains out.

CHAPTER FIFTY-EIGHT

Three months later

"It's highly irregular," the circuit judge was saying as he paced around the sheriff's office. Standing in a tight-lipped row, Reece, Ira, and Bessy dare not meet his glowering gaze. In the doorway, Miriam Clapham and Frank Morrison, the senior bank-teller looked on with apprehension.

"You," said the judge, pointing towards Morrison, "you say the bank manager is out of town?"

"He is, your honor, and as far as I know he won't be back for another six weeks."

"Highly irregular," said the judge again. "I should call in a United States Marshal, you understand?"

Everyone nodded.

"Most ..." He moved behind the desk and pulled open a drawer. "Irregular." He sat down and produced a piece of paper. "I'll pen a telegram, see if I can summon a marshal before fall. I understand the snows come early in these parts?"

"They can do, your honor," said Bessy.

"Yes, well, I have no choice ... what with the bank manager not being here. As he's the most senior professional, I would have only his word as recommendation..."

"Mr Morrison here," said Miriam Clapham, "is by far the

most upstanding citizen we have in Whitewater right now, your honor."

The judge studied the diminutive bank-teller for several moments. "I'm sure he is, but even so..."

"Why not telegram Mrs Swanson, the bank manager," continued Mrs Clapham with renewed energy, "he will vouch for Mr Morrison here, put your mind at rest. We'd receive the reply within a day."

"You know where's he's staying?"

"Adelphi Hotel, Kansas City," said Morrison.

"The Adelphi?" The judge sat back, pen drumming on his lower lip. He appeared impressed. "Very well, I'll do that. In the meantime, we continue as usual."

"Usual?" put in Reece with a tiny snigger. "What's that exactly?"

"Reece, isn't it?"

"Yes, your honor," replied the gunfighter, touching the brim of his hat.

"And you're the one who blew down the mine?"

"And helped divert the stream, your honor," put in Bessy quickly.

"The stream that's been poisoning this town for years and years," added Mrs Clapham.

"The *usual*, Mr Reece, is whoever's been doing the job of sheriff since the dreadful circumstances that befell this town continues to do just that."

"That'll be Mr Reece, your honor," said Bessy.

"Yes ..." The judge now took to tapping his teeth with the quill pen. "Let me compose this telegram then if you'd be so good ma'am, I'd like you to put me up in the finest room you have at your guesthouse."

Bessy gave a small bow. "It'll be my honor, your ... honor."

Someone laughed. The judge did not.

. . .

The following afternoon they stood on the steps of the sheriff's office, the circuit judge stepping back after pinning the badge to Reece's shirt. He grunted and turned away. The others gathered there erupted into cheers of celebration, all of them taking turns to pump Reece's hand. All except Bessy, who planted a large kiss on his cheek. Blinking, Reece felt his face burning. Then, with no warning, she grabbed him and kissed him fully on the lips.

The cheering grew even louder than ever.

Dear reader,

We hope you enjoyed reading *Milky Trail To Death*. Please take a moment to leave a review, even if it's a short one. Your opinion is important to us.

Discover more books by Stuart G. Yates at https://www. nextchapter.pub/authors/stuart-g-yates

Want to know when one of our books is free or discounted? Join the newsletter at http://eepurl.com/bqqB3H

Best regards,

Stuart G. Yates and the Next Chapter Team

ABOUT THE AUTHOR

What could have caused those entering the mine in this story to hallucinate and act so strangely?

In Ancient Greece, many would visit the oracle at Delphi to seek answers to questions. What was this curious gift she possessed that enabled her to look into the future? A recent report by the geologist Jelle De Boer, concludes that hallucinogenic gases seeped up through cracks in the ground at the site, causing the high-priestess, the Pythia, to slip into a trance and utter her famed prophecies. Greece sits upon several tectonic plates and when these move, the sweet smelling ethylene gas seeps out and is absorbed by the surrounding rocks. As Boer states, "gases that came through the fractures" almost certainly induced an euphoric state upon the oracle, helping her to foresee the future and guide her visitors – including Alexander the Great – to whatever fates awaited them.

If this could have happened in Greece, then why not in the American West some one hundred and fifty years ago?

As always, I will leave this for you to puzzle over, dear reader.

I hope you enjoyed this Western. I have tried to make it somewhat different from the norm and, if I have succeeded, perhaps you could leave a review on Amazon? It doesn't need to be too long and should take you only a few moments to complete. Reviews are the lifeblood for novelists and one of the best ways of driving readers to an author's books. In addition, if you enjoy Westerns, why not sample some of the other works I have written in this genre? You can find them all on my Amazon page. I love Westerns and enjoy writing them. I hope you enjoy reading them! Thanks to everyone for all your support. I appreciate it very much.

SG Yates, spring, 2021.

Milky Trail To Death
ISBN: 978-4-86750-676-9

Published by
Next Chapter
1-60-20 Minami-Otsuka
170-0005 Toshima-Ku, Tokyo
+818035793528

22nd September 2021

Lightning Source UK Ltd.
Milton Keynes UK
UKHW010013131222
413832UK00004BA/97

9 784867 506769